CW00602430

MY SECRET FANTASIES

Edited by Maria Isabel Pita

MY SECRET FANTASIES

Copyright ©2004 by Magic Carpet Books, Inc.

All Rights Reserved

No part of this book may be reproduced,
stored in a retrieval system, or transmitted in any form,
by any means, including mechanical, electronic,
photocopying, recording or otherwise, without
prior written permission from the publisher and author.

First Magic Carpet Books, Inc. edition August 2004

Published in 2004

Manufactured in the United States of America
Published by Magic Carpet Books, Inc.

Magic Carpet Books, Inc.
PO Box 473
New Milford, CT 06776

Library of Congress Cataloging in Publication Date

My Secret Fantisies Edited by Maria Isabel Pita
ISBN # 0-9755331-2-6

Book Design: P. Ruggieri

CONTENTS

1. Megan – In the Woods

Last year at the age of thirty, I finally decided I was sick of the city rat race – too much dirt and stress and too many subway perverts – so I made plans to move out of the city to a small town near the Canadian border. My friends helped me out by referring me to small companies who used freelance writers so it didn't matter where I lived, and I was planning to work on my half-finished novel as well. Peace and quiet were just what I needed to inspire me.

The move was none too smooth, but after six months I already loved the relaxed ease of small-town life. Everyone was so friendly, and the country was absolutely beautiful. A doe and her fawn often stepped out of the woods to graze near my cabin right in front of my window! The downside of rural life was that my nearest neighbor was an hour's drive away. Forget about telephones; there were no phone lines out here at all, so I invested in a CB radio in case of an emergency. After I figured out how to work the thing, I introduced myself to my nearest neighbor and we began having long conversations over the radio. He had an incredibly sexy voice, and we joked about paying each other a neighborly visit. Finally, after a few weeks of CB chatter, we each agreed to drive fifty miles to a restaurant in town and meet face to face.

When I saw a tall, handsome man waiting inside the door, I could scarcely dare hope it was him. He looked at me, I stared at him, and we just stood there awkwardly. Then at last he broke the ice. 'Megan?' he asked, and a cold, frightened place inside me I hadn't even realized was there melted away forever and I knew everything was going to be all right.

Once we had been seated, he smiled and said, 'My real name is John. How does it feel to finally see another fellow human being?'

It felt great, especially because he was such a fine example of a human being. John was a tall, muscular man with blond hair and amazing crystal-clear blue eyes. I found myself continuing to mysteriously melt inside wondering what he would be like in bed. Since moving up here, I had been in a perpetual state of horniness; often drifting off into sexual fantasies I could do nothing about in my isolated environment. I had been channeling all my sexual energy into my novel, and that was getting a bit old...

After dinner and a few hours of pleasant conversation where we seemed to talk about everything and nothing, I knew we were both dreading the long drive home alone. I thought fast, and made a decision. 'Why not come over to my house?' I asked boldly. 'We can keep each other warm.'

'You mean you'd rather have me than a quilt and space heater?' he teased. 'Well, I guess I'd better be a good neighbor.'

An hour later – after very little conversation as we both silently anticipated what was to come – we reached my little cabin. As he sat on my couch, I could tell we were both having a hard time keeping our hands off each other. It had been so long! His well-defined ass, hard muscles and the bulge in his crotch were making my pussy hot with longing, and my nipples stood provocatively out against my sweatshirt. They were so hard they managed to make a noticeable impression on the thick cotton, and I'm sure David noticed them.

'So, Megan, why do you want to live out here in the sticks?' he inquired.

I told him how much I disliked the city and about the novel I was writing. 'Besides, it's not totally isolated out here,' I replied with a promising smile.

'You really aren't lonely?' he asked as he moved closer. 'Do you want me to leave?' One of his hands ran boldly up and down my inner thighs, pushing my skirt up higher.

By way of an answer, I lay submissively down on the couch as his hand crept slowly towards my wet sex. Of course I didn't want him to leave! If he left now, I would die!

He ran his slightly rough fingertips along my slit, holding my eyes as he gradually delved deeper inside, until two of his thick, hard digits reached the spot inside me desperately aching for his attention. A moan escaped my lips as he touched my clit. Then, gently pushing my legs apart, he dipped his head and licked my labia. Now it was his tongue that found my clitoris and teased it, at first slowly, and then faster and more firmly as I begged him not to stop.

He sat up, impatiently pulled off my sweatshirt, and began sucking my nipples, flicking his tongue over one of them gently while his fingers tugged and pinched the other. My own fingers were sliding in and out of my pussy now as I rode a cresting wave of exquisite pleasure. 'Oh, God, this feels so good,' I moaned in his ear.

'I'm glad,' he whispered back, and then kissed me, thrusting his hot tongue into my mouth while his thumb made circular motions on my throbbing love button. I moaned again and again as he slid two of his fingers deeper and deeper inside of me, and then I came violently, with him groaning his satisfaction at my writhing pleasure.

No longer starving for a climax, I was now in the grip of another intense hunger – I had to have him inside me! He must have read my mind, because he stood up and slowly took off his corduroy trousers, letting me enjoy the sight of him stripping himself naked before me. His chest was huge, and accented by a thick growth of curly blond hair. I was helplessly aroused again, this time by his gloriously big dick. I quickly sat up and took it in my mouth, running my tongue over its glistening tip and caressing the head with the insides of my cheeks and the back of my throat. It was scarcely possible, but his rapid breathing and deep moans made me lust after him even more. Finally, he shoved me back across the couch, and I reached up to slip my arms around his neck and kiss him as he rammed his big cock into my slick pussy. He pumped his rending erection in and out of my eagerly juicing hole until I could scarcely breathe from the depth of the pleasure his penetrations filled me with. His groans were driving me wild as we rocked together in a frenzy of desire. The ecstasy I experienced was so intense I was almost afraid I would lose consciousness. When I started coming I couldn't seem to stop; I had five orgasms at least as he thrust faster and harder in the violent throes of his own release.

We awoke up hours later to a bright, clear day lying in each other's arms on the couch. John had a long drive back to his house, and I smiled as I lay there listening to him shower and dress. Then I heard him moving around in the kitchen, but felt too languid to get up and go investigate what he was doing.

He returned bearing coffee and toast for both of us, and we had a companionable breakfast together, thoroughly enjoying each other's company.

'How did you learn to become so domestic?' I asked curiously.

'I live alone,' he replied. 'It was either learn to make toast or perish. Now, if you would be so kind as to walk me to the door; I need to go out and make some money.'

We exchanged a long, lingering kiss on the threshold as his hands ran hungrily up and down my body, promising much more pleasure to come. I shivered from the delicious combination of the cold air outside and the deep warmth of his touch.

'You're so sweet,' he said, his eyes meeting mine. 'Can I come back tonight?'

You bet he could! 'Of course,' I replied, somehow managing to keep the naked eagerness out of my voice. I stood at the door as he revved up the engine of his truck, letting it warm up for a bit. Then he gave me a wave and started down the long snow-covered road. As I watched him go, I thought, I'm going to like living in the wilderness!

2. Fran – Sharing

I got to my continuing education class a little late last week, remembering that Charles – the man who sits next to me – told me that if I ever needed to copy his notes, he'd be more than happy to stay after class with me. Charles took the neatest notes I had ever seen, so I decided I'd take him up on his offer.

'Sorry, Fran, but I have to meet a friend for dinner in ten minutes,' he said when I talked to him after class. 'How about Saturday afternoon? We could meet at my apartment, or something.'

'That would be great, Charles, I really appreciate it.'

'No problem.' He whipped out a piece of paper and wrote down his address.

I arrived at Charles' apartment at noon on Saturday. When I knocked on his door, I got no answer. A moment later, I saw him running up the steps. I couldn't help noticing that through his tight running shorts – which clung to his pelvis like a second layer of skin – the outline of his penis was clearly visible.

'Hi,' he gasped, smiling, 'I wasn't expecting you till later.'

'I'm sorry. Want me to come back?'

'Oh, no, that's all right. We didn't set up any specific time. I was just coming back from my late-morning jog. Come on in.' His notebook was sitting on top of the stereo. 'Here,' he said, handing it to me. 'I hope you don't mind, but I feel kind of, well… I'm really hot. I'm gonna jump in the shower for five minutes. Okay?'

'Of course, go ahead,' I told him, 'and take your time, please.' I could not believe how attracted I was to him at that point; I had never really thought of Charles as anything but a classmate before. I watched lustfully as his broad shoulders and tight buns disappeared behind the bathroom door.

Once I heard the shower running, I had to restrain myself from boldly walking into the bathroom. I imagined how great it would be to see him in the shower, not to mention being in the shower with him! Then I imagined him beside me, breathing heavily the way he was when he ran up the steps, only this time I'd be the cause of his shortness of breath.

Five minutes later, just as he had promised, Charles finished his shower and emerged from the bathroom, his lean hips enticingly wrapped in a wet dark-blue towel. He walked past me where I sat at his small dining room table, heading towards what appeared to be his bedroom. But on the threshold, he suddenly turned around and asked, 'Did you get the handout Professor Melville gave out in class?' He walked towards me again.

All I could think about at that moment was how good his freshly shampooed hair smelled, and how much I wanted him to lose his grip on the towel.

Without waiting for my answer, he pulled a piece of paper out of the front of his notebook and tossed it onto the table in front of me.

I unfolded it, and quickly began copying its contents into my note-book, struggling to concentrate as I felt him watching me. I yearned to look up and meet his eyes, but I resisted, and finally he walked away.

I stole a quick peek at him as he moved around in his bedroom, and I wondered if he had deliberately left the door open so I could watch him. As he bent down to rummage through a drawer, I caught a glimpse of his ass beneath the towel. For a breathtaking moment, his balls and penis were in full view. I gasped at the sight of him, and he must have heard me because he turned around, gazing at me with those gorgeous eyes that for some reason I'd never noticed before. He was smiling.

My heart raced as I watched him walking towards me again. He stood beside me, lifted my face up towards his, and bent over to kiss me.

The sweet ache that bloomed between my legs amazed me as his tongue darted into my mouth. I stood up, and willingly let him pull my jeans and panties down. When they were off, he slid his hands up and down my calves, moving slowly up to my thighs. His teasing was driving me crazy. I grabbed his head with both hands and pulled his face up to my pussy, sighing with pleasure as his hard features penetrated the tender folds of my sex. And while his tongue teased my clitoris, his hands continued exploring my legs, a dual action that had me moaning and whimpering with delight, especially when he moved his caresses to my belly; slipping his hands up beneath my shirt to cradle my bra-free breasts. His lips sucked my clit, and I bucked against his face as a shiver of approaching ecstasy ran up and down my spine. Once again I took hold of his head and guided his mouth to where it felt the best, and after just a few more minutes of his devoted oral attentions, I climaxed, spreading my legs so he could furiously work his tongue up into the wetness flowing from me.

After I regained my composure, I noticed he was still wearing his towel. As he straightened up in front of me, I put my hand on his chest and gently raked my fingernails down his firm body to his athlete's muscular belly. I reached for the towel fastened at his waist, and gently pulled it off.

Smiling, he lay on his back on the carpet, his legs slightly spread, and I eagerly knelt between them so I could hungrily suck his balls, which leapt with excitement against my lips. I turned so my hips were within his reach, and while I sucked him off, he grabbed hold of my thighs and teased two fingers up inside of me, then a third one. He slid them in and out of my pussy, increasing the force of his penetrations and sending almost painful flashes of arousal up through my pelvis to my breasts and then down my spine. Finally, I couldn't wait anymore; I lay on my back beside him, my legs spread wide apart. He understood immediately what I wanted and rolled on top of me, burying his long erection deep inside my cunt with one well-aimed thrust. His energetic penetrations sent waves of pleasure crashing through my blood as I raised my hips up to collide with his on each of his downward thrusts. And as our momentum increased, I had an orgasm the likes of which I had never experienced before. He quickly followed me, groaning as he whipped out of me and pumped streaming jets of hot cum over my throbbing mound.

'I never had any study partners like you when I went to college,' I remarked breathlessly.

'I bet you would have gotten straight A's if you had,' he teased, smiling.

3. Alison – A Real Workout

I had fantasized about Steve forever even though I pretended not to because we were only friends. Yet what woman could continue to resist a six-foot tall man with black hair, vivid blue eyes, and the body of Adonis? To top it all off, he had a great sense of humor, too, and if it's true that people who are in good shape have better sex, I was in for a treat if we ever slept together. I know he was in good shape because I met Steve in the weight room of our apartment complex. At first it was just a coincidence we had the same workout schedule, but soon we began checking up on each other and arranging times to meet so we could exercise together. We enjoyed each other's company. We spent a great deal of time discussing our woes with current lovers, asking each other for help and advice.

Despite how attractive he was, I was determined to think of Steve only as a friend – no dating, no stolen kisses, no sex, nothing; I was afraid of ruining our wonderful friendship. Then I began having sexual dreams about him. Usually, I'm a forthright person, but what was I supposed to do now, go up to him and say, 'Hey, it's just occurred to me that I desperately want your body and I'm going to go crazy if I keep telling myself otherwise'? He would probably run for the hills. I was at a complete loss what to do about my helpless infatuation.

Fortunately for me, Steve had very few inhibitions, and one evening he did what I had only dared to dream of doing myself…

We met in the weight room as usual, and I had to struggle to keep myself from staring, because he was looking particularly devastating. He was wearing tight black bicycle shorts and a red tank top. The outfit left little to the imagination, outlining his muscular physique and drawing my attention to the bulge between his powerful thighs.

The sight of him was driving me wild. I had to run my perspiring hands over my legs before I could pick up my weights. My pussy was wet, but at least there was no way he could know that, and I could only pray my hardened nipples wouldn't draw his attention through my sport's bra. As though my body wasn't in hyper-drive, we began our workouts as usual, laughing and joking the whole time.

Then, gradually, I noticed a difference in his behavior. His eyes kept straying over my nearly naked body. I was wearing a turquoise-and-pink-striped tank top with tight matching shorts. Since it was warm in the weight room, and I felt comfortable with him, I hadn't worn tights. His gaze made me feel hotter than any workout ever had, and his hands… he kept touching me, as often as possible, which was decidedly different since most of the time we worked out alone, only helping each other with the really difficult lifts. But that evening he was constantly at my side with his hands grazing up my waist, and then innocently along the sides of my breasts, as he gave me friendly suggestions on how to improve my form. Needless to say, I was almost out of my head with lust. My eyes devoured him as I returned his touches; every chance I got I touched his warm, sweat-slick body. Then I even dared to slip my hands down his back and very briefly, as if by accident, caress the firm curve of his buttocks. He had the finest ass I had ever seen on a man, and when I felt how tight it was, I almost lost it. Breathing deeply, I bent over to adjust the weights for my final exercise.

'Alison…' he whispered behind me.

Startled, I began turning around to see if he needed help with a weight. Suddenly, his hands gripped my waist, and then boldly, slowly, caressed my ass. 'Steve?' my voice was calculatedly bewildered, yet intensely excited.

'I'm sorry, Alison,' he said, his voice thick with desire. He pressed his pelvis directly against my nether cheeks, and I felt his erection straining to be released. His hands wandered up my torso, almost searing my breasts as they pushed my tank up out of the way. I moaned as he began lightly pinching both my nipples while his lips kissed my shoulders and neck. 'Oh, Alison,' he breathed, and suddenly spanked me, once, then twice, as if punishing me for how much he desired me.

My pussy was so hot, I almost thought I would come when he smacked my ass again a third time, and suddenly I couldn't take how much I wanted him. I turned frantically around, and hungrily yanked his tank top over his head before struggling with his tight bike pants. 'I've wanted your body for so long!' I gasped as I finally got him naked and could gaze in wonder at his erection. I immediately knelt before him and eagerly swallowed the beautiful muscle of his penis, taking as much as I could hold into my mouth. Then I slowly licked his head and worked my clinging lips down to his tender balls, feeling him tremble beneath my every lick and suck.

'Oh, God,' he pleaded as he pulled me to my feet so he could yank my shorts down. 'I can't wait, Alison...'

'I can't wait either,' I agreed breathlessly.

He sat down on the nearest weight bench, and without hesitation pulled me down on top of him, plunging his hard-on deep into my pussy. I held onto the back of his head as he began lifting my hips up and down around his rigid cock in a swift, fierce rhythm. And all the while our hands and lips were busy; the passion we had ignored for so long had finally burst and we were going crazy over each other.

'I'm sorry,' he said through clenched teeth, 'I can't hold back...' Frantically his mouth and tongue sought my breasts as one of his hands splayed over my stomach and his thumb began stroking my clitoris. 'Put your hands over your head,' he commanded. 'Hold onto the bar and ride me... that's it, ride my cock with your tight little cunt, baby.'

I joyfully obeyed him, getting the workout of my life as I ground my hips up and down around his untiring hard-on. My whole body was as tight as a violin string waiting for that one special note that would send my senses into a magnificent crescendo. 'Steve...' my voice broke, and my hands came to rest helplessly on his head.

'Do I have to tie your wrists to the bar?' he threatened.

I moaned and raised my arms over my head again; my body was completely his to command. I was terrified someone would walk into the weight room and discover us, but somehow this fear only intensified the profound pleasure I was taking in his penetrations.

'Come for me, Alison, I want you to make yourself come for me…'

His whispered words shook me to the core. I was going to lose it, but not alone. I arched my back, taking him as deep inside my pussy as was physically possible.

'Alison, no!' he gasped, and his whole body tensed. He flung his head back, and I felt the explosion of his pleasure deep in my pelvis. His hands gripped my hips like a vice as he ejaculated. I was completely lost in the sensations of our violent love-making; the moment his cock began pulsing inside me, my body lost control and I climaxed feeling as though I was blasting off into space on the most violent ecstasy I had ever experienced.

A few minutes later, I stopped moaning and gradually regained my senses. I was wrapped tightly in Steve's arms, and I could feel his breath on my forehead as his lips started to kiss his way down to mine.

'Some workout,' he remarked huskily.

'No pain, no gain,' I caressed his slick, hard chest.

'If that was pain, I think I'm in heaven.' He kissed me again, and then laughed.

I looked down, and burst out laughing, too.

We were both still wearing our socks and sneakers.

4. Jan – Home Alone

Last Friday night I sat home alone while my husband, Bob, was across town helping his brother put a new set of breaks on his Olds. A phone call at nine-forty-five assured me he would be home no later than midnight. Typical; so often Bob was off on some errand of mercy fixing a neighbor's broken dishwasher or repairing a relative's car. He's just that type of guy – the kind that is only too eager to help out family and friends while he takes me for granted. After nearly ten years, you'd think I would have become resigned to Bob's idiosyncrasies, but I hadn't. Not when it means I spend my evenings alone so much of the time.

By eleven o'clock, with sultry images of Don Johnson still fresh in my mind from an old rerun of *Miami Vice*, I was faced with nothing more erotic than the late night news and an hour-and-a-half of sexual frustration awaiting Bob's return. The idea of slipping into the bedroom with my vibrator became more enticing with each passing moment. A short while later, I lay naked in the middle of our king-size bed, the long, thick undulating 'penis' obeying the commands of my hand moving with hard, pounding strokes between the moist folds of my sex lips.

As my body tensed in anticipation of my second orgasm, the doorbell sounded an unwelcome interruption. With a muffled curse, I stashed my plastic lover beneath a pillow and reluctantly rolled out of bed, impatiently slipping into my robe and carelessly knotting the sash. Angrily, I stomped down the hallway to the front door, intent on scolding Bob for forgetting his house key. But my angry scowl and gruff rebuke vanished when I opened the door to find not my husband, but my neighbor's teenage son standing out on the porch.

For an instant, Ryan appeared both startled by the suddenness with which I yanked open the door, and the look of displeasure on my face. But when my expression changed from annoyance to surprise, softening into one of recognition, he returned my smile with a lopsided, boyish grin.

'Don't tell me, let me guess,' he began in a voice much too deep for an eighteen-year-old. 'The old man's off on another mission of mercy and, as usual, you're home all alone with no one to tuck you in.' A smile of sarcastic amusement now curled his sensuous lips, sparking a mocking gleam in his blue eyes.

Over the course of the last six years, I had watched Ryan grow from a gangly, tow-headed youth into a tall, attractive man. I had witnessed his interests evolve from skate-boards and video games to cars, football and girls. His fascination for carburetors and fuel pumps had him constantly hanging around the house, for my husband's knowledge of automotive engines is something of a legend in our neighborhood. Over the years, Ryan had developed a fairly accurate picture of the situation between Bob and me. Nevertheless, the shrewdness of his deduction and the confidence with which he made it were a little unsettling. For some strange reason, I found myself becoming defensive, and feeling the need to champion Bob's compulsion to play the knight-errant, thereby excusing his frequent absences.

'You make it sound as if Bob's never home, which you know isn't true,' I heard myself saying still unsure why I felt compelled to justify my husband's actions. 'And don't knock Bob's desire to help out now and then. You'll be thankful for it the next time you need a hand.' Yet after I finished my little speech, I was faced with a disquieting thought. Ryan never stopped by unless he needed to talk to Bob or to enlist his aid in a little automotive repair work. Surely Ryan had known before stopping by that Bob wasn't home. Bob's battered blue truck was gone from the driveway, a sure sign he was off somewhere. 'What do you want?' I tried to sound casual even though my mind was racing light years ahead. Somehow, I already knew the reason for Ryan's visit, and secretly I prayed I hadn't missed my guess.

Ryan's smile deepened noticeably, and his compelling gaze drifted slowly, arrogantly, down the front of the short robe covering, but not entirely concealing, my ripe, naked body beneath it. I felt disturbing warmth suffuse my face as I watched this virile young man boldly gauge my reaction to his seductive appraisal. While he was surveying my attire, or lack thereof, all I could think about was how scantily dressed I was. But now that his sharp blue eyes were fixed on mine, I noticed how riveting his stare was.

'Do you really want to be alone tonight, Jan?' he asked, a huskiness to his voice that made me suspect he'd anticipated my answer. He had never addressed me formally. Since the first day we met – despite the twelve-year difference in our ages – he had always used my first name casually. Yet hearing him call me Jan in such a low, seductive tone sent shivers down my spine. My stomach knotted with excitement.

'No, I don't want to be alone,' I admitted, 'but…. but I… Bob will be home shortly,' I stammered. The element of danger filled me with excitement.

'Then we shouldn't be wasting time standing here talking,' he answered calmly, his smile vanishing and taking with it some of his cocky, youthful charm. With the graceful assurance of a man in his physical and sexual prime, Ryan stepped across the threshold of my home, forcing me to move back into the living room and allow him access. While he paused to close the door, my retreat continued, fueled by a strange need to challenge this young Adonis; to test his intent and make certain he wasn't just all talk.

My eyes met his boldly as my backward steps carried me farther from him, until my progress was halted abruptly when I came up against the couch. Falling clumsily onto the cushion, my legs parted in an accidental but explicit and provocative display of my dark pubic hair. I could feel the pink, swollen lips of my pussy wet with the juices of the solitary orgasm I had just given myself in the bedroom. Yet a gasp of surprise had barely passed my lips when Ryan appeared over me, having moved swiftly across the room to take full advantage of my predicament. Before I could right myself, he dropped to his knees between my outstretched legs, and braced his broad shoulders beneath my thighs. Strong hands eagerly sandwiched themselves between my ass and the sofa cushion as he lifted my hips, roughly kneading the firm flesh of my bottom cheeks. For a long moment his eyes blazed into mine, glowing with a savage hunger, and something more... a primitive exhilaration at knowing he was in control and I was completely at his mercy.

A thrill of desire sliced through me like a knife as I read the message in his expression. My eyes fluttered closed, and then slowly opened again in a gesture of submission; a silent signal to him that I knew what was coming and wanted it as much as he did. There was no answering look; none was needed. His head dipped between my open legs and I felt the hot, probing stabs of his tongue between the folds of my sex and against my clitoris.

My breathing quickened to match the pounding of my heart. The deep moan that rose from my throat forced my head back as my entire awareness focused on the heat between my legs and the greedy thrusts of Ryan's tongue into my cunt. My clit throbbed insistently beneath his avid wet caresses, inviting the delicious nibbling of his teeth. And every time his relentless tongue worked its way up into my hot hole, I cried out as he attacked it with the feral hunger, driving his tongue into me as far as was humanly possible; tongue-fucking me until my whole body began to tremble.

'Oh, yes, eat me, eat me!' I gasped, filling my hands with his soft blond hair and pushing his face deeper into my pulsing core.

'No, baby, you're gonna eat me now,' he commanded hoarsely, rising to his feet and reaching for the zipper of his blue jeans. By the time he had pushed it down my hands were already there to peel back the flaps of denim. And as he worked the jeans down past his hips, I tugged at his briefs, feverishly seeking his hard cock.

The moment his erection sprang to life before me, I captured its smooth, bulbous head between my lips, drinking in the strong, erotic scent of his manhood, and savoring the salty taste of the slick pearl droplet crowning his cock's velvet tip. I heard him suck a hissing breath between his teeth as I drew his full-grown organ greedily into my mouth, taking him deeper, all the way into the tight confines of my throat, until my nose was nestled in the golden hair at the base of his shaft.

'God damn, Jan, you've got the whole damn thing!' he exclaimed in amazement. Then he pulled his hips back, withdrawing several inches of his turgid cock from between my lips, only to suddenly thrust his hips forward again and fill my mouth. He began fucking my mouth like a cunt, and instinctively I matched his driving motion, keeping pace with his accelerating tempo, impelled by an overpowering desire to devour him as he had devoured me.

Suddenly, I felt him stiffen as he fought to suppress the shudder rippling through his lean body. He grabbed my hair with both hands, stilling the piston-like movements of my head as he drew a deep, steadying breath. For several long moments we remained motionless as he struggled for control. Finally, his fingers released their painful grip on my hair and he eased his hard, purplish cock from between my lips.

When I tilted my head back to gaze questioningly into his passion-darkened eyes, he returned my look of confusion with a sly, confident grin. 'I'm gonna fuck that juicy cunt of yours now,' he told me in a throaty whisper, his hands fastening themselves to my shoulders as he guided me back up onto the couch. Tearing at the sash holding my robe closed, his strong fingers possessively claimed my breasts as he moved to cover me with his young, sinewy body. One of his long, muscular legs parted my thighs as his moist mouth anchored itself to one of my stiff nipples. I could feel the hungry sucking action of his lips deep down in my womb, and I raised my hips in a wordless entreaty for him to satisfy my bottomless need. At his forceful entry, a throaty moan was ripped from my throat, bringing his mouth up to mine in a savage kiss.

As Ryan pounded into me, rocking my body with each ramming stroke of his cock, ardent words of praise punctuated with erotic profanity filled my ears. Compliments on the firmness of my breasts and the slenderness of my body were interspersed with raunchy taunts of 'bitch' and 'cunt' in a delicious, amatory blend of kindness and cruelty, love and hate, as powerfully erotic as the contrast between his tender kisses on my neck and the frenzied slapping of his cool balls against my hot vulva.

A tightening sensation deep within my pelvis was the only warning

I had of the powerful orgasm that suddenly swept my awareness away for a few blinding moments. Wave after delirious wave of ecstasy crashed through my body, coaxing gasping cries of exquisite agony from me as Ryan ejaculated explosively inside me, his hard, throbbing dick swelling against the imprisoning walls of my pussy as he filled me with his young molten river of cum.

Spent and exhausted, he collapsed heavily on top of me, dreamily murmuring tender, loving words in my ear. Then, reluctantly, he climbed off the couch, admiration and satisfaction glowing in the blue eyes surveying my naked form as he pulled up his jeans, and zipped them closed.

The glare of headlights flashed across the living room drapes as a truck pulled into the driveway – Bob's truck.

Ryan directed a knowing smile my way, and gave me a sassy wink. 'The next time Bob takes off on one of his errands of mercy, I'll be back to perform one of my own,' he promised. Then without another word, he headed for the back door.

5. Diana – Hard Study

There,' I sighed, dropping my brush wearily into the can of turpentine. 'It's finished. Want to take a look, Steve?'

I sank to the floor of my studio as my model stepped off his stand and approached the large painting. It was possibly the finest work I'd done so far. Steve's handsome face and muscular body loomed up from the canvas in a blaze of color, the brushwork thick and hasty, capturing his strong facial features – the broad forehead and straight nose, the large, intelligent eyes and full, sensual lips. His face was mysterious, his body taut and strong. The whole painting vibrated with Steve's knowing, sexy aura.

His face lit up with pleasure as he considered the wet canvas. I was smiling as well, because now that the painting was finished, and Steve was no longer my model, I could do what I had been dying to do for the past three months, ever since he wandered into my studio and told me he wanted to pose for some extra cash. I had hesitated; he was far too good-looking for me to trust myself around. Still, he was a student and he needed money and something about him made me want to paint him. He was young and vibrant, he radiated life, and he definitely radiated sex. I'd kept my hands to myself these past few months, but now I wanted to savor the delights of his body firsthand, without thinking of composition.

I rose from the floor and touched his arm. 'Do you like it?' I asked, smiling up at his face.

He nodded. 'Very much… you caught something in me, in my face…' He groped for words.

'I know,' I replied, boldly running my hands down his chest to his abdomen.

He shuddered, and his penis began to swell as his breaths quickened.

We didn't speak. Although Steve hadn't yet touched me, countless times I had imagined his strong hands on my breasts cupping their soft heaviness, his chest crushing them as he probed my mouth with his warm, insistent tongue…

'Diana…' his voice brought me out of my reverie. His blue eyes sparkled and his mouth turned up in that knowing, mysterious smile of his. He ran the fingers of one hand through my hair, and then abruptly buried his face in the side of my neck. His warm breath moistened my skin and a hot ache spread up from between my thighs into my belly as his hard penis pressed against me. I couldn't resist; I had to close my hand possessively around the warmth of his erection.

'Diana,' he repeated in a whisper, and then suddenly he was pulling my faded sweatshirt up over my head and running his hands from my shoulders to my breasts in one slow, light caress. I arched my back in pleasure as he lifted my breasts, his thumbs tickling my nipples and his eyes smiling at me dreamily. He reached down between my legs, rubbing my hot pussy through the tight denim of my jeans.

'Mm,' I murmured, spreading my legs farther apart. My sex felt like a blooming flower straining towards the hot sun.

'Take off your jeans,' he murmured.

My fingers fumbled for the zipper, but at last I was naked before him, the slickness between my legs betraying my desire to feel him inside me.

He pushed me gently down onto the floor, and knelt before me. I closed my eyes, moaning with gratitude as I felt his firm, moist tongue exploring my wet sex; gently licking the smooth inner lips of my slit before lightly nibbling my clitoris. I spread my legs farther apart as he delicately, insistently, flicked the tip of his tongue against my knob. When he pushed two, then three fingers up inside me, I felt my pussy clench around them. I dimly heard myself making sounds I'd never made with a man before as his strong fingers and talented tongue swiftly released me, allowing me to tremble around them as he eagerly lapped the flow of sweetness from between my thighs.

When I opened my eyes, Steve was lying beside me, his bright eyes studying my face. 'Ready for some more?' he asked quietly.

I was.

He moved on top of me, and the sight of his cock head teasingly probing the outside of my vaginal lips was too much for me. I grabbed his hips and pushed him down inside me, gasping as I felt his warmth fill me deep and hard. Our eyes met and held, and as he thrust vigorously in and out of my grateful pussy, it wasn't long before I felt his body tense, preparing for its release as I wrapped my legs around his hips.

'Oh, yes, don't stop,' he whispered, and then his whole body tensed as he ejaculated, filling me with so much cum it slowly trickled out of me, painting white trails down the insides of my thighs. Yet he kept driving in and out of me, watching me steadily as he deliberately rubbed his body against my throbbing clit, so that I came again.

We lay in each other's arms for a long time afterwards. He stroked my back lazily, his eyes closed, while I looked at the painting I had just finished. 'I knew you'd make love as well as you pose,' I mumbled sleepily.

'I hope you let me pose for you again real soon.'

And he has, at least a dozen times now, and each time he gets better and better. Sex is, indeed, an art form.

6. Savanna — Soap Stud

'What a day!' I said, as I threw my purse down on the bed. 'I need a shower. Traveling always makes me feel dirty.'

'Me, too,' Bill agreed. He dropped our suitcases and loosened his tie.

I was excited about coming to the Convention with Bill. We hadn't known each other long, but I was beginning to fall for his laughing blue eyes and his easy-going, sensitive ways. He made me feel special. The trip to Seattle had been tiring, and I was relieved when we finally checked into our motel room. I wanted to get out of my clothes, get clean, and relax before the opening session that evening.

He took me into his arms, kissing my lips as he stroked my hair. 'Yeah, let's take a shower,' he said.

Bill and I had made love a couple of times, but we had never showered together. I had showered with a guy once when I was in college and it was... well, that's a whole disaster story in itself, but Bill had a great body, and the thought of soaping him up made me smile.

'Sure,' I said. I put my rings and beads on the nightstand while he got rid of his coat. I began to take off my blouse, but he took hold of my hands. He looked down at my breasts, and lightly caressed the lace cups of my bra. Meanwhile, I opened his shirt, pleased by how hard his nipples became beneath my touch.

He pulled me into his arms and kissed me for a long time. I felt my brassiere loosen and shrugged off my shirt, allowing him to slowly unveil my breasts as if they were sculptures. 'They're beautiful,' he whispered.

'Too small,' I protested shyly.

'No, small breasts are sexy. I love them.' My nipples jutted out in response as he flicked his thumbs over them. Then he pinched my left peak with his lips, pulling gently at it, and then with more force, until I moaned. The muscles in my vagina clenched as I felt myself juicing in response. Oh, how I wanted him already! Impatiently, I unzipped his pants and yanked them down. The bulge in his underpants made me want to rip them off him, but I had to wait since he was busy removing my skirt. 'A garter belt and stockings!' he said in surprise. 'And no panties... Mm, I like it!' He parted the outer lips of my labia with his fingertips as I spread my legs slightly to give him a better view. His face glowed like a child's gazing at a Christmas tree. Seemingly mesmerized, he fingered my inner lips, and when he touched my clitoris, my whole body tensed and my pelvis thrust forward. I was so turned on all I wanted was more; I wanted to drag him over to the bed and forget all about the shower.

He stood up, and I quickly tugged down his underpants. His penis and balls leapt out at me – so big! I put my hand around the shaft, which was unbelievably hard, yet the tip was deliciously soft.

'Sexy as they are, I want you to take off your stockings and garter belt,' he commanded.

I obeyed him, and then grabbed his erection again and gently led him into the bathroom by it.

We turned on the shower, and when the water was the right temperature, we stepped into the tub and he began soaping me up. Our naked bodies pressed together as he put his arms around me and lathered my back, and then my ass, lingering over its soft, luscious curves. He washed my breasts for a long time, and the sweet tension returned to my pelvis; I wanted to make love so bad it hurt.

He started soaping my thighs, and pressed the slick hard bar of soap against my labia. The tightness was building inside me, branching out from my sex into my thighs, then back and up to my breasts. I pushed down against his hand as he worked the soap up to my clitoris, and then two fingers (or was it three) from his other hand slid easily up into my slippery hole. A pulse of hot pleasure shot through me with every thrust of his hand and my pelvis banged greedily against his firm palm.

I stayed on the edge so long I almost couldn't stand it; I wanted to come so much, and yet I also wanted to linger in the exhilaration gripping me as he lathered my clit and finger-fucked my pussy relentlessly. Then everything inside me seemed to let go at once, and I went limp from the force of the orgasm that ripped through me. Afterwards, I felt totally relaxed, all the tensions of the long trip flowing out of me with the rushing water. I think I would have collapsed if Bill hadn't stood up and held me against him.

And he wasn't finished with me yet. His fingers found my clitoris again, and satisfied as I was, I wanted to come again as he began stroking my quivering button. The pleasure welled up from my crotch in ever-tightening pulses, until a second, incredible orgasm swelled through me, leaving me utterly exhausted.

'Please,' I gasped, 'enough.'

'Okay,' he said, 'but now it's my turn.'

We traded places beneath the shower, and I soaped him up all over. When I tweaked his nipples, his penis went rigid and poked at my belly button. I took a long time washing his genitals, which felt gloriously heavy in my hands. I couldn't wait to get out of the shower and get him to bed. I dragged him out, and still dripping wet, we fell onto the mattress and made love again until I climaxed a third time, after which my clitoris was almost too sensitive to be touched. Bill came inside me – I could feel the hot pulses of sperm shooting out of his pulsing penis – and then collapsed by my side. Damp and drowsy, I drifted off in the afterglow of pleasure.

We both slept until we had to hurry and dress for the opening session of the Convention. I always thought you were supposed to take a shower after making love, but we had already showered. Bill's lips smelled faintly of my love juices as I kissed him. Would anyone else notice? I hoped so. Let them eat their hearts out!

7. Heather – The Cabana

I tilted my head up to the blazing sun, letting the balmy breeze waft my hair up away from the nape of my neck.

'Ah,' I sighed languidly as I lay back against the chaise lounge, two feet away from the sky-blue water of the Olympic-sized swimming pool. I reached for the large glass of icy soda by my side, and took a sip. This was the life – being married to Clinton Weber, president of a top hotel chain based in Miami. This was truly a fairy-tale life. Although I'm thirty-five-years-old and Clinton is sixty, we have a wonderful relationship. We had been married now for four years, and I was looking forward to many, many more years together. Sexually, however, we were incompatible; Clinton wasn't that interested in sex anymore, and I had to fight the impulse to do as all my rich friends were doing and have affairs. But I wouldn't do it, at least not yet...

'Excuse me,' said a deep male voice.

Startled, I nearly dropped my drink. Lowering my sunglasses, I peered over them into the face of the most handsome man I had ever laid eyes on. His skin was tanned a light gold, and his sun-streaked, sandy-blond hair looked so touchable my fingers instantly ached to caress it. His dark-blue eyes, with deep laugh-lines radiating from their corners, smiled at me. He could have been anywhere from twenty-five to my age. He was shirtless, and it was obvious he worked out because his muscles, though not too large, were clearly defined. He wore faded jeans that clung like a second skin to his slender hips and thighs. The man emanated sexuality, and it was definitely wafting my way.

'I didn't know anyone would be out here while I cleaned the pool,' he explained, eyeing my body, which was barely concealed by my skimpy black bikini.

'Well, you can just work around me,' I answered a bit testily. Who did he think he was, anyway?

He just stared at me blankly for a moment, and then moved on to begin cleaning the pool.

I settled back down in my lounger, but only on the outside. Inside, I was already hot with desire. I had not felt like this in quite some time. I opened my eyes behind my sunglasses and watched him. He was bending over, reaching for the sweep in the pool. I could see the whiteness of his skin where his jeans dipped down just above the sweet crevice of his gorgeous ass. I shuddered inwardly. I could feel lust beginning to dampen my bikini bottom. I squirmed a little against the lounge.

I had only closed my eyes for a moment it seemed when a shadow passed over me. Opening my eyes again, I was startled to once again find the pool man standing over me. 'What do you want?' I asked him a bit breathlessly.

'I just wondered if you could spare a glass of cold water,' he replied. 'I guess I could get it from the hose, but a glass with ice sure would be nice.' He let his eyes – those deep-blue eyes – roam boldly over my breasts and between my slightly spread legs.

'Yes, I suppose I could get you a glass of ice water,' I sighed. What was it with this man? How dared he stare at me as if I was naked? I rose to fulfill his request, and he reached out and grasped my sun-browned arm to steady me as I slipped into my high-heeled sandals. His touch felt like fire.

'I think maybe I should get your glass of water from the cabana… if you don't mind,' I said in a faint voice. Damn! Why was I acting this way? I should be in control. He was the hired help, after all.

He let go of my arm, and walked slowly behind me as I led the way to the cabana. My arm was still tingling where he had gripped me. I opened the door and we stepped inside the dark, cool building. The heavy drapes were pulled closed. The furnishings consisted of a large brass bar with four stools and a comfy sofa with a matching love seat.

I walked over to the bar to get a glass, but before I could reach it he grasped my arm again and turned me slowly to face him. Looking deep into my eyes, he bent to kiss me. He parted his lips and touched the tip of my tongue with his. Suddenly, I felt as though I had had two vodka nad tonics and not just soda.

When I did not protest, his kiss deepened boldly. 'I'm going to make love to you,' he whispered. One of his hands caressed my Lycra-covered mound, feeling for the dampness he must sense was there, probing with the tip of his finger and tracing the full outlines of my labia. We backed over to the sofa, and all the while his mouth was on mine and his hand was working my pussy.

I lay submissively down across the cushions and peeled off my bikini bottoms for him, flinging them aside carelessly. I spread my legs and let him gaze at my glistening sex. I held my breath waiting for him to touch me where I needed it most, but he just stared. Then at last he reached down and untied my top, sliding the delicate material away from my breasts and off my body.

'Turn over, honey,' he whispered.

I complied, feeling mysteriously weak from the intensity of the desire I was experiencing. I got up on my hands and knees, thrusting my ass up into the air towards him, and I moaned in delicious expectation as he began stroking my tender cheeks. And all the time I could feel his eyes feasting on the sight of my fat little pudenda visible between my wide-spread thighs. Then suddenly I felt a stiff, but tender probing at the exquisitely hot heart of my pussy, and knew he was making love to me with his tongue. I became almost delirious with pleasure as he lapped at my vulva from behind. By the time I heard him kick off his sandals and slide off his jeans, I wanted his cock inside me more than I had ever wanted anything in my life.

'Open your mouth, sweetie,' he said huskily, stepping around in front of me where I knelt doggie-style on the couch.

I stuck my tongue out and licked his head. The pre-cum on its tip tasted sweet, and I wanted more. Yet after a few minutes of sucking him noisily, like a starving animal, I knew I had to feel him inside me soon. He took my silent cue and stepped behind me again, forcefully gripping my hips. His beautiful cock plunged deep into my cunt with one driving stroke and filled me up like I'd never been filled up before. He dove into my pussy from behind over and over again, banging me like the slut I wanted to be for him, his fingers branded into my skin as he watched himself diving in and out of my tight wet hole.

'I'm going to come with you, baby!' he said fiercely, and began fucking me even harder, his erection pulsing bigger and thicker until I felt his cum drenching my cervix, a sensation that sent me careening into my own mind drowning climax...

'Heather, are you all right?' asked a familiar voice. 'Wake up.'

I opened my eyes. My husband was leaning over me where I lay face-down on the chaise lounge by the pool.

'Huh? What...?' I mumbled dazedly, rising up on my elbows.

'You were groaning,' he said, rubbing my slightly burned back with cool, soothing hands. 'I just got home from the club and came out to greet you.'

'I guess I was dreaming,' I replied, gazing around the empty pool grounds. It had seemed so real...

'Well, let's get inside before you burn.' He gathered up my towel and empty glass.

Once in the privacy of my bathroom, I stripped off my bikini. I felt sore, tender and very satisfied, yet it must have been a dream...

8. Nina – Student Teacher

Last week I turned forty, yet after a long, hard look in the mirror this morning, I still think I look pretty damn good. True, there are a few tiny wrinkles around my eyes and a couple of gray hairs, but so what? I'm a professor with tenure, and the house I bought in my thirties for a mere forty-six thousand dollars is now estimated to be worth six times that amount. But the best part about being forty is my sex drive; it's stronger than it ever was when I was in my twenties and thirties. I find myself turning around to stare when I see a good-looking male student on campus, and I even try to imagine what some of them are like in bed.

And there's this one particular student, Jeff, I find hard to get off my mind. He's in my Tuesday-Thursday Calculus Class and sits in the front row. When the semester first began, I thought of him as a 'nice young man', but then I began noticing how sexy his features were and how great he looked in tight jeans. A couple of times I even lost my train of thought during my lectures whenever our eyes met.

About two months ago, Jeff approached me after class. 'I'm having trouble understanding differential equations,' he said. 'Do you think you could give me some help?'

I couldn't believe my ears. Here's my chance, I thought. Still, I had a lesson plan I had to get done, so I replied briskly, 'I don't have time right now, but I can meet you later... let's say at around nine o'clock tonight at the Math Center, if that's good for you.'

'Nine o'clock is fine,' he replied, and smiled. 'Thanks.'

I had every intention of spending our time together tutoring him, and nothing more. But before I left to meet him, I dabbed some French perfume behind my ears and replaced my cotton briefs with satin bikini panties. I wasn't planning for anything to happen, but I wanted to be prepared, just in case.

Jeff met me promptly at nine o'clock. He was wearing a pair of snug-fitting jeans, as usual. The room was almost totally silent with the exception of two students talking softly in the back. The Center would be closing soon, but I had a key and could stay if I wanted to, and since Jeff needed help, I would not hesitate to use this privilege. After all, I didn't want him to flunk my class.

We sat down together at one of the front tables. I reached across him to grab a pencil, and my breast brushed against his chest. I was wearing a sweater, but the slightest contact with him was still enough to get me intensely aroused. I turned my head to see if the other two students were still there. They had left.

I gave Jeff a few problems for him to do on his own, and watched him, making helpful comments as he struggled to solve them.

'These are impossible!' he exclaimed with a laugh.

'Come on, now, Jeff,' I scolded him teasingly. 'Here, let me give you a little hint.'

He kept his eyes fixed on mine, and then moved his head closer just as I looked at him, so that our lips accidentally brushed in a soft kiss.

He drew back with an astonished look on his face. 'I'm sorry!' he gasped.

'It's okay,' I reassured him quietly. 'Please, come back here.'

He looked at me for a moment, and then we kissed again, this time deliberately. His tongue slowly parted my lips, and I caught my breath as a flood of desire hit me in the pit of my stomach. I longed for him to touch me; to slide his hands up the front of my sweater, to nibble on my neck, and I pushed my body urgently into his side. His big arms enveloped me as his hands caressed my back and his tongue probed my mouth.

'Stop for just a second,' I whispered as I got up and walked to the door of the room. I locked it with my personal key, and pulled down the shades over the narrow window. 'That's much better.' I smiled as I returned to my seat, and to his lips. My breasts ached, craving his attention so. At long last, he began to pull at my sweater, carefully lifting it up over my head. He slipped his hands into my silky bra, and trapped one of my nipples between his fingertips.

'So beautiful,' he whispered as he circled it, and another hot flash of desire ignited deep in my pussy. I moved back slightly so I could slip his T-shirt over his head, and marveled at his thick patch of chest hair. My vagina was hot and wet. I squirmed against him and drew my leg up across his leg, pressing my vulva against his thigh. I writhed into him, rubbing my wet sex hard against his leg.

After a few minutes of this, I slipped out of my chair and sank to my knees. Without wasting any time, I fumbled with the rest of his clothing, and then mine. When we were naked, I looked into his face, and then down at his crotch. What I saw made me moan with lust. His impressive penis was fully erect, and as I fondled, he groaned with satisfaction. Before I could protest (not that I wanted to) he pushed me gently to the floor, and at once his skilled fingers were sliding inside my slick hole. 'You're so wet,' he whispered in wonder.

I opened my legs wide, allowing him a better view of my sex.

'I want to please you so much,' he told me seriously, looking into my eyes. He replaced his fingers with his tongue, and as it rubbed against my clit, I let out a moan of pure pleasure. With every flick of his tongue a charge went through me, making everything inside of me exquisitely tight as I thrust my crotch up to meet his face. I had been on the edge for so long that the urge to come was overpowering, but I wanted to prolong this wonderful encounter. My body stiffened as I sought to contain my orgasm, but I just couldn't hold it back any longer… I moaned helplessly as I climaxed.

A sweetly triumphant look on his face, Jeff lifted himself up beside me. He kissed me softly, and I tweaked his nipples ever so gently. His still-erect penis was pressed hard against my leg. 'I've got to have you now,' he whispered against my neck as he spread himself on top of me and prepared to enter me. The weight of his body made me feel secure and warm, and my pussy was more than ready for him. He eased his thick erection inside me as I lifted my legs and wrapped them around his back so he could sink deep.

'Does that feel good?' he asked as he began moving, plunging into my hole with mounting passion, faster and harder.

All I could do was moan in response as I felt another orgasm cresting inside my pelvis. And just as I came, I felt his young hot spunk drenching my cervix.

He rolled over beside me and took me in his arms. We were both wonderfully drained, and all I could think of was how vibrant he had just made me feel. I would have loved to simply drift off to sleep in his arms, but I knew we had to leave the building before someone found us like that. I chuckled to myself.

'I never did get to go over differential equations with you,' I said.

'How about tomorrow night?' my clever student replied.

9. Kelly – A Big Favor

A small favor… before he's even opened his mouth, his eyes have let me know it's coming, one of Cliff's small favors. How can I refuse him, the way his eyes take on that mischievous gleam and he grabs at my belt loops and pulls me his way? He knows it all too well that I can't resist. And anyway, these frequent 'favors' of his can be a lot of fun. He may be an irrepressibly horny guy, sure, but I'm horny, too.

So there's this old friend of his in the living room at this very moment. I've barely met him, this poor friend. He's so lonely. Couldn't I just help, be of some assistance to the poor guy? 'He's got the hots for you, Kelly,' Cliff whispers, burrowing his fingers with athletic verve into the cheeks of my ass. Suddenly, I'm a bit less dry than I was just a moment before. 'Really hot!' he continues in his most enticing growl, giving my ass a sudden hard smack with his open hand, 'and I assure you, he's got the equipment. Brian may be in a slow spell right now, but,' he takes my lower lip in his teeth and murmurs, 'he's a champion, expert training, tried and true.'

In all his days, Cliff has probably never been turned down for anything. So how can I break his track record? Meanwhile, I've gotten so excited I can barely stand still. 'Of course,' I murmur. 'I'll go change into something a little more… shall we say, permissive?'

'You're just as debauched as I am,' he replies, spanking me again, this time approvingly, and of course he's right. Together we carry the sodas and chips back out to the living room, startling his witless and well-hung buddy.

'Kelly's going to go change,' Cliff announces, passing his fingers with tantalizing languor down my neck, over my shoulders, and across my nipples, which spring to attention.

'I won't be long,' I say, gazing into Brian's eyes with a look that sends a visible shiver down his spine. I head for the bedroom, aware of two pairs of hungry eyes devouring every swing of my hips.

I'm not too long in the bedroom; my fingers fly and my head reels with the possibilities. The underwear goes at once, nothing but thigh-high black fishnet stockings, nothing between my throbbing cunt and those two hunks but a sticky coating of lust. A gauzy camisole, easily removed, with a perfect view of my large breasts, and a tight black mini skirt slit so far up the side there won't be any secrets among us. Then I slip on gleaming black high-heels.

One last look in the mirror… five minutes and my whole ensemble should be scattered across the floor.

When I saunter back into the living room, Brian makes no attempt to hide the smile that races from one ear to the other. Especially when, with a wink at Cliff, I don't take the empty chair, but sidle up to Brian's, leaning one bent knee on the arm and offering him the gorgeous panorama of my pussy.

'So, Brian,' I say in my huskiest voice, 'what do you do for a living?'

He puts down his drink, clamps my offered thigh with both hands, and his fingers drift toward the pleasure zone. 'Who the hell cares?' he manages to breathe in reply, and I dive toward his lips and thrust my tongue between them. This is all the encouragement our bashful friend requires. I groan with desire as his fingers plunge deep into my cunt, tugging at my throbbing clitoris; furiously stroking it until it's dripping with juice. My head spins as we kiss each other like we're starving.

Abruptly, he removes his fingers and my heart skips a beat. He replaces them with his tongue, and I eagerly lap up the sweet hot milk that swathes his digits hoping that soon I can get my lips on his honey-tipped rod.

I feel Cliff behind me, his rock-hard bulge pressed into the small of my back as his hands deftly disrobe me. First my skirt, one short zipper at the side, and he flings it away, then two simple buttons on the camisole easily exposing my breasts. Brian licks the tips of my tits with confident and furious strokes, nibbling on my nipples with such teasing precision that I groan out loud. This is too much for any woman to endure.

'Come on,' I moan before I can stop myself, 'let's fuck!' and my fingers tug at his belt buckle.

'Slow down a little there, Kelly,' Brian drawls, pushing himself and me from the chair. Seeing him at his full height, his prick clearly outlined and stiff inside his jeans, and with Cliff standing behind me, nibbling on my neck and kneading my nipples with his fingers, I wonder if I can hold out much longer. Again I grope at Brian's belt, and with unsteady fingers ease the zipper down, tearing off his jeans and sinking to my knees to taste my lover's oldest friend's gorgeous glistening rod. Cliff keeps right in step with me, dropping to his knees behind me, the three of us panting with excitement. Reaching behind with one hand, I stroke and cradle every delicious contour of Cliff's hard dick, while with the other hand I get a good grip on Brian's erection. I caress the moist head, the warm shaft and cool balls, with my lips and ecstatic tongue, at the same time moaning with delight at the feel of Cliff's expert fingers working in my cunt. Doing a favor never felt so good and never tasted so sweet.

Brian gently pushes my head away. 'Okay, Kelly,' he says in a throaty whisper, 'I'm ready. Are you?' Without removing his burning gaze from mine, he carefully peels off the rest of his clothes and then stretches out on his back on the carpet, his muscles relaxed except for his glorious hard-on. I straddle him wearing only the stockings, my dagger-like heels ground firmly in the rug. I stare into his eyes and smile coyly, teasing.

'You know I'm ready,' I say, and my gaze moves down from his face to his cock. I can feel its heat. I give us both another moment's torturous delay, and then eagerly descend toward the prize, leaving Cliff's fingers to trail behind. Slowly, fighting the impulse to impale myself on him all at once, I ease myself down, taking only his head inside me before I ease back up, again and again parting the lips of my pussy with the tender tip of dick, savoring the sweet anticipation.

I sink a little deeper... my thighs begin to quiver with the effort of restraint. I massage his chest, and my thumb and forefingers toy with his nipples, inspiring him to grab a firm hold of my own stiff peaks and tug at them with a corkscrew twist. In a wave of delirious desire, I arch my back and thrust down hard, plunging and grinding until I feel the whole of my insides filled with him. At this very instant, as my mouth gasps wide with the shock of the pleasure, Cliff's familiar and tasty prick is in front of my face and I need no directions. I take the whole of Cliff's cock in my mouth, running my tongue hard against it. Falling into perfect synch with Brian and Cliff, I slowly ease back to the delectable head of each man, and then thrust again.

The three of us are groaning and sighing. I feel no boundaries, no limits to our combined ecstasy. When Cliff explodes inside my mouth, it's as if I just came; as if his cock and my tongue are the same; as if his come is my mouth's own nectar. Then Brian cries out loud, flooding my insides and encouraging me to scream as I climax with him.

***

Brian takes off the next morning. Back in the kitchen, dishrag in his hand, Cliff smiles his sweetest smile. 'Brian's a happy man again,' he tells me.

'I'm glad,' I say. 'He ought to be.'

'You looked like you were having fun yourself.'

'I had lots of fun,' I admit.

'So it wasn't such a big favor, then?'

'It wasn't a favor at all,' I assure him, returning his smile and meaning it. 'What are friends for?'

10. Mara — The Wild West

The sign read, *Thar ain't no place 'round this place like this place, so this must be the place. Twin Oaks Dude Ranch.* This dream vacation marked the end of two years of mourning for my husband, who had died painfully young of a massive heart attack. I was determined to enjoy myself in the old Wild West setting I had always dreamed of and forget the rat-race of the city, at least for a week, anyway. I checked into my own private little log cabin and unpacked.

***

The next morning I was up and ready early, or so I thought. I got to the stable yard just in time to grab the last horse for the breakfast-on-the-trail ride. It had been years since I had ridden, and being out of practice really showed as I clambered rather ungracefully into the saddle.

'Need some help?' a husky voice asked. It belonged to the handsome hunk of a cowboy holding my horse. From my lofty perch, I studied him for a moment. Tousled sandy hair barely showed from under the cowboy hat. Steel-gray eyes twinkled in the morning sun, and his wide grin was nearly blinding. I knew what he was thinking, 'Greenhorn' but I found myself wishing it was something else.

'Yes,' I answered, 'my stirrups are too long.' I knew perfectly well how to adjust them, but I couldn't resist the temptation to have him do it. And as he did so, his wide shoulders and arms rippled under the threadbare western shirt, making me long to rip open those pearl snaps.

'Is that okay?' he asked.

'Huh? Oh, yes, that's fine, thank you,' I replied. He walked away toward his own waiting horse and I admired his backside – small, tight, and muscular covered by faded jeans. He grabbed his saddle horn, and without the aid of the stirrups swung lightly onto his tall steed. Was he showing off for me?

Just then my horse started off of its own accord. The other riders were already down the trail, leaving us behind. I let the eager animal trot to catch up with them, and became painfully aware I had forgotten to put on my bra. I'm no small-chested woman, and my bouncing breasts did not escape the attention of the cowboy as he passed me at a gallop.

'Kick 'em!' he yelled.

I did, and we quickly caught up to the others. I slowed my mount to a walk, but the cowboy rode on ahead, leaving me last in line. The fresh air and lovely scenery were intoxicating, but my thoughts soon drifted back to the exquisite man in jeans, and before long I was far behind again. Then, just as we rounded the mountain, a rabbit suddenly jumped across the trail and startled my horse.

The next thing I knew I was on my back being shaken vigorously by the shoulders. Something was shading my face. Was it...? Yes, it was the cowboy. He favored me with that same broad smile, but his cool gray eyes weren't meeting mine – they were directed lower, and I realized my blouse had been ripped open, revealing my naked breasts.

'You all right?' he inquired, still smiling.

'I think so,' I muttered.

'Your horse took off for the barn, so you'll have to ride double with me. I'll take you back to your cabin,' he said, and I could have been a feather for all the effort this man made to pick me up and put me on his horse. Then, holding the saddle horn, he vaulted up behind me. As he did so, a strong arm brushed lightly against my bared breasts, and a small gasp escaped my lips as my nipples rose to attention.

'You married?' he whispered in my ear.

'Widowed,' I said, feeling a thrill begin between my legs. 'And you?'

'Divorced,' he answered, and we fell silent. The rocking motion of the horse made the saddle rub my pussy into an almost painful state of desire. Could I be mistaken, or was that an erection poking me in the back? His breath seemed to sound heavier in my ear.

'Nice tits....' his voice quivered.

I grasped one of his hands and placed it over one of my exposed breasts. His rough, callused index finger felt like a cat's tongue on my nipple, sending ripples of electricity through my body, and I moaned softly as his hot, moist lips buried themselves in the hollow of my neck.

We finally reached our destination, and leaving the horse to graze, he whisked me off the saddle, carried me into the cabin, and kicked the door shut behind us. I could wait no longer; the pearl snaps parted easily beneath my eager grasp, and his western shirt fell to the floor.

'My turn,' he said as he laid his hat on the bedside table. Deftly, he unbuttoned what was left of my blouse, and slowly pushed it off my shoulders, kissing and licking every inch of skin he revealed. He was driving me crazy with his mouth! My pussy ached to be filled by him, but still he lingered, lightly tracing circles around my aureoles with his tongue. I almost came from the anticipation as I dug my nails into his back.

After what seemed an eternity, he unzipped my pants and coaxed them, along with my panties, down over my hips, following their descent with his tongue. As the cowboy removed my boots, he kissed my feet, but then I stepped out of my pants and took charge. Bending over, I inhaled deeply and pressed my open lips against his jeans, which were stretched tight by an impressive erection. Then I straightened up and unbuckled his leather belt, fastened by a large silver buckle that read, *Champion Saddle Rider.* This was going to be a wild ride of a different sort! I whisked the belt through the loops and stared aggressively up into his expectant eyes. Holding the belt taut at both ends, I placed it across the beautiful bare chest before me, and pushed until he fell back across the bed. Without a moment's hesitation, I straddled his strong thighs and pulled his zipper down, my breasts swaying with the movement. At last his big cock was set free of its cloth prison, and my eyes went wide at the glorious sight. He lifted his hips off the bed so I could pull his jeans down to his knees. Then, still straddling him, I parted his legs just enough to gain access to the inside of his thighs, which I lovingly licked and kissed, working my way up toward his crotch. By the time I got there, he was practically begging for mercy. Gently, I drew his balls up just a little and licked them.

He moaned, 'Your tongue feels so good...'

I twirled it around the smooth purple head of his cock. I licked and sucked passionately on his dick. He was close to coming, but he wanted me to share his pleasure, so we moved into a 69 position. His tongue explored my pussy lips, and then he began slowly sucking at my swollen clit as his hands massaged my ass cheeks. I tasted his pre-cum as I ground my hips into his face, and our movements became frenzied. He let out a low moan just as his liquid burst forth, the waves of his ecstasy washing over my lips and into my mouth. I licked him dry like a hungry feline, and then we rested for a moment. His dick remained firm, and we were both ready for more. Yet I wanted to feel his hot mouth again, so I twisted my body around and placed my wet pussy above his face. He sucked my clit and darted a finger, then another one, into my slippery passage. Waves of delight crashed through my body and shook me like a rag doll.

Limp with pleasure, I rolled over onto my back and my lover repositioned himself above me. As the head of his penis penetrated me, my sex stretched open and a feeling of warmth spread through me. My back arched, and I wrapped my legs around his back to draw him in all the way down inside me. My nails dug into his rock-hard biceps as his crotch at last met mine, and he began beating his hips against mine in smooth, hard strokes.

My legs loosened their grip on the cowboy's waist as he began riding me, slowly at first but rapidly gaining momentum, until we were both at the wild, galloping brink of orgasm. Then suddenly he slowed his pace. Searching, his fingers explored my labia stretched wide around his erection until his thumb found my clitoris. I lifted my hips to meet his hand, and let my legs relax until my knees were close to my shoulders, enabling me to watch his dick sliding in and out. His thrusts built up tempo again, and he sustained the fast, driving rhythm, rubbing my clit with every penetration until we reached a crescendo of passion that spilled us both over the edge at the same time.

He collapsed into my arms and tenderly kissed my lips, holding me close. I ran my fingers through his silky hair, and gently nibbled his earlobe.

'The name's Kenny,' he said quietly. 'If there's anything I can do to make your stay here more enjoyable, just let me know.'

This was definitely going to be the best vacation I had ever had.

11. Sheila — Play It For Me

He didn't know I had arrived. He stood with his back to the door, facing the microphone. He was putting the record on the turntable when I slipped up behind him and gently blew in his ear.

He jumped, but then smiled when he saw it was me. 'It's about time you got here,' he said.

'Well, I had to wait until everyone left.'

'Hold on a minute…' He turned his back to me again and put on his headphones. He flipped the mike switch, and a red light glowed out in the hall. His voice was smooth, like French vanilla ice cream on a warm summer day. I closed my eyes and let the sound of it wash over me. Standing so close I could feel the heat from his body radiating towards me. The lines he spoke were unrehearsed and yet flowed as though he had said them a thousand times before. The words didn't matter; it was the way he said them. He could even make the weather forecast sound sexy.

The red light went out and he took off the headphones. Without saying another word he reached for me and our bodies molded together. Yes 'molded' was definitely the right word. As trite as it may sound, I really was putty in his hands. His lips began tracing delicate circles on the skin of my neck as his hands explored the curve of my back.

'Talk to me,' I whispered.

He laughed softly and said I was only dating him for his voice as he continued caressing any bare skin he could find with his lips and tongue.

'You're so talented,' I sighed. I couldn't wait any longer; I began to unbutton his shirt.

He leaned back and looked at me devilishly.

I reached his belly button and began stroking his chest lightly, taking great joy in running my fingertips through the soft hair covering his pectoral muscles before tracing the line of hair down to where it disappeared into the top of his jeans.

'Hey, you'd better hold it right there,' he warned. 'I still have thirty minutes left on the air.'

I smiled the special grin that means I'm intensely horny, and he laughed again deeply. He didn't know it yet, but he had just given me quite an idea. The song was ending. A commercial break was up next, so while he worked, I sat on a stool behind him and planned my attack. The sound of his voice was doing incredible things to my pussy.

He cued up a record and a slow rhythmic beat filled the studio. I recognized it immediately. What an excellent choice for what I had in mind! I wasted no time. The minute he swung himself away from the board and faced me again, I began tugging his shirt out of his pants. He tried to stop me, but I looked deeply into his eyes and kindled the fire I knew was smoldering inside him. He couldn't resist me anymore. Besides, I knew he would enjoy the adventure as much as I. I blew softly around his nipples, and felt them harden in response. His hands slid down my back and then up beneath my shirt. Even though we ran the risk of being caught, he tugged at my bra clasp, unhooking it with ease.

My chest heaved as his hands cradled my naked breasts, my tongue hungering to caress the line of hair leading down into his jeans. It was getting more and more difficult to remain seated on the stool as he worked his magic on me, and I strained to go lower. I reached for the snap at the top of his jeans, and he stopped what he was doing for a moment to grasp my hands.

'What if someone comes?' he asked.

'That's what I'm hoping for,' I replied playfully.

He smiled, and let go of my hands. As I unsnapped his jeans, and slowly pulled down the zipper, the song began to fade. He pulled away from me, and reached the control board just in time to cue up the next record. I had roughly four minutes, and then he'd have to go back on the air. He turned back towards me, and lowered his head to enjoy with his lips the full, heavy treasures his hands had been previously exploring. Low moans emanated from deep within me. What he was doing to me was exquisite torture, but there was no stopping him. His fingers had found the soft cleft between my legs and were massaging it through my jeans. He quickly undid my button-fly, and despite the fact that my pants were skintight, his talented fingers worked their way down between my mound and the clinging denim and into my panties, making me gasp in surprise.

'You're so wet,' he whispered. He began circling my clitoris with his talented fingertips, and we shifted positions a little so he could maneuver better. He slid two fingers up into my moist slit while he kept remorselessly stimulating my clit with his thumb. My sex was firmly cradled in his hand, and the divine pressure began building inside me. I could feel my labial lips blossoming and my clitoris growing hard as a seed ready to burst. My hips responded to the rhythm of his finger fucking as I eased my body up and down around his digits sliding in and out of my slick hole. It was incredible. I never wanted that record to end. My whole body grew tense and I blocked out the music, the studio, and the rest of the world, my juices flowing into his hand. He picked up the pace knowing I was close to climaxing. I arched towards him as ecstatic pulses flooded my pelvis and took my breath away. Afterwards, I leaned weakly against him, panting gratefully.

'Damn!' he cursed as the song began fading. He whirled around to the board, pulled the commercials he needed to run, cleared his throat, and flipped on the microphone. He announced the name of the songs he had just played, sounding only a little bit flustered.

He continued talking as I positioned myself in front of him. The pitch of his voice rose slightly as he realized what I had in mind. I lowered his jeans and underpants just enough to get to the center of his desire. He almost sighed as I released his cock from its confining quarters. Time was of the essence; I wanted him to lose control while the microphone was on and the whole city listened in unknowingly. My lips kissed his head, delicately at first and then with more urgency as I slid the full length of his erection into my warm, loving mouth. He closed his eyes as my tongue swirled around his rigid shaft and my hand massaged his tender balls. Finally, he cut to a commercial and turned off the mike.

'You're going to get me fired!' he gasped.

'Do you want me to stop?' I managed to mumble with my mouth full of his cock.

'Not on your life,' he whispered. He turned the mike back on after the commercial, and kept talking. I heard the erotic sounds I knew he was dying to make in every syllable he spoke. He announced who he was, and that his shift was almost over. He told the audience who was coming up next, and read a live promotion spot for an upcoming event. As he announced the time and the station call letters, he shook gently and moaned audibly. There was no explanation needed, at least not for me, but if you were listening that night, you might have wondered what happened as that song came on, the one that's now our song.

12. Kim – Private Get Together

I'm in the Army Reserves. You might wonder why I signed up in the first place. After all, the only sensual pleasures involved (and they are very limited ones at that) consist of masticating the lousy food and collapsing in a heap at the end of another sweaty day. But the army gives me both a sense of adventure and of belonging. Coming from a broken home, I grew up accustomed to change and always yearned for stability. Besides, I owe a lot to good old Uncle Sam, including my college education. If I hadn't joined up right after high school, who knows, I might still be slinging hash. That's what I did on weekends when I was a teenager. Slinging hash and wishing I was popular enough to get dates.

But that was then, and this is now. Being a military woman is part of my life. For two weeks every summer, my unit packs up and heads for some God-forsaken, tick-infested forest. I thought this year would be the same as any other, but I was wrong. The great outdoors lived up to its name, all right. I got enough insect bites to last me a long while, but I also met someone who knew how to scratch my itch.

There was this new guy in one of the other units that went into training with us. I like to see a guy in training, that way I get a sense of whether he has real stamina. I'm not interested in heavy combat, just one-on-one contact; the kind of action that definitely doesn't require a uniform. And I could see right away this guy had what it takes – skin so smooth it looked polished, and a well-developed chest I imagined myself climbing up or sliding down. Yes sir, this guy was getting under my skin.

We flirted for a week. I was a train dispatcher and he worked on the railroad. Sometimes I would watch him from the cabin as he hammered at the track. Sweat would trickle down his brow and then his chest, and finally disappear into his pants. He gleamed in the sun, his muscles flexing every time he let the hammer land. Sometimes, he'd catch me staring at him. He'd smile slyly and resume hammering. I'd turn away, embarrassed.

You can bet I made sure I stood in front of him in the chow line. I'd purposely stall so he would have to come up behind me, the bulge in his pants touching my buttocks, and ask me to please move forward. Oh, yeah, I thought, it would be fun to have him beg for it. I'd turn around and face him, lick my lips and answer snappily, 'Of course, soldier!'

As the days slogged by, our tolerance for this kid's stuff dwindled. We had to fulfill our mutual desire, so we made plans to meet in the mess tent after lights-out.

As I crept past my sleeping bunkmates, I started to worry he wouldn't be there, but I mustered up my courage and made it past the officers' tent to what we had jokingly designated the 'demilitarized zone.'

When I pulled back the flap of the mess tent, I saw his big chest, bare and waiting for me along with the rest of his beautifully toned body in skimpy khaki shorts. My heart pounded like a hammer as I sashayed over to him, taking my time. I stood directly in front of him, bold as brass, my nipples poking through my T-shirt. I was only there a second before he grabbed the back of my head and thrust his searching tongue into my mouth. At the same time he guided my hand to his fully erect cock.

Before long his large hands tunneled beneath my flimsy T-shirt. My breasts were aching for his touch and he knew it. He squeezed them playfully, rolled them around, and rubbed my nipples between his thumb and forefinger. Then he lifted my T-shirt so he could get a full view.

'You have a beautiful body,' he whispered. 'I wanted you from the first day I saw you.' Then, taking a gentle bite of a nipple, he added, 'You taste delicious, so sweet, good enough to eat!' By that time my pussy was wet beyond imagining. He sucked and licked my tits with a trained thoroughness I found thrilling. I pushed my crotch against one of his thighs, and almost bestial sounds emanated from his throat as I massaged his penis and balls. I kept at it steadily, knowing I would be fully rewarded for my work, breathless with anticipation.

He lifted me onto one of the picnic tables and proceeded to pull off my shorts. Seeing that I wasn't wearing any panties, he chuckled devilishly. I slapped his face in fun.

'I think you need to be restrained,' he said, giving me a little peck on the mouth that successfully distracted me while he snatched up my discarded T-shirt, and deftly used it to quickly tie my wrists behind my back.

'What are you doing?' I gasped, as if I didn't know, and didn't love losing the control I value so much in other parts of my life.

'Just relax and enjoy it,' he muttered. Kneeling before me, he began kissing and licking the insides of my thighs, teasing me with anticipation of feeling his lips and tongue on my cunt. It was all I could do to contain myself when his head finally made it between my legs. Obviously, skilled cunnilingus was part of his personal arsenal, and I succumbed willingly, totally. I felt like shoving his face into my crotch until he couldn't breathe, but obviously I couldn't since my hands were tied behind my back, which somehow made the pleasure even more intense.

After I climaxed helplessly into his arrogantly gratified mouth, I summoned my strength and wriggled my wrists free. I urged him back across the table, and promptly yanking his shorts down out of my way began returning his oral favors. He moaned, obviously pleased with my onslaught. Yet just as I was hitting my stride, he startled me by sitting up.

'I want you now!' he breathed. He pulled me onto the table with him, rolled on top of me, and with one sure stroke filled my cunt with his rampant cock. We writhed together, slowly at first, then he accelerated the pace and I grabbed his buttocks to push him even deeper inside me. His thrusts were so violent I wanted to scream in ecstasy and let the whole world know what I was feeling, but caught up in a frenzy of lust, I was still lucid enough to remember that was against regulations. I gripped his nipples with my mouth and sucked good and hard as his eyes flashed above my face with an animal-like intensity I had never seen before. He lifted my legs off the table, supporting my ankles on his powerful shoulders as he and plunged into me with ferocious virility. He felt my pussy tightening around him, and quickened his pace as we came explosively together.

'Basic training was never this much fun,' he gasped, collapsing on top of me.

13. Diedra – Snow Day

The morning was damp and cold, not a great day for getting out of bed and going to work.

Once I arrived at the office, my coworkers and I watched the snow falling. We were hoping to leave work early. Because I lived nearby, I had offered the use of my foldout couch to colleagues who lived farther away, but no one seemed too worried.

By three o'clock, however, six inches of snow had fallen and the highway patrol began closing some roads. That's when I got the interoffice call.

'Hi, it's Ken,' the male voice said. 'I think I'd like to take you up on your offer. Is that foldout couch still vacant?'

'No problem,' I replied. Ken was one of the most attractive men in the office. I'd always had a 'hands off' policy about male coworkers, yet it was snowing, and surely one night on my foldout couch wouldn't hurt...

A little later I went to Ken's office to ask if he'd be ready to leave early. I was getting nervous about driving in the snow, not to mention about having him as an overnight guest.

'I'm ready right now,' he said. 'Let's go.'

During the drive home, I found out he was intelligent and funny as well as handsome. We arrived too soon, and I was still feeling a bit shy as I unlocked my apartment.

'Make yourself comfortable,' I said as I walked into the kitchen and turned up the thermostat. 'The heat should kick in in a few minutes. Want some hot chocolate?'

'You bet.' His brown eyes were shining, and his cheeks were attractively flushed from the cold. He made me think of a little boy coming in after playing in the snow.

As I put water on to boil, I thought about the night yet to come. We had about seven more hours until bedtime, and I started thinking about how I could get Ken off my foldout couch and into my bedroom. As I was to discover, I wouldn't have to wait until dark...

I returned to the living room with the hot chocolate only to find the lights dimmed and the radio playing a low jazzy tune. Ken was sitting on the couch with his jacket lying beside him and his tie loosened. He looked very comfortable; the whole atmosphere had turned from cold and dreary to warm and cozy.

'Here,' I said, 'something hot for a cold day.' I handed him the warm mug, kicked off my shoes and sat down beside him. 'This is nice,' I added, watching the snow falling outside through the living-room window.

'Mm,' he agreed, and took my free hand in his, 'but you're nicer.' Then he took my mug from me, and set it down along with his on the coffee table in front of us. He cupped my face in his warm hands, caressing my cheeks with his thumbs before tracing the full outline of my lower lip. When I didn't protest, he rested his mouth over mine and kissed me gently.

I returned his kiss eagerly, and it deepened as his hands gently cupped my breasts through my cotton blouse. He alternated between stroking my nipples poking through the soft material with his thumbs, and squeezing them, making my pussy ache with excitement. With his left hand he unbuttoned my white blouse while his right hand expertly unhooked my bra.

'Nice,' he murmured in response to the lacy white cups. 'This is certainly a surprise. You just never know about your coworkers.' He kissed and bit my neck while continuing to tease my nipples with his thumbs. Finally he lowered his head to suck on them, squeezing and biting gently. 'We should both get out of our wet clothes,' he suggested.

I stood up. 'Come here,' I said, and led him into my bedroom.

I turned on my bedside lamp and it cast a soft glow around the room. Pulling him close, I kissed him again, running my hands up and down his back before hungrily cupping his firm buttocks. I ground my pelvis into his, and my arousal intensified as I felt his erection pressing against my belly. I ran my hand up the front of his trousers, unbuttoned them, and pulled them down, sinking to my knees before him. His penis was straining against his black briefs, and I kissed it through the damp cotton.

'I can't wait anymore,' he said as I stroked his cock through his briefs with the base of my palm. I had mercy and pulled them down, grasping his beautiful shaft with my left hand while gently cupping his scrotum with the other. I heard his breathing become uneven as I captured his balls in my mouth, and it wasn't long before I felt them tightening, but I didn't want him to come before I could feel his hot, hard dick in my pussy.

As if reading my mind, he pulled me back up to my feet and began stroking my pussy with his hand, testing with his fingers to see how wet I was. Determining that I was more than ready for him, he shoved me onto the bed, spread himself on top of me, and thrust his straining erection all the way inside my slick hole. He moved against me fast and hard, and I literally began seeing stars behind my closed eyelids as I gripped his penis with the walls of my sex, sucking him in deeper and deeper... until he was pumping his hips against me fast as he could. And just as I reached my peak I felt him explode with me, flooding my inner space with the hot white shooting stars of his cum.

'What a way to spend a winter afternoon,' I murmured sleepily a few hours later as together we sat wrapped in a blanket on the couch watching the snow fall silently outside.

'I think we need another snow day tomorrow,' he agreed, smiling as he kissed me.

14. Sally – Birthday Present

It's impossible not be distracted in the bar of Armond's, restaurant for the rich, famous and important. My aunt and I were meeting for lunch. I was waiting for her at the bar talking to a guy who must have dropped from heaven. He looked Nordic, with blue eyes and dusty blond hair. His clothes were well-cut and I could tell they concealed fluid, rippling muscles. Soon I was tongue-tied and edged away from him to find my aunt's reserved table.

'I see you met Sam,' my Aunt Flora said later. 'Isn't he exquisite?'

'He seemed to have a nice personality,' I responded demurely. 'He said he was meeting a client here.' I blushed, playing with my heavy silver fork.

Aunt Flora emitted a melodious, elegant stream of laughter. 'Client? I must remember that,' she declared, unfolding her napkin.

'What is he?' I asked, thinking of the possibilities. Lawyer? Stockbroker? Maybe an executive?

'About five hundred dollars a night,' Aunt Flora replied blithely.

'You mean…?'

'One of the finest.' She sipped her wine.

'Well, if you really want to know what I want for my birth-day…' I hinted casually. The mark of a truly elegant woman is her ability to both understand and ignore innuendo, so I suspected Aunt Flora caught my meaning even though she didn't appear to.

***

One night as I dusted off my phone, I thought about my aunt. Alone and lonely, I envied her; she always seemed to get what she wanted. She never seemed to worry about not having a good time. On the other hand, my important 'dates' were with books and exams. I could be found in libraries and laboratories dressed in Aunt Flora's hand-me-downs. I looked nice, but inspiring? Entrancing? I sighed as I sank into a chair with my heavy textbooks. Another fascinating night lay before me. Then the doorbell rang. I got up and opened the door a crack. Sam was standing out on the landing, and suddenly I couldn't seem to breathe.

'You must have the wrong address,' I said reluctantly, looking past the chain at him.

He was dressed for work in a silk suit. 'I'm sure I have the right place,' he insisted quietly. 'You are Sally, aren't you?'

I nodded.

'Your aunt sent me.'

'She hired you... to come here?' I stammered.

'Yes, to be with you.' He smiled.

I let him in. I felt nervous, but also excited. No matter what the circumstances were, he was a man I desired; my pussy was beginning to get warm and moist. Still, I couldn't hide my flustered shyness. 'This is definitely too weird for me,' I muttered.

'Why? Men have been doing this for thousands of years,' he countered suavely. 'Why should women be denied satisfying life's most fulfilling drive?' Already he was undressing me with his eyes.

A logical little voice was speaking inside my head cajolingly. 'Sophie, you have the worst record of short dates in history. This is a golden opportunity. This one is paid to stay.'

'This is a lovely room,' he remarked politely.

'Thank you,' I replied, patting the edge of my foldaway couch. 'Help me unfold this?' I requested.

'If I may suggest, I thought we could dance first.'

I blushed. 'Um, okay, I'll put on some music...' I chose a soft jazz CD at random, and tried not to hold myself too stiffly as he took me in his arms. His elegant suit made me feel even shabbier in my simple white cotton housedress. Yet as we danced, his hand slowly caressing my spine, I began to feel relaxed and beautiful and I almost forgot he was an actor performing a professional role. He was very skillful. He made me forget my books, my exams, and, most of all, the poor image I had of myself.

'I don't often date women as beautiful as you,' he said quietly. 'I don't often date, actually.'

'What do you mean, *date*? Isn't this more of a business relationship?'

'Oh, that's right, your aunt sent me…' He had an odd look on his face.

I kissed him to get things moving.

He pulled my dress up over my head and tossed it away. His hands were warm and felt wonderful as they caressed my breasts while I boldly unbuttoned his shirt, and then timidly stroked his naked chest. He really kissed me then, his tender tongue exploring my mouth as his hard arms pressed me against him.

I had always thought of my breasts as average, but he treated them with reverence. He kissed just the nipples first, and then nibbled them a moment before bringing his mouth down on as much flesh as possible, his tongue moving in a circular pattern that sent warm flashes of pleasure through my body. Then one of his hands caressed the moist warmth of my pussy through my cotton panties. I gasped as he sank to his knees before me, and pressed his face full against my vulva. I didn't resist as he slipped my panties down my legs, holding them open so I could step out of them. My legs were trembling as his lips found my clit, alternating between kissing it and tonguing the full length of my slit. I moaned in delight, feeling the need for more; I wanted all of his naked body touching and filling mine.

He stood up, grabbed some pillows off the couch, and tossed them onto the floor. 'Lay down,' he instructed, and I immediately did as he said, mesmerized by his confidence and beauty. I rested my head on the pillows and looked up at him as he slid out of his expensive suit. My breath caught at the sight of his perfect body, and when he knelt between my legs, I could hardly stand the anticipation.

'Close your eyes,' he said, and I whimpered in surprise as he suddenly wrapped a silky cloth around my head, plunging me into a darkness that mysteriously heightened all my other senses. 'Have you ever been blindfolded before?' he asked me quietly.

'No,' I replied faintly.

'Don't be frightened. This way you'll feel everything more intensely without worrying about how you look. All you'll know is what you're feeling. I want you to let yourself go for me, Sally.'

I gasped as I felt the tender head of his cock kiss my sex lips. I raised my hips to try and capture him, and it was true – not being able to see what was happening made the sensation of his erection sliding into me almost unbearably intense.

Our bodies moved together naturally, hungrily. I had never felt so turned on before; it was like a subtle fire was blazing through my flesh and burning away all my thoughts. As I lay blindly pinned beneath his straining muscles, a velvet cocoon of sensations surrounded me as a pure, deep pleasure massaged away all my tensions and insecurities. I climaxed in sweet, sharp bursts, the darkness behind my eyelids alive with the star-like flashes of my mental synapses.

My euphoria gradually ebbed like a tide, but he was still vigorously riding the waves of our pleasure between my thighs, diving in and out of me as though his life depended on it. Then his whole body tensed and I felt him achieve his own breathless release deep in my pussy.

Afterwards, he gently removed the blindfold and lay relaxed beside me. Our legs were still intertwined, rubbing together slowly, languidly, my head pillowed against the soft down of his chest. It wasn't like snuggling with my favorite giant teddy bear, this was much better. I had to remember to thank Aunt Flora for her gift. It was exactly what I had needed.

***

Two days later, I was having lunch with Aunt Flora again. 'Well, I certainly enjoyed your gift, darling aunt,' I told her. 'I only wish I hadn't had to return him.'

'Return him?' Her face, usually so composed, registered surprise. 'My dear, what on earth are you talking about?'

15. Chloe – Paradise

After working two jobs nonstop all year, I thought it was about time I took a vacation. My girlfriends and I had been planning this trip for months, and now it was finally happening. We had decided to spend a week in Cancun, Mexico to get away from the miserable, rainy, humid spring we were experiencing in Southampton, Long Island.

When Gabrielle, Ashley, Ally and I, finally arrived in Cancun after going through Customs and unpacking, our first order of business was to hit the beach. The powdery white sand and crystal-clear water were intoxicating. It seemed as though I had stepped into a dream. Not only was the atmosphere gorgeous, but so were the men. There were quite a few beautiful, bronzed male bodies on the beach that day.

I applied a liberal amount of sunscreen and settled into my beach chair. Then I saw him. He was about six-foot-three and built like a Greek god with perfect muscle definition. His long dark hair looked soft and sexy as it blew back from his sculptured face and down over his broad shoulders in the gentle breeze. His ultramarine-blue eyes, with long, dark eyelashes, were looking right at me, and he was heading in my direction! I suddenly became acutely aware of how fish-belly white I was compared to his golden bronzed physique. I immediately became quite flustered and broke his enchanting gaze, bending my head to sip my Tequila Sunrise. I thought he had walked right by me, but then I felt his large, warm hand come to rest on my shoulder as he knelt beside my chair.

'Is it your first day here?' he asked, smiling.

'Isn't it obvious?' I held up my pale arm next to his bronzed one.

As our conversation continued, I learned his name was Zack and that he was a local nightclub owner. As he talked, I began to notice a tingling sensation spreading throughout my body, and it seemed to be drawing us together almost magnetically. I wanted to press my naked body against his smooth, oiled skin and probe my tongue between his lips...

'Want to go to a private party at my club?' he asked. 'It's called Blue Thunder.'

I told him my friends and I would have to discuss our plans and that if everyone agreed, we would stop by later that evening.

As he got up to leave, he ran his palm down the length of my arm, and pulled my hand up to his warm lips. 'I hope I see you tonight,' he said.

***

As it turned out, our plans for the evening did not include going to Blue Thunder. The girls and I decided to go out to dinner at the hotel's nightclub-restaurant, and ended up staying there for the rest of the evening. We had met a group of nice-looking men who kept us on the dance floor all night. Gabrielle, Ashley, and Ally seemed to be enjoying themselves thoroughly, but my thoughts kept wandering to Zack. When the club closed at four a.m., they headed back to our hotel room. I told the girls to go ahead without me. I said I just wanted to take a short walk.

My walk led me right past Blue Thunder, but all the lights were out. I turned around and started walking down the moonlit beach back toward my hotel, and then I sensed someone walking behind me. My first instinct was to run, but instead I froze in place, my nipples erect with fear. Before I knew it, strong arms engulfed my body and turned me around. I came face-to- face with Zack.

'Better late than never,' he said, holding me so tightly against his solid body I could feel his penis stiffening through his lightweight trousers. He wasn't wearing shoes or a shirt, and his long hair rested lightly on his shoulders. I could feel my pussy begin to juice in anticipation as he kissed me passionately on my neck, face and mouth while I ran my fingers through his silky hair. Before I knew it, I had pulled him down onto the sand. Talk about being overwhelmed by passion! I had absolutely no desire to control myself.

I began kissing his neck and his chest, moaning feverishly, and he let me indulge myself before rolling me over onto my back in the cool sand. He began peeling off my clothes and kissing my exposed flesh with a hot, eager mouth. I caressed his hard cock through his pants, the heat of lust deepening between my thighs. I eagerly pulled off his slacks and let my fingers wander through his soft pubic hair to his thick shaft and down to his heavy balls. He sat up, taking a long look at my naked body in the moonlight before he began planting hot kisses on my neck, breasts, and stomach. Everything – the moonlight, the sound of the waves, and his hard body on mine – was making the night a fantasy come true.

When his mouth finally reached my moist sex, I thought I would come immediately. He ran his tongue around my clitoris in small teasing circles, slowly and skillfully bringing me to a tremendous orgasm that seemed to last forever; returning in fresh new waves every time his tongue darted around my throbbing knob. After that I thought all energy would be drained from my body, but I was wrong. Before I knew it I was ready for more, and I almost literally pounced on him. I turned him over and slowly began rubbing my naked body up and down against his hardness. Then I quickly mounted his erection and began riding him wildly. He grabbed my ass and pulled me tighter against him, and I slowed down as his moans deepened. But just as I thought he was going to come, he rolled me over onto my back again. A second orgasm rose swiftly inside me as I dug my nails into his ass while he drove himself into my pussy with the stamina of an athlete. As the white-hot ecstasy seared my flesh, he reached beneath me and cupped my buttocks in his hands and we bucked together in the throes of a simultaneous climax.

He brushed the hair from my face with the back of his hand as we lay on the sand enjoying the cool ocean breeze caressing our perspiring bodies.

'Ready for a swim?' he asked me finally.

I smiled back at him, but before I could reply, he swept me up into his arms and carried me toward the ocean. He put me down at the water's edge, and the waves rolled in gently around our ankles. We stood there a moment watching the beginning of the sunrise on the horizon, and I knew this was going to be the best vacation ever.

16. Patricia — Omnivore

I've always hated grocery shopping, but it was worse now that I was only cooking for one. Widowed at thirty-three after thirteen years of marriage, I had made plenty of adjustments to a new lifestyle. The only things that remained were grocery shopping and carrying out the garbage on Wednesdays.

Lost in thought in the frozen food section (did I want to nuke a microwave dinner or just fix a salad?) I jumped when I felt a hand on my shoulder.

'Mrs. P, is that you?' a deep voice asked.

I turned and looked up into the hazel eyes of a tall, red-headed man. He was smiling as if he knew me, and since all of my journalism students had called me Mrs. P from the first day I started teaching, I knew this hunk had to be a former student. 'You have the advantage,' I said. 'I know you must be one of my students, but I don't remember who.'

'Oh, sorry, I'm Greg. Greg Johnson, class of '95. I was one of the co-editors of the yearbook.'

'Oh, sure, Greg, I remember you, though I didn't recognize you. You look fantastic! What are you doing now?'

'I work in public relations,' he replied, his eyes staring deeply into mine. 'You really inspired me to go into the field, Mrs. P. I've always wanted to thank you.'

I reached out and touched his arm, and felt a charge go through my hand all the way down to my pussy. 'Well, Greg, I'm just glad I could be there to get you started. You always were a talented young man.' Did he feel that electricity between us or was it all in my sex-starved mind?

'You know, Mrs. P., I would have recognized you anywhere. You're still as good-looking as I remember you. God, I had such a crush on you!' He chuckled deep in his throat. 'I used to make up excuses to stay after school and spend a few extra minutes alone with you.' He bent over and whispered in my ear, his lips grazing my hair, 'And you're even sexier now than I remember.' He grasped my elbow, and began pushing my cart along with me down the frozen food aisle. 'So what of Mr. P?' he went on. 'You're apparently only cooking for one now, judging by your cart here.'

'My husband died two years ago, Greg,' I informed him in my best lecture voice. 'Before you start asking questions, I'll answer them.' And I went into the speech I had repeated a million times in the last two years.

When I finished he said, 'Can I ask you something, teacher?' He bent his tall frame and whispered in my ear again, 'Have you ever made love with one of your students?' Before I could answer, he began pushing the cart again. 'Shall we go through the express line?'

I didn't say anything.

The six-block walk to my home seemed endless. Under the brown bag of groceries he carried in his arms, I could see the bulge in his crotch. My hands shook as I opened the door. He set the bag down on the kitchen counter, then wrapped his arms around me and lightly brushed my lips with his. I tried driving my tongue between his teeth, but he pulled back and whispered, 'Patience, patience, teacher, we've got all night. You need some romance.'

'Just who's the teacher here?' I asked breathlessly.

'Quiet,' he urged as he slowly kissed every inch of my face and neck.

I led him into my bedroom. We sat together on the edge of the bed, and I tried to push him down, kissing him desperately.

'Patience, patience…' He continued his slow exploration of my neck with his mouth, gradually moving down into my cleavage. I groaned, and a rush of desire dampened my panties. But when I tried to unbutton his shirt, he pulled my hands away. 'You've got beautiful breasts,' he said.

He slid his hand up my skirt. 'My, you're a wet little thing,' he murmured feeling my moist panties. He unhooked my bra, and pushed my sweater up around my neck, burying his face between my breasts. Then he sucked one of my nipples like a newborn baby, roughly fingering my hot sex through the wet cotton.

'Recess is over, young man,' I declared, pulling him to his feet. He moaned as I reached down and unbuckled his belt, unzipping his fly and releasing his rigid cock. 'It's time to pay attention to what the teacher is doing.' I had us both naked in a matter of seconds. He shivered when I massaged my tits against his firm belly as my mouth moved down to his crotch. My tongue flicked teasingly in and out of his belly button, and then I slid my lips past his penis to nibble on his inner thigh.

He growled and tried to grab for my face.

'No,' I said in a stern voice. 'The first thing you have to learn is that the teacher is in change. Now I'm giving *you* a lesson in patience.'

'Yes, ma'am,' he said obligingly.

Yet I found I couldn't resist him for long, and he groaned with pleasure as I sucked on the head of his hard-on. I slowly slid more of him into my mouth, feasting on the taste of his pleasure. Then I abandoned his cock for a moment to greedily tongue his tender scrotum. I took first one, then the other heavy sack into my mouth as he groaned again. I licked the tender area between his balls, then slid up his body and rubbed his erection between my heavy breasts.

'Good boy,' I cooed. 'Now it's time to take your final. Show the teacher what you've learned.'

He pulled me to my feet, shoved me onto my back across the bed, and lifting my legs up around his chest plunged his erection into my welcoming pussy.

I gasped beneath his violent thrusts, and almost at once an orgasm overwhelmed me.

'You're so tight!' he gasped. 'You're going to make me come in seconds!' He drove his cock as hard and as deep as he could into my grateful cunt, banging me with all the glorious energy of youth as orgasm after orgasm blinded me. God, it had been so long! Then I felt his hot sperm drenching my cervix and I climaxed again right along with him. Afterwards, I felt young and alive for the first time in years.

'Well, teacher, do I pass?'

I looked up into his bright eyes and smiled. 'You've shown a great deal of improvement in your work, Greg, a fine effort, but I think some private tutoring is in order. Shall we say three times a week to begin with?'

17. Sophia — The Bass Player

There's nothing unusual about my sex life except that I don't have one. You've heard of common-law marriage, right? After seven months of celibacy, I felt I could qualify as a common-law virgin. It was one of those sexual slumps that not even shopping could alleviate. But I sweated it out, and finally got my reward.

I knew the moment I saw him that I was going to have him. I met him at a bar. My roommate and I decided to go out one night to visit a few bars, drink, dance, and attract as many available men as possible. We were decked out to the hilt, and we hit all our favorite nightspots. One of the best things about one particular bar is the live band and the variety of men who grace the stage. On this particular night, Ron was playing bass, larger than life and strumming his way into my fantasies.

The man was gorgeous. Dark hair, dark skin, and sensuous features accented by a black tank-top, a red jacket, and black boots beneath bulge-hugging black Spandex pants. I could feel my juices begin to flow just looking at him and hearing him play. Then our eyes met.

He looked out across the crowd almost as if he could feel my eyes scorching his lithe frame. Our eyes locked. Hastily, I lowered mine, feeling shy, nervous, and incredibly aroused all at once. Brushing a hand over my taut breasts, I tried to soothe the ache this man was creating in me. Then I looked up again. His tongue was running over his lips as he followed my hand's movement across my breasts. Again our eyes met, now with complete understanding and raw, burning desire.

My heart leapt into my throat as the band took a break. Trying to look blasé, I engaged in casual conversation with my roommate. As much as I was hoping for the contact, I jumped in surprise as I felt a warm hand on my back and a deep voice inquire, 'Can I buy you ladies a drink?'

I turned, and felt the full force of his masculinity up close. He was overwhelming. The smell of warm, vibrant, musky man infiltrated my brain even as it busily took inventory – gorgeous chest, lean legs yet well muscled, and his tight pants showed he was well formed as well as generously endowed. Dizzily, my eyes met his. They were alight with amusement. My cheeks turned red as I realized that while I had been taking 'inventory' the pleasantries of normal introductory conversation had continued without me.

His hazel eyes twinkled. 'So, Sophia, what do you do?'

'I'm a… bank teller,' I stumbled over my words. 'I'm sorry, I didn't catch your name,' I lied.

'Ron,' he said as he shook my hand.

'Oh,' I muttered inanely, totally bewitched by him.

We talked for a few minutes, and then he left to finish the last set of the evening.

After dancing a few times, I stepped outside to get some relief from the smoky bar. I heard the band finish, and let my mind drift to Ron. I was hoping to see him before I left. In the next instant, I felt warm arms wrap around my waist, and lips caressed my neck as a voice murmured, 'Hi, Sophia.'

My body shivered in uninhibited response as my buttocks snuggled back against his hardening sex. His hands came up to fondle my breasts, and he pulled me in tighter against him.

I turned in his arms, and molded myself to his body.

Without hesitation, Ron tilted my chin up and kissed me. Sinuously, our tongues entwined, dancing and retreating in one of the most sensual kisses I had ever experienced. It made me think of warm bodies, secret wet places, and hard-driving sex.

His lips trailed down my throat. 'Oh, God,' he moaned against my damp flesh. 'Please come back to my hotel with me. It'll be so good! No, it'll be fucking fantastic.'

Wordlessly, I nodded, and went back inside the bar to tell my roommate I wouldn't be going home with her. Then Ron and I hopped into a taxi and drove to his hotel. The ride there was most enjoyable as he caressed the tops of my stockings and my silky garters beneath my mini-skirt.

'I love women who wear garters,' he whispered as his index finger slipped past my panties and fingered my wet labia. I stifled a moan of ecstasy as I buried my face in his warm neck. Playfully, he rubbed my clit, and then slipped two fingers into my yielding sex, giving my juicing walls something to grab onto. I bit his neck, and desperate to get some of my own I reached down for his groin. He moaned as I caressed his penis through the sleek material.

The minute the door to his suite closed behind us, our lips were locked, fingers fumbling and clothes flying left and right until at last we were lying naked on the bed.

'You feel so good, so warm,' I moaned as I caressed his powerful chest. Between my legs I could feel the head of his cock nestled at the entrance to my pussy, probing gently. My mouth opened to admit his tongue as my hand went down to guide his erection inside me. 'Fuck me!' I begged.

'Ride me,' he commanded, his hands gripping my hips, and in perfect unison we thrust against each other. His strong bass player's fingers dug into my buttocks, alternately squeezing and stroking me.

'I'm going to come!' I gasped. The minute the words were out of my mouth, he jerked us up into a sitting position and clamped his mouth down around one of my nipples as I straddled him. His cock was almost painfully deep inside me now, and I could feel his body straining, trying to get even deeper inside me even as the ecstatic clenching of my pussy made him climax with me. He savagely bit my nipple as a grunt of satisfaction escaped him, and I could feel his prick pulsing inside me as his cum filled me. Then we collapsed into each other's arms with mutual sighs of satisfaction.

'Wonderful,' he murmured.

'Definitely deserves an encore,' I agreed.

18. Margaret — Choreography

The studio was almost dark; only one dim bulb cast an intimate glow on the mirrored walls. Jack and I had been working for several hours on the *pas de deux* I was creating as the climax of my new dance piece set to Ravel's *Bolero*. I had dismissed the rest of my company so I could work alone with Jack. Ironing out the intricate choreography I envisioned was a slow and tedious process; I didn't want everyone waiting around watching me think. The subdued lighting was for effect, but Jack and I did not have to imagine the steamy heat we were trying to create. At 9:45 p.m., it was still a sultry eighty degrees.

Let me back up a bit… I'm a choreographer with my own company, which until the beginning of last year was entirely female. This was not by choice. Good male dancers are rare in my part of the country and therefore in great demand. When Jack first walked into my studio in response to my ad, I knew he was perfect for the job. Now if he could only dance, I thought. At about six feet, Jack is solidly built in a way that is particular to dancers, with long legs that can do wonders. Although he embodies a wonderful mix of boyish charm and sudden, intense sexiness, I had been careful to keep the relationship strictly professional. That doesn't mean I hadn't imagined what he would be like in bed, but Jack's respect for my work, and the easy friendship that had developed between us, made me reluctant to do anything to disturb our rapport. At times, this proved to be very difficult. The other night, it proved impossible…

There was something different in the way he held me that night. He looked at me with clear blue eyes that made me hot in a way I couldn't resist. I tried to ignore it, focusing on the fact that I had no idea where I wanted this dance piece to go. Finally, with a cry of frustration, I broke away from him and moved to my sound system to turn off the tape.

'Maybe we should just call it quits for tonight,' I suggested, noting the small trickles of sweat running down his bare chest and disappearing into his loose cotton pants.

There was that look again, and though subtle, it made me fully aware of the skimpiness of my attire. To beat the heat, I had put on a close-fitting half top that clung to my breasts and a pair of dance trunks, omitting the tights.

Jack wasn't ready to quit. 'I've got an idea,' he said. 'Why don't we put the music on and just start improvising. Maybe we'll get nothing, but on the other hand, it could lead to something good.'

I had nothing to lose but time, so I rewound the tape deck.

'Wait!' he said as I was about to start the music, 'I'll be right back.' He headed for the bathroom. When he returned, I noticed he had rolled up the waistband of his pants a few times, which accentuated his crotch. For the hundredth time, I pictured what this beautiful man would look like naked, and a shiver ran through me like an ice cube caressing my skin.

'I'm ready now,' he said, and I switched on the music. I turned to him and we began circling each other, the fluidity of the music lifting me up to another plane. His hand reached out to me as I turned, and gradually our bodies were pressed together. We had practiced this part many times before, and this was the point from which I could not seem to continue. I snuggled myself into him, groin against groin. When I did, I realized he had removed his dance belt and was naked beneath his thin pants. The feel of his cock rubbing against me took me by surprise, making me falter for a moment. Then I glanced at his face and that look was there again. He turned me around abruptly and stood behind me so we were both facing the mirror. A slow smile spread across my face as his hand skimmed over my breasts, across my taut stomach, and down to my crotch, where it stopped and cradled my pussy as our hips gently swayed to the pulsing rhythm of the erotic music.

I ran my fingertips lightly down his forearm to where his fingers were gently rubbing my clitoris through the fabric of my dance trunks. Taking his hand, I slowly brought it up to my waist and guided it inside the elastic to where I could finally feel his flesh on mine. We continued gazing at each other in the mirror, our rhythm never missing a beat even as I moaned in response to the wondrous sensations coursing through my body. Reaching behind me, my hands found his slim hips. I pressed him against my buttocks and began rocking my pelvis back and forth. I could feel his cock growing and hardening against me, and his quickening breath told me he was enjoying my choreography.

With my hands still on his hips, I started pulling gently on his pants, bringing them with me as I sank to my knees. Still watching his face in the mirror, I saw him close his eyes as the soft material made its way over his swollen cock, replaced by the sensation of my hair brushing over and around him. I sensed he was on the brink of losing control as he followed me down to his knees, turning me so we were facing each other. We stared at each other. There seemed to be a dome of electricity surrounding us; binding our minds and bodies together as he slowly peeled off my dance uniform.

We remained naked on our knees as if in prayer, each basking in the beauty of the other. The music had ended. There was no sound now except for our quiet breathing. I slowly spread myself back across the wooden floor, bringing my arms up over my head. I brought my knees up to face the ceiling, and spread them ever so slightly in an invitation, my tongue passing over my dry lips in anticipation as he penetrated me with just the tip of his erection.

'Now,' I said, and pushed my hips up to meet his downward thrust. We kept our rhythm slow and steady at first. He was watching me with such intensity I felt as if he were studying my heart as well as my body. Our union gradually became more urgent, our erotic dance falling into a harder, faster tempo, filling my mind; blotting out everything except for the pleasure of the intense friction between us making its way up from my sex to possess my entire being. But it felt so good to have him inside me after wanting him for so long that I wanted it to last forever, so I forced myself to slow down.

'Not so fast,' I whispered. 'We have all the time in the world.'

'I can't help myself,' he confessed, but complied with my request.

I closed my eyes and concentrated on the feel of his erection sliding slowly in and out of my slick hole. And as we moved in unison, the heat of our bodies made us glossy with perspiration. I kissed his neck and tasted his saltiness with pleasure.

'It feels so good!' I sighed. 'I don't want to stop, not ever...' I was so excited I suddenly wanted to be on top. I pushed him off me and squatted over him, slowly impaling myself on him. I gasped from the incredible sensation of being completely filled and lost control as I swiftly raised and lowered myself over his thick hard-on.

And he was apparently enjoying it as much as I was; his eyes were squeezed shut, and through gritted teeth he muttered, 'Don't stop. God, don't stop!'

I had no intention of stopping until we both came together. Already I could feel my orgasm building, and I knew it was going to be one of the best I'd ever had. I whispered, 'Give it to me! I want it!' and watched him as he climaxed. He looked so beautiful that I cried out as well, my body overloaded with pleasure.

After a few moments during which we lay side-by-side catching our breath, Jack pushed himself up just enough to look at my face. 'I've wanted to do that for a long time,' he confessed. 'Are you sorry it happened?'

'If that's your idea of improvisation,' I smiled as I brought his face down towards mine, 'this *pas de deux* could be a long time in the making.'

19. Leslie – Career Move

It had been six years since I'd seen Carl. My high school fantasy man, Carl had run cross-country and been on the Academic Decathlon in his senior year. In other words, not only did he possess the brilliance of a top engineer, he also had the best ass in my home town. I recall sitting behind him in class and dreaming of how wonderful it would be to be with him; to be a part of his life. I'd become flushed with warmth and hoped no one would notice, especially Carl. Back then I would have died from embarrassment.

Since high school, I had moved to a new town, completed college, and lived two years of life as an accomplished businesswoman. I'd had several lovers, some of them very good, who initiated me into womanhood. They taught me how to enjoy my body and how to enjoy sex, something I had never been able to do before. They left me an experienced and sensuous creature. Yet something had always seemed to be missing, and I just couldn't put my finger on it.

After working at a business near my college for two years, I decided I needed a change of scenery. A colleague told me about an opening at a well-established company near my home town, and I applied. The executives jumped at the chance to inject some new blood into the company and hired me almost immediately. Excited, I packed my things and moved back home.

One day I was shopping at the local grocery store, casually picking out a grapefruit in the produce section. Out of the corner of my eye I caught sight of a lean, tan body near the apple display. My heart leapt into my throat as I realized I was looking directly at Carl. He was different, yet he'd only changed for the better. His strong, corded arms moved easily as he picked out some apples. Running shorts clung scantily to his sun-darkened thighs, making my pussy tighten and juice just at the sight. His legs were incredible in their muscled splendor, veins and tendons running down to his well-worn running shoes. Gone was the awkwardness of youth. Having passed through adolescence, Carl was now a man. And what a man! For an instant, our eyes met, then breaking the gaze he slowly looked me up and down, and I could not prevent a deep blush from spreading over my cheeks.

'Don't I know you?' he asked. 'Oh, man, I know that sounds corny, but I'm sure I know you…' he stammered.

'Um, we went to high school together. I'm Leslie. Does that sound familiar?'

'Leslie from Economics class? Oh, my God, I can't believe it.'

We talked about high school for a few minutes. 'Would you like to have dinner with me, Leslie? I mean, we could go over old times and stuff.'

'Well, I really have to get my new apartment in order. I only moved in two days ago and I'm getting sick of living out of boxes,' I replied, not wanting to appear too eager.

'Please, let me help. I'll bring over Chinese.'

'Well…'

'Please don't refuse, Leslie.'

'Okay. The address is Twelve State Street. Six o'clock. And I love shrimp fried rice.' Smiling demurely, I sauntered off to the frozen food section feeling his eyes on me the whole time.

***

Somehow, I made it to six o'clock. Dressed in a 'little black dress' I waited eagerly, knowing Carl would be on time. At exactly 6:01, the bell rang.

'Come in,' I said, any other conversation choked from my throat as I looked at him. He was dressed in a tight black turtleneck and black jeans. I had to restrain myself from touching his broad shoulders as he shrugged off his coat after handing me a large bag of takeout Chinese and a bottle of wine.

'You look great, Leslie,' he said earnestly, 'but that's not much of an outfit for unpacking.'

I gave him what I thought was a knowing look. Little did he know I didn't plan on doing any unpacking that evening.

As he looked around him, he seemed surprised. 'The place looks great even with boxes. Could I have a tour?'

'Well, okay, but promise you'll keep in mind it's still in the process of transformation.'

'I promise,' he said as he winked at me.

I deposited the food and wine on my small dining room table and quickly led him through my small yet cozy apartment. Pure adrenaline coursed through my veins in sweet anticipation. I was having dinner with Carl, and hopefully dessert, too!

Dinner went by slowly, too slowly for me. After only a few egg rolls, I decided I just couldn't wait any longer. I had to make a move if he wasn't going to. 'Carl, I think we've had enough food for now. I'm ready for a more filling meal.' I stood up and leaned across the table towards him, looking directly into his eyes as I reached my hand out to his.

He grasped it. His palm was sweaty. 'Leslie, I...'

'Don't say another word unless you want me to stop,' I whispered.

'No, God no, it's just that, well, I can't believe it. You were such a kid in high school.'

'That was the past. Let's concentrate on tonight.'

I led him into the bedroom. We fumbled at each other's clothing like inexperienced teenagers, making things even more exciting. Finally, we stood before each other naked. He pulled my body towards his as I slowly caressed his shoulders, enjoying their broad firmness, and my pulse quickened as I felt the hardness of his cock prodding my belly. My juices began trickling down my inner thighs I was so aroused as he wrapped his powerful arms around me, crushing my breasts against his smooth chest. His warm, insistent tongue explored my mouth as he ran his strong hands up and down my back, making me want to melt into him. Then he suddenly knelt, parted my pussy lips with his fingers, and brushed my clitoris ever so softly with the tip of his tongue. Gradually he probed deeper and deeper, skillfully teasing me into ecstasy.

Suddenly, I felt an intense need to feel his cock inside me. Urging him back up, I grasped his hard-on with a gentle yet insistent hand. 'I want you inside me,' I whispered in his ear. 'Make love to me!'

He swept me off my feet and spread me tenderly across the bed. Grasping his hips, I pulled him down on top of me, and gasped as his thick long cock slowly, ever so slowly, filled me up. He fucked me with deep, luxurious strokes, penetrating to my very depths, and I moved with him in exquisite rhythm... gradually moving faster and faster, working my vaginal muscles and massaging his hard-on until both of us reached the peak of pleasure together and he ejaculated violently inside me, shooting his hot cum into my cunt as an orgasm ripped through me that felt breathtakingly endless.

We clung to each other, spent and content as I breathed in his delicious scent. Basking in the afterglow, I realized that Carl, my high school fantasy man, was all I had imagined he would be. Talk about a high school reunion.

20. Marin — Home Run

I joined the company softball team, a coed group, half men and half women, for two reasons. First, it was a good way to stay in shape. I have a great body, but I have to work hard to keep it that way. Second, it seemed to me a great way to meet sexy guys. And, believe me, there were plenty of them there on the mound.

Ironically, it wasn't any of the players who attracted me as much as the coach of the team. Hank, in his early forties, worked out every day, so he had no hint of a middle-age bulge. He was lean and muscular, and he moved with the supple grace of a panther. When he hit the softball, the muscles in his upper back and shoulders rippled, and when he ran the bases, the muscles in his thighs stood out. He had black hair, the kind that shows highlights of blue, gray eyes and a firm mouth.

I didn't realize he had even noticed me until he asked me last week if I'd like to stay after practice. 'Maybe I can help you with your swing,' he said.

This was my chance. I wiped my perspiring forehead with my bandanna and answered, 'Well, I could sure use the practice. I guess I could stay a little longer.'

'Oh, come on, you can't be that tired out.'

I made a face. 'You think so? Then you try standing out in right field for a few hours with the sun beating down on your head.'

He looked at me with mock ferocity. 'I have,' he retorted. 'I used to play semi-pro. Or didn't I tell you?' By now I could tell he was as attracted to me as I was to him. His eyes were slightly narrowed as they traveled up and down my tight T-shirt and cutoff jeans. 'So, are we going to practice or what, Marin?'

I was feeling a little reckless. 'I'll stay if we can rest a little first,' I suggested. 'I need some water.' I walked back to the team cooler and poured some of the cold water down my parched throat. It tasted so clear and good that I wanted to feel some on my body, too. I began dripping the cool water along my arms, all over my face, and between my breasts.

Hank just stood there, not doing anything, just staring. I noticed his shorts were filled with a promising bulge as I walked back toward him and picked up my bat, hitting it in the dust a few times like I'd seen other players do. 'I'm ready!' I declared.

***

After practice, everyone disappeared and Hank and I were left alone on the field. As you can imagine, it didn't take him long at all to show me how to swing the bat by putting his arms, with their huge biceps, around me. He held me close, and I could feel his heart beating against my back and his swelling cock nestling into the crack of my ass. I wiggled my backside against his shaft, and was rewarded by feeling it twitch in response.

He nuzzled my neck. 'Shall we go into the dugout?' he asked.

My throat was already tight so I just nodded, and followed him.

He yanked off my t-shirt and my sports bra followed, the cool breeze drifting over my nipples as he admired my breasts for a moment. But that wasn't the wind that made my nipples stiff and rigid; it was Hank's fingers as he grazed them gently between his thumb and forefinger. Then he took my stiff peaks one after other into his mouth and nibbled on them as if they were luscious grapes. Before I knew it I was completely naked and lying face-down on the hard bench, one leg draped over each side of it as Hank fondled my soft ass.

'God, you're beautiful', he murmured, and suddenly spanked me.

'Mm!' I moaned as he caressed my burning cheeks. There was something very voluptuous about being exposed like this to him. He was my coach, and this was a much more entertaining form of discipline.

He spanked me again with his hard open hand, making the cheeks of my ass flame and quiver in response. 'Do you like that?' he whispered.

I moaned.

He spanked me again, and then with his strong hands lifted my hips slightly, so I could feel every inch of his silky erection slowly penetrating me, and making me gasp with pleasure at this intense contrast of sensations. Holding me firmly by the hips, he yanked my whole body towards him, filling my hot pussy with a cock that felt almost as hard as his bat. I yelped and whimpered as his thick hard-on stretched my tight little slot open around it, pummeling me ruthlessly and filling me with his devastating dimensions. I rested my cheek against the bench, my eyes closed as I moaned.

After a while he flipped me over and lifted my legs so I could rest my ankles on his shoulders. He leaned forward and lodged the head of his cock in my creaming hole.

'Oh, yes,' I murmured. 'Yes!'

Once again, inch by inch, his big smooth length disappeared inside my soaking-wet sex. I could feel my juices trickling down into my butt crack as with massive strength he rammed his flesh bat home over and over again. He thrust into me with deep and powerful strokes, biting my neck and kissing my lips. He gripped my ankles as he pounded into me, my legs high in the air as my ass bounced against the bench beneath his onslaught. He grunted each time he thrust and I trembled on the brink of a climax the whole time. At last I felt my pussy contract with ecstasy, and my orgasm was intensified by the sensation of his ejaculation deep inside me.

He kissed me hard and held me tightly against him. 'That was great,' he said dazedly as my long nails scraped across his back.

'I think I need a lot more coaching,' I replied. 'Don't you?'

21. Alana — Basic Equipment

'Hi,' I finally said to him one day after watching his every move in our evening photography class for over a month.

'Hello,' he replied with a sly smile, his attentive hazel eyes gazing directly into my gray ones. He then sat down at the desk next to me, glancing over surreptitiously as if to see my reaction. I stared shyly down at my notes, hoping he couldn't see my trembling hand. I smelled the faint, pleasant scent of his cologne as he leaned over. 'Are you enjoying this class so far?' he inquired.

I nodded. I turned my head to look at him, and noticed he was as gorgeous close up as he was from far away, the only way I'd seen him so far. He was Mediterranean, I decided. Along with those beautiful eyes he had soft-looking coffee-colored hair cut short, and a sensual smile that would knock any level-headed woman off her feet. 'I'm Alana,' I finally managed to say.

'Nice to meet you, Alana, I'm Nathaniel, Nathan for short.' He took my small hand in his considerably larger, warm one, and shook it firmly. Then class began, ending that wonderful, magical handshake, and we were absorbed in the world of photography and film for over an hour. I studied Nathan's profile in the half-light of the film projector. More than once, his eyes met mine.

After class I stood up, and he jumped quickly to his feet, helping me into my coat. 'That was a very interesting class, don't you think?' he murmured to me from behind. The intimate tone of his voice made me want him more than ever.

'Yes, very interesting,' I agreed. 'I'm really beginning to love photography.' We walked out of the classroom together. 'I just wish I had more equipment to work with.'

'Would you like to come up to my apartment and see my equipment – my photography equipment, that is.' He chucked, and then blushed slightly.

I accepted his offer, feeling a twinge of delight in my stomach. We strolled to his apartment, which turned out only to be four blocks away. As we walked, I wondered just what kind of 'equipment' I was going to see.

It was in the elevator that things began to heat up. On the short ride to the fifth floor, I suddenly felt his strong arms come around me from behind and his soft lips caress my neck with a sweet passion. I turned, still in his arms, and met his lips with mine. Our tongues touched briefly, then tangled together as if in battle. The elevator door opened abruptly, and to my surprise Nathan lifted me up in his arms and carried me all the way to his apartment, still kissing me feverishly.

'I want you… I want to make love to you, Alana.' He broke contact with me suddenly, as if waiting for my response.

Staring directly into his eyes, I was growing weak with desire. With trembling hands, I began to undress myself, watching him intently. I got as far as my blouse when he stepped in to assist me. He didn't touch my breasts, but he ran his strong hands smoothly over my back, unsnapping my bra and tossing it to the floor. I felt almost too exposed as he stared at my bare chest, touching my bosom with his eyes but not his hands.

'Do you like what you see?' I asked softly.

'You're beautiful,' he murmured, smiling back at me.

Still mesmerized by his eyes and hypnotized by his soft voice, I let him unzip my skirt; I stepped out of it and stood naked before him except for my high heels.

'Leave them on,' he muttered as he ran his hands over my buttocks.

I responded by lying back across his sofa and beckoning him to me. He lay gently on top of me, and I wrapped my legs around him tightly. The bulge inside his jeans told me he wanted me, and I was as eager as he was. I smiled as he looked over my entire body, completely naked in his arms. His eyes took in every curve, lingering on my slightly spread legs.

'You're so beautiful,' he whispered, 'even more so than I could ever have imagined.'

I sat up and urged him to stand before me so I could unzip his jeans, and pull them down slowly. By now, he was trembling visibly. I then proceeded to strip the rest of his clothes off him, wanting him even more as I saw more of his muscular physique. He stiffened and became incredibly hard as I fondled his balls and his cock with my hands. I squirmed on the sofa cushion, wanting release but not wanting the sweet tension to end.

'I want you inside me,' I finally gasped, and he obediently joined me on the sofa again and shoved three fingers inside my wetness, pushing them in and sliding them out again faster and faster as I groaned with pleasure and quickly climaxed, crying out in ecstasy.

I opened my eyes. Nathan was leaning over me, brushing a loose strand of hair away from my face. His body was solid over mine; his hard cock pulsated just outside my damp opening. I wrapped my legs around him, and pushed him inside me. He thrust his rigid shaft into my warm hole again and again and we both came fiercely, our bodies meshing into one single entity of flesh. He moaned deeply as his hot cum filled me.

We relaxed for a few moments afterwards, not speaking. Then he sighed, picked me up in his arms, and carried me to the bathroom, nuzzling me to him as he turned on the shower.

'I'm glad I got this chance to make use of all your, um, equipment,' I whispered, smiling.

22. Moira – Sun Shower

It's another hot and sultry Sunday afternoon in central Virginia. To get some relief from the humidity, I decide to go with some friends on a tubing trip down the river. Wearing a black T-shirt, army shorts, and sneakers, I wade into the shallow water and climb into the large, black rubber inner tube floating on the surface. My bottom hangs down in the warm water, which seeps through my cotton shorts, my legs and shoulders dangling over the tube as I sip a frosty can of beer. It's the perfect summer holiday for an exhausted college student, and I feel good floating down the river in the gentle sunshine. I relax as we move slowly along the water; I study the trees by the shore and drink my beer, letting time go by...

Suddenly there's a rumble of thunder, and myriads of tiny raindrops cascade from the sky, gently but insistently tapping against my skin. Damn! Up in the heavens I see a white flash of lightning like a loose thread against a patch of gray cloth. I paddle frantically with my hands and feet, reaching the shore as the sky opens up and the trickle becomes a downpour. I climb up the muddy bank, dragging my tube behind me, and realize my friends have drifted ahead of me; I am alone. Or am I? A strange sense tells me I'm not... suddenly a wet hand touches my shoulder, causing a surge of adrenaline and a clenching of fear in my stomach. I turn around quickly, ready to defend myself, and look straight into a pair of dark-brown, innocent, but intensely sensuous, eyes. Like me, he is soaking wet – this tall, sun-tanned muscular stranger with wild dark hair. Looped through his arm is an inner tube. He, too, is seeking shelter from the driving rain, and he whispers an apology for frightening me.

I am ashamed of my fear and my appearance, but feel titillated when I look down and see my drenched shirt clinging to my breasts and my erect nipples. Following my gaze, he approaches me. I step back instinctively, but a second later I mysteriously relax and allow him to get close. His wet, taut torso touches mine, and blood rushes to my clitoris in a mad flood as I swallow in wicked anticipation.

'I want it so bad,' I hear myself say to this young man whose name I don't even know, acknowledging my thought even as I speak it out loud.

He smiles a devilish grin, and gently pulls my shirt up around my neck, trapping me in it as he kisses my chest and throat, his hands and lips touching me light as feathers. Finally, he pulls the shirt up over my head and leads me beneath the shelter of some trees where the driving rain falls only in gentle, caressing trickles. Slowly, he unbuttons and unzips my shorts and pulls them off me. Then he sits on a tree stump and pulls me down onto his lap, rubbing between my thighs with one hand while he cradles me against him. For a moment he stops to admire the lines of my body, and like a greedy child I peel his blue T-shirt up away from his chest as though I'm unwrapping a candy bar. He kisses my mouth, forming a tight seal between us before probing deeply with his tongue. I'm so hot and wet at the same time I could scream. I reach down for the drawstring of his bathing shorts, and feel him growing hard against me.

With his strong arms he picks me up and spreads me across the ground. He spreads my legs and kisses my breasts, sucking delicately on each nipple. A rumble of thunder causes me to tremble in anticipation as he makes his way down to my navel, showering me with kisses. I savor the delicate pleasure, moaning as he positions his head between my legs and begins licking and kissing my sex. His tongue slides along my labia into my pussy, and I writhe against the ground, unable to control my body's responses to his oral skill.

'Relax and let me do my stuff,' he whispers. He straddles me, making light circles around my nipples with his fingertips. Then he reaches for a condom in the packet of his wet shorts, and I giggle at his Boy Scout preparedness as he unrolls it over his long, hard cock as I watch in fascination. He positions himself over me, his hard-on slapping the insides of my thighs, and I feel a rush of pure lust. He slides halfway into my cunt, then places his hands on my shoulders as he drives his dick deep inside me. I cry out from the almost unbearable fulfillment as he thrusts and thrusts and thrusts, and soon I can feel him coming as my own orgasm floods me deep and slow as a river overflowing, cleansing my tension-filled body.

As he softens up and pulls out of me, he takes his weight off my body and lies down beside me, placing my leg over his waist and holding me in an embrace as we both drift into a luscious sleep, entwined as one.

I wake to a gentle kiss on my cheek. The rain has stopped, and for several minutes we sit up together naked watching the steam rise from the river and pairs of dragonflies mating and fluttering about. We talk quietly, and then he helps me get dressed. Together we climb into our inner tubes, and as we float gently down the river, I wonder if this afternoon really ever happened.

'I hope you're not too late to catch up with your friends,' he says apologetically.

'I really don't mind at all,' I reply with a smile. 'Let's just sit back and relax for a while.'

23. Michelle – The Anniversary

I massaged my temples, and then childishly threw a pencil across my office, watching without interest as it bounced from the wall to the file cabinet to the thickly carpeted floor.

I had had it. A recent job promotion had given me more money, but much less time at home, more headaches and a short fuse. Shouting matches with my husband and three daughters were frequent and getting worse. As for sex, I didn't seem to have the time or energy to enjoy it anymore. I had made the mistake of letting the job run me instead of the other way around. That flash of insight was accompanied by a decision.

My secretary scuttled past the open door.

'Annie!' I barked, instantly regretting my tone of voice as she hurried in with a wary expression; she was as harried as I. Softening my voice, I went on as soon as she seated herself, pen and pad ready. 'Call my beauty salon and tell Frankie I want a noon appointment for the works – hair, hands, feet, face. Next, get in touch with that little boutique around the corner. I'll be in after I get out of the salon. Tell Grace I want a black dress – sexy, not trashy. I'm taking the afternoon and weekend off.' I raised a hand to halt her protest. 'I have a date tonight and nothing is going to interfere. Understand?' She snapped her mouth shut and merely nodded. 'If you absolutely must reach me before Monday, leave a message on my answering machine at home, but it had better be an emergency.' I leaned back in my chair and smiled at her for what must have been the first time in weeks. 'We're going to make some changes around this place, beginning with me.' I was noticing a slight tingle between my legs and enjoyed it. Tonight was the night!

***

Hours of pampering later, I was reveling in girlish excitement as I was escorted to a suggestively dark corner booth in a dimly lit restaurant. A tall, handsome man with dark-blond hair greeted me, his bright smile warming my blood.

'God, you look terrific,' he said, his eyes greedily roaming over my curves. He kissed my cheek and stood aside to let me slide across the semi-circular booth.

'Why, thank you, Eric,' I replied calmly, successfully thwarting the urge to giggle. I squeezed his hand. 'It seems ages since I've seen you.' Though he was nearly forty, he was just as attractive as he had been twenty years before. In fact, I thought as I took in the generous sprinkling of gray in his hair, he was even more attractive now. His blue eyes sparkled as they came to rest on my stiffening nipples.

'Cold?' he asked with false innocence.

'No,' I sighed as I placed my hand on his thigh. 'Actually, I'm quite warm.' As his arm encircled my shoulders, his hand brushed the strap of my dress, sending it gliding slowly down my arm. The top half of my breast lay revealed with just a hint of brown aureole peeking above the cloth, perilously held up by my erect nipple. I left it as it was, and increased the pressure on his firm thigh, glad the tablecloth provided a bit of privacy.

An exotically dark young waiter with liquid bedroom eyes appeared, offering menus and stealthy glances at my chest. As Eric ordered wine, the waiter repeatedly took cautious peeks in my direction, fearing, or hoping, my dress would reveal more. Purposely, I took a long, deep breath and squelched the urge to stretch as the waiter, now fascinated, openly gawked.

Eric pulled his arm from around my shoulders to better handle the over-sized menu and, in doing so, his elbow brushed the remaining strap from its place. I turned toward him slightly, and my right breast brushed against his scratchy suit, raising little goose bumps of pleasure down my arm and further stiffening my nipples. As he made a distinct effort to study the menu, I caressed his thigh, slowly working my way nearer his crotch and the erection rising there. Slipping his arm around me again, he squeezed my shoulders, making my tits jiggle temptingly as the entranced waiter continued watching. Eric was speaking, ordering our food, but the waiter seemed more interested in my round, firm bosom. I felt Eric's fingers moving sensuously downward over my collarbone and near the softness of my cleavage. He increased his pressure slightly, which raised my nipple from behind the fabric of my dress. It popped free, pointing directly at the young waiter, who promptly fled.

As I made a move to cover the freed aureole, Eric touched my hand and whispered, 'Why bother? No one can see us.' He made certain of it by blowing out the single candle which lit our table. I was already beyond modesty anyway. We could have stripped off all our clothes and fucked ourselves silly right there on top of the table for all I cared. I was hot and getting hotter by the minute.

I lifted my right leg, placing it over his knee, and my pussy lips were so wet they parted with a faint smacking sound. My juices were flowing; my cunt hungry for attention. I surprised Eric by unzipping his fly, allowing his eight inches to burst free of their confines. A drop of pre-cum met my hand as I wrapped my fingers around his head. Then, rubbing my fingers over the dish of fresh butter the waiter had so generously provided for other purposes, I lubricated my hand and felt Eric's body stiffen as I grasped his swollen member. Closing my hand tightly around its base, I began a slow upward movement, relaxing my grip as my fist traveled nearer his sensitive ridge. Moaning, he buried his head in my hair, muffling his ragged breathing. Meanwhile, one of his hands worked its way up my inner thigh with a deliberate slowness calculated to drive me wild. Eventually reaching its destination, his sharp intake of breath was his only outward sign of pleasure at finding my pussy not only unfettered by underwear, but unadorned by its usual soft curly bush. The urgent movement of his fingers inside me told me it had been well worth the time and effort to shave the hair from around my sex.

Eric was in the midst of a controlled frenzy, and I moved my hips to meet his stiff fingers plunging deep into my hot and hungry hole. His teeth bit into the side of my neck and I stifled a moan, my head falling back against cool leather seat. His fingers kept rhythmically gliding in and out of my slick sex, and then his thumb began rubbing my clitoris, gently circling it and caressing the soft wet folds of flesh around it. It felt so good! Suddenly, I opened my eyes and saw our waiter standing mesmerized before our table. The young man's eyes were half closed, as if he was experiencing the heat of our sexual arousal himself. He made a move to leave once he was aware that I was watching him, but I smiled at him and he stayed, a line of perspiration popping out on his upper lip.

Eric's cock was as stiff as an iron rod in my hand, the two big blood vessels which ran up both sides of his dick pulsing wildly. I knew he was near orgasm, and I found myself moving more slowly around his penetrating fingers. Looking directly into the eyes of the waiter, I whispered to Eric, 'Rub my clit, baby, rub it hard! I want to come all over your hand.'

A deep groan vibrated in my ear as his cock spurted forth a stream of cum as he shivered and gasped like a fish out of water. And as his spunk drenched my hand, my vaginal muscles tightened spasmodically, greedily clamping around his fingers as his thumb continued circling my throbbing clitoris. The restaurant sounds were muffled by the roar of blood through my head as I climaxed, and then my mind and body were filled with a peaceful, dreamy quiet.

Moments later, I cautiously opened my eyes. The waiter had disappeared and Eric was sipping his wine.

'Hungry?' he asked, as if we had only just arrived. He looked around impatiently. 'Where's the waiter? I'm starved! By the way, when do we have to pick up the girls at your sister's house?'

'Not until tomorrow afternoon,' I replied.

'Ah, there you are!' Eric declared as the waiter reappeared. 'Bring us another bottle of wine. It's our fifteenth wedding anniversary and we're celebrating.'

I distinctly heard the young man mutter, 'No shit!' under his breath as he left.

Eric and I exchanged shocked expressions, and then laughed happily.

24. Brenda – Forever

The sound of the waves splashing against the rocks below our room woke me from my deep sleep. I lay there quietly with my head resting on his chest, the soft hairs tickling my face. He looked so handsome, so peaceful. I loved these special moments when we were alone together. I lay there memorizing every feature of his face – his long lashes, the outline of his jaw, the strength of his forehead, the softness of his lips. Each moment we spent together made my love for him grow stronger, and I knew deep in my heart that I would never know a love like this again.

I smiled as I remembered the night we had just spent together. It had started off with a promise; his promise of an evening I would never forget. He picked me up at work. His body in a double-breasted suit was amazing. He wore clothes like a model. 'Ready for a great weekend?' he asked as his lips reached for mine and my arms instinctively slipped around his neck to pull him closer. We drove for a couple of hours, neither of us saying much. We were anticipating the time alone away from the distractions of work and family.

We arrived at our rented beach house while the sun was still perched on the horizon. We both stopped, awed by the light show playing before us. I started to reach for our suitcase, but he protested. 'No work at all this weekend for you. I'll do it.' I wasn't going to argue; I let him carry the bags into the house while I locked up the car. He came back and swept me off my feet, carrying me up to the front door.

The house was dark except for an eerie glow coming from the bedroom. As he carried me in there, I saw candles spread around the room. The bed looked as if it were glowing. Beautiful black lingerie lay across the mattress. 'What is this?' I asked.

'I bought it for you,' he said.

I smiled, thinking how silly he must have looked shopping for lingerie.

A champagne bottle was placed by the side of the bed. He set me down and poured champagne into two glasses then made a toast. 'To us, forever and ever!'

We drank most of the bottle before he began kissing me. I tasted the wine on his tongue and I felt his hardness growing against me. He stopped abruptly and said, 'Put on your lingerie.' He stepped back and watched as I undressed, and then redressed. His eyes glowed with appreciation. 'You're the most beautiful woman I've ever seen,' he whispered as he held me close.

I made a wet trail with my lips to his dick as I undressed him. Then he lay back across the bed, his clothes on the floor, his cock hard and ready for me. My juices were flowing as I straddled him, and slowly eased myself down around him. He gasped as I engulfed him, his erection filling me. I rubbed my clitoris against him as I picked up the pace. His hands were squeezing my breasts, but as I climaxed, he gripped my hips and pumped wildly. We rode each other like this for a few minutes, each thrust sending orgasmic waves rushing through me. Finally he tensed up, his face a mask of concentration as he came, moaning, his beloved cum filling me. Then we held each other tenderly as moonlight flooded the bedroom.

***

The next morning as bright rays of sunlight penetrated through the open window I could feel the damp night air beginning to warm up. He took a deep breath and stirred awake, his eyes meeting mine as they opened. We exchanged a smile, and he placed a loving kiss on my forehead. His arms closed tightly around my waist, lifting me on top of his warm, naked body. It felt wonderful to rest against him as his hands grasped my buttocks tightly and I felt his hardness rising up against my pelvis. My pulse began to race as his tongue brushed my lips and then explored my mouth. Swiftly, he rolled me onto my back, the weight of his body pinning me down as my heart pounded with excitement. He held my face in his hands, kissing my lips ever so lightly. His tongue glided slowly down my neck, sending a tingling sensation along my spine. He continued his journey down my body, taking each of my breasts in his hands and caressing one nipple between his thumb and forefinger while gently sucking on the other. Then he trailed his fingers and tongue down my stomach, and my pussy ached as a sweet wetness seeped down my inner thighs. Suddenly, he lifted my legs over his shoulders and brushed his lips against my clit. A deep yearning consumed me as his tongue licked up every drop of my arousal. Then two of his strong fingers entered me even as his tongue continued probing, and the feeling was irresistible. My body writhed with pleasure as I climaxed, and the rhythm of his tongue and fingers slowed to a gentle pace, bringing me down slowly and extending the thrill of my orgasm.

As I lay there, my body awash in a haze of contentment, he kissed me passionately. Soon, though, he grabbed my hand and guided me into the bathroom, where the warm water of the shower relaxed our bodies. I kissed him fervently, holding his body close to mine as the pulse of the water beat against us. I took the bar of soap and rubbed it against his chest and shoulders, then down to his tight stomach muscles. I rubbed my breasts against him as I slipped my hands around his waist and soaped up his firm buttocks. The soap was slippery, and the friction between our bodies made us shiver with excitement as we playfully massaged each other. I loved the feeling of his tight ass in my hands as I pressed him against me, and the sensation of his fingers rubbing small circles around my nipples, which were taut with desire. Slipping gently down his soap-slick body, letting my hard nipples brush against his skin, I delicately massaged his thighs and balls as I took his penis into my mouth. My tongue lapped against him as I slowly began a smooth rhythm. His buttocks tightened and I could feel the tension rising in him; it wasn't long before his pleasure filled my mouth. Finally, our passion spent for the moment, we embraced tightly as we kissed long and ardently.

As we dressed for our day on the beach, our eyes barely left each other. We made our way down to the water's edge, our picnic basket in his hand. Spreading our blanket across the warm sand, we nibbled on fruit, cheese and crackers, and sipped wine. When we had finished our feast, we sat in each other's arms watching the waves breaking against the shore. Looking deeply into my eyes, he whispered softly that the love he had always dreamed of he had found with me.

25. Julia – Research Assistant

I had been working on a college term paper last semester and had spent all my spare time at the library, partly to research eighteenth-century art, and partly because Kerry, the assistant librarian, worked at the reference desk. I had noticed him the first time he was there. I had been impressed by the way he pulled together even the most obscure information on any topic. I was also impressed with his intelligent, sparkling green eyes and his nice ass, very obvious in his tight-fitting jeans. I would always sit at the table closest to the reference desk.

After a few weeks I found myself paying more attention to Kerry than to my research. The more I heard his soft mellifluous voice and watched him move, the more turned on I got. I used every excuse I could think of to go to the reference desk to ask him for something. He would hand information to me, and I would make sure our fingers touched. I wanted him badly; however, a library is not a place where one can pursue lustful desires. I chalked Kerry up as a never-to-be-fulfilled sexual fantasy. I would never know the touch of his lips, the feel of his hands or the sensation of his naked body against mine. All I would ever know about Kerry was that he knew his card catalogs almost by heart.

Suddenly, my reverie was broken by a hand touching my shoulder. The suddenness of the intrusion into my fantasy startled me, and I jumped. Then I heard Kerry's voice say, 'I'm sorry, I didn't mean to scare you. You had such a strange, faraway look on your face, I got worried. Is anything wrong?' Those intelligent eyes of his were looking into my very soul. I hoped he couldn't tell I had just been imagining him naked.

'I'm fine…' I cleared my throat. 'I was just thinking about the project I'm working on.' Impulsively, I put my hand over his before he had a chance to move it off my shoulder. 'Thanks for caring,' I added. 'It's nice to know someone's around who's willing to help.' I smiled at him, my most alluring and flirtatious smile.

'No bother at all,' he assured me, returning my smile. He removed his hand, and returned to the reference desk. That had probably been my one and only chance to initiate any kind of personal contact between us, and I'd blown it.

I continued with my studies until it was time for the library to close. I lingered over what I was doing while the few remaining people left. He walked over to where I was sitting. 'You know that information you asked me for but that I didn't have? Well, I've located what I think you want. It's down in the basement with the obscure reference books. If you don't mind staying I could show it to you and see if it's what you need.'

Was he really talking about reference material or was this conversation about what I had been lusting after all this time? I looked around. It seemed we were the only two people in the library. 'Isn't the library manager going to want to lock up and go home?' I asked.

His smile was different. 'I'm locking up tonight, and I certainly don't mind staying if you don't.'

I felt a shiver run down my spine.

'If you'll come down to the basement with me, I'll show you what I have,' he repeated.

'Sounds good to me.' I sincerely hoped books weren't the only thing on his mind.

We walked to the back of the stacks, and down the stairs to the basement. I had pictured it as being gloomy, with decades of dust covering everything, but instead there was a large employee lounge and lunch room, and several other rooms containing stacks and stacks of neatly maintained books. He showed me into the lounge, and motioned toward the couch. 'Sit down and make yourself comfortable. I'll be right back.'

I kicked off my shoes and waited for his return, scarcely daring to hope.

It seemed like an eternity, but in reality it was only about five minutes, when I finally heard Kerry returning. He had two books in his hands, but instead of handing them to me he sat down beside me on the couch. His nearness was making me crazy; sensations were rushing through my body out of control. My panties were getting wet, my nipples were hard, and my breathing was becoming shallow. He was talking to me, but I wasn't listening, all my attention concentrated on my body and on trying to get myself under control so I didn't come off as some sex-starved fool. Suddenly, what he was saying filtered through to my consciousness. '…I've wanted to be alone with you for a long time.' I looked at him, and he was looking at me, eyes narrowed with desire. That was all the encouragement I needed. I leaned forward to kiss him, and as our lips met I felt an urgent ache surge through my pussy. I pressed my breasts against his chest, letting his tongue explore my mouth. He leaned me back across the couch and slowly unbuttoned my blouse, cupping my breasts in his hands.

I massaged his chest and shoulders while removing his shirt. He kissed my neck and throat, and then moved his mouth down to my breasts. He kissed each nipple in turn, alternately sucking on them as he pulled off my pants, quickly unzipping his own jeans and slipping them off.

I massaged his beautiful ass, his warm buns deliciously filling my hands as he moved his own hand down between my legs. He seemed to know by my wetness how sensitive my clitoris would be, so he proceeded carefully, slowly drawing his fingertips through the moisture between my labial lips, and then very gently touching my knob. I jumped a little, but then moved my pussy up against his hand. He slowly stroked my sex while sucking on my breasts, and I reached for his penis in response, finding it fully erect. I wrapped my fingers around his shaft and began slowly moving up and down its glorious length, passionately pumping him with my fist. He was massaging my clit more firmly with his thumb now and my pussy was getting hotter and wetter by the second.

'Feel good?' he asked.

I nodded breathlessly.

His lips reached for mine and I eagerly took his tongue into my mouth. He poised himself above me as I opened my legs wide to receive him. He inserted his erection into my opening, driving it down as far as possible before he began pumping rhythmically against me. His penetrations felt incredible. We moved together slowly at first, and then faster and faster, until out hips were beating against each other's with reckless abandon. My vaginal muscles hugged his cock, massaging him to orgasm, longing to consume him entirely. I prayed he had enough stamina to last for a while longer, because I wanted to orgasm with him; already I could feel my pleasure building irresistibly. And as he drove into me harder and faster, I came so intensely my body crossed that fine line between pleasure and pain. I grabbed his ass and squeezed it violently as I climaxed and this seemed to intensify his pleasure, because I heard him moaning, a low sensual sound. I had never felt a man thrust so hard for so long; his staying power was not to be believed. Suddenly, I realized he was slowing down, trying to hold off his own release.

He breathed in my ear, 'Come on, baby, just one more time, come just once more for me...'

His encouragement propelled me over the edge again as he banged me wildly. I could feel him moving closer and closer to his own release, and he gave one last hard, deep push as he exploded.

We lay there in each other's arms for several minutes, exhausted. Finally, he spoke. 'You have no idea how incredible it felt to me when you came. I wish I could have lasted longer so you could have come again and again. Maybe next time. There *will* be a next time, won't there?'

I don't need to fantasize about Kerry anymore, and I'm looking forward to doing much, much more 'research' with him. When we're together, the library isn't a place to be quiet!

26. Nancy – Dream Lover

I still have a hard time believing this ever happened to me. Maybe that's why I've written it down; if I tell someone, it'll all seem real.

It was a typical Friday night. I went out with a few girlfriends for drinks after work, then went home and watched an X-rated video I had rented. It seemed too erotic to watch alone, but I was too comfortable on the couch to rev up my vibrator, so I just kept telling myself a little frustration would make the sex even better when it did happen.

After the movie, I climbed naked onto my crisp bed sheets. The evening was pleasant, so I left my first floor windows open. I remember turning and searching for the blankets in the middle of the night. My skin felt cool and moist. My arms crossed in front of my nipples, which were erect because of the cold. Suddenly, a warm feeling overcame my arms, legs, breasts – my entire body. And then came a tingling sensation beginning at the bottom of my feet and working its way up my legs to my sex. The center of my body felt hot and cold at the same time. Then like a knife heat sliced through my core. It felt wonderful; I wanted it to hold me and fill me forever. My hand curled into what felt like a mat of thick hair and I longed to merge with whatever was embracing me. My body was filled with warmth and I could feel the imprint of a delicious weight against my breasts, tummy and beneath my chin. I curled to one side, trying to find the sensation again, but didn't know how. Something cold touched my nipples and I sat up, suddenly wide awake, confused as to whether I had been having an erotic dream or if someone had been teasing me while I slept.

'Hold on,' a man's voice whispered in the dark, and a mouth closed over one of my nipples. I gasped at the sensation as it suckled my breast, sucking on the nipples. The mouth moved down to my stomach, and lingered on my sensitive hipbones. Then a tongue slipped into my pussy, causing me to arch my back and cry out with pleasure. It licked me gently, lapping my labial lips, winding my body tight as a string.

'Nancy,' he murmured soothingly, and continued eating me. 'You're so hot and sweet, Nancy.' His voice was deep and dark as the night. 'Let go and come for me, Nancy.' He plunged his tongue in and out of my slick hole, tasting and savoring my juices. One of his hands moved down and caressed my inner thighs, and the dual caress sent me skyrocketing into convulsion after convulsion...

I was shaken to the core of my being. I had been released and felt fresh and new. My body was so relaxed I thought I could sleep, though I wanted more. Suddenly, he moved up my body and kissed my lips. We tongued each other for a long time, and I could taste myself on his mouth. He finally lifted his head and my eyes tried desperately to discern his features in the darkness, but there was no light in my room.

At his urging, my hand encircled his manhood. He was perfect. Not huge, just right. His erection filled my palm, surging with a life of its own, growing warmer and harder as I stroked it. I moved my fist up and down his hard-on, a little more tightly with each stroke, and he lay on top of me.

'Nancy, you make me crazy,' he whispered as he penetrated me slowly. He pushed into me gently, letting me feel his thick fullness, making me crazy with the need to feel him as deep inside me as he could go.

'Please,' I spoke for the first time, my hands moving to his powerful shoulders to pull him closer to me. 'I need you...'

With a groan he sank down hard, and my pleasure intensified with his every thrust. I matched his rhythm, building my pleasure up until it was sharp enough that a second climax sliced through me. I wanted him to feel the same pleasure. I wanted him to have the greatest orgasm ever, but it was too late. My body convulsed in his arms and once more I found overwhelming release and a remarkable ensuing peace...

I woke up the next morning and he was gone. His taste and smell lingered on the sheets. I've asked myself why on earth I allowed a man

I didn't know, a man who had broken into my apartment, to do what he did to me. After all, I place a strong value on sex and do not consider myself easy, but his magical hands warmed me to the core of my being. His mouth and tongue sent me soaring to a place I had never known existed before. And his lovemaking was so extraordinary the memories will hold me for many a lonely night to come.

27. Valerie – Special of the Day

I worked as a waitress at a truck stop for about a year while finishing college. It had always been my personal policy never to date any of the clientele, especially the truck drivers. Frankly, I was scared of them. Not because of how they looked – big, bad and bawdy – but because I saw them as transient. So, bored though I was, I stuck to dates with the lackluster men I met on campus.

Everyone at work knew how I felt about socializing with the patrons. I made it pretty clear; never flirting with any of them no matter how 'nice' they looked to my co-workers, or how big a tip some guy would try to tempt me with. I held my head high and kept the strings of my apron firmly knotted. But when a fellow waitress, Bobbie Jo, whispered in my ear that the trucker in booth six wanted my phone number, I took a moment to jot it down on a paper napkin. The kitchen crew watched, mouths agape, as I thrust the napkin into her hand.

Earlier, when I was serving someone else, I saw him from the corner of my eye, and what I saw, I liked. He was gorgeous, with every muscle of his well-defined body visible through his jeans and western shirt. For once, I thought mischievously, I'll throw caution to the wind.

Bobbie Jo gave him the paper napkin with my name and number on it, and he glanced up from his newspaper. He met my gaze with green eyes that held flecks of gold and a hint of humor. Good, I thought, smiling to myself, we can laugh together, too. I stood there unable to move as his eyes slowly scanned every inch of my body, lingering longest on my apron-clad torso. His wink let me know I passed the inspection with flying colors.

It was a few seconds before I could regain enough composure to take down my next order. My legs and voice were both shaking. I couldn't remember the Special of the Day to save my life.

The trucker-with-a-difference sidled up to me. Denim grazed the ruffles of my gingham apron. 'My name is Guy, Guy Huffine,' he informed me in a heavy Cajun accent. I imagined jambalaya-flavored kisses in the moonlight and bouncing on the bayou. 'I'm parked next to the first driving barrier in the front.'

I turned and nodded to him, totally disregarding my other customers. Luckily for me (and several hungry people) Suzie, a real sweetheart and a pro all the way, silently took over. Her cheerful chatter extolled the virtues of meat loaf and mashed potatoes. Guy took my arm gently, and led me away from reality. He was smiling in the same self-assured way he had exhibited earlier as he left the diner ahead of me as I went in search of my boss. My pulse and heartbeat were racing, and there was a faint roaring in my ears. My panties were moist at the crotch. My mouth felt dry; I could barely manage to tell my supervisor I was leaving early.

'Tylene, I feel sick and need to go home now,' I said in a quavering voice.

'Well, your shift is almost over, and you do look rather flushed,' she observed sympathetically.

After three or four tries, I managed to pull open the door of my locker. I grabbed my purse, and had a quick check in the mirror.

Guy was waiting for me beside his truck. He let me know where he was going. 'I'm headed for Houston, San Antonio, and then back to New Orleans, where I live.'

'Okay,' I said. 'Can you pick me up at the Holiday Inn next door? I can't leave my car here for two or three days.'

I couldn't believe this was happening. I could lose my reputation – not to mention my job – if anyone found out about this. But there was no way I could stop what was already out of hand. Thank God I had a small suitcase already packed in my car for the upcoming weekend at my mother's house, which wasn't going to happen now, but at least I didn't have to waste any precious time deciding what to take.

Before I knew it, Guy and I were traveling down the interstate headed toward Houston. Though I hadn't drunk anything all day except colas, I was totally intoxicated.

'How do you feel about roadside parks?' His question seemed to come out of the blue. Since leaving the truck stop, neither of us had said a word.

'I don't have any objection to them.' I was trying to sound nonchalant, but I just didn't make it.

The truck came to an abrupt stop outside of Beaumont City limits at the roadside park. Guy turned, and let his hand glide down over my hair, gathering it all at the nape of my neck and gazing at me. Then in one swift motion his mouth came down on mine, hard and demanding. I responded; my lips and tongue greedy for his. His grip gradually softened; his caresses became soothing, tantalizing. I felt his powerful arms lift me into his sleeper, and I sighed as he spread his body across the full length of mine, so that I was acutely aware of his need for me. We undressed each other with an urgency that left us panting. Our hands explored each other's naked bodies, becoming more and more familiar; less and less the strangers we had been just an hour before. I could feel his muscles twitching beneath the touch of my hands as I slid them down his back. I rested my palms in the indentations made by the muscles in his buttocks. We squeezed each other, first gently, and then more firmly, pulling close together.

'I'm going to make you think you'll die if you don't have me.' His breath felt warm against the side of my face as his fingers tweaked my nipple.

'But I want you deep inside me now!' I couldn't look at him as I said this.

He kissed the side of my neck and shoulders tenderly, taking love bites along the way. When he got to my breasts, he avoided my erect nipples even when I maneuvered one close to his mouth. He chuckled softly; he was teasing me on purpose. His fingers slid between my legs and discovered absolute wetness. My attention was focused on the movement of his hand down there when he suddenly grasped one of my taut, aching nipples between his lips. My body leapt from the shock and I cried out as his thumb began massaging my clitoris. I raised and lowered my hips, hoping he would get the hint, but he continued sucking my nipple and caressing my clit. My back arched and I trembled, slipping into a haze of pleasure as his head found its way down between my legs and I felt the warm strokes of his tongue on my vulva. Then at last he positioned his cock between my legs, and in one desperate thrust I brought my pussy up around his beautiful hard-on. My arms and legs gripped his body like a vise, afraid he would pull away, but instead he rocked forward, completing the union of our bodies. I gripped his buttocks with both hands, forcing him deeper and deeper inside me. He was moaning, and even the sounds of his lovemaking had a sweet southern tang.

Using what seemed like every ounce of my strength, I rolled forward so I was on top of him. 'Relax,' I whispered, 'and let me do the work.' I slid off his body and lowered my mouth over his erection, slick now with my own sweet-tasting juices.

'No, I want to come inside you,' he protested.

I ignored him; it was my turn to tease him. Delighting in this reversal, I tightened and loosened the grip of my lips on his shaft as he clutched the mattress with both hands. I went down on him for as long as he had eaten me. Finally he grabbed me and rolled me onto my back again, ramming his cock into my cunt and grinding himself against me. The heat from his ejaculation acted as a tranquilizer, slowing our frenzied movements to a halt, and I laid my head contentedly on his shoulder.

'I hope you weren't planning to go anywhere,' he smiled.

'This weekend?' I mumbled.

'No, for the rest of your life.'

28. Ruth – Roommates

It's always been hair for me, and as I grew up, my interest only increased. I'm moved by the feel of a man's hair against my naked skin. My fascination is not with the quantity of the hair involved, it's all about quality – curl, coarseness, smoothness, whatever. Often, while conversing with men, my eyes wander toward their crowning glory and so do my fantasies.

Six months after arriving in France where I was attending school, I found myself depressed and dateless. Too much studying had left me without time to discover the renowned prowess of the French lover, a distraction I'd long looked forward to. Celibacy began to weigh heavily on me and my libido was rebelling in a big way.

Then Stephan moved in. He needed a roommate for financial reasons, and the flat I shared with Shauna, an Irish student, had space to spare. He was the ideal housemate, with a sweet disposition and a marvelous sense of humor. But most of all, he had dark, lustrous hair that curled down to the middle of his back. It was lust at first sight for me, but I virtually ignored him for weeks, not wanting to complicate our domestic situation.

And then it happened. I was in the living room studying by the fire after Shauna retired for the night. Stephan had fallen asleep on the couch as usual. Finding it difficult to concentrate on the history of the French Fifth Republic, I rested my eyes on him. His burnished black tresses caught the light of the fire in a way that made me ache.

I thought that maybe if I just touched his hair lightly he wouldn't wake up. Creeping toward the couch, I reached out a trembling hand and toyed with the very ends of his luscious locks. He didn't move. Holding my breath, I caressed him more boldly. He moaned softly, and rolled onto his back. I gazed down at his crotch, and with delicious shock saw my own desire reflected there. Stephan's T-shirt was hiked up above his boxer shorts, and the exposed tangle of his ebony body hair made me bite my lip. With one hand still caressing his tresses, I assumed a kneeling position beside the couch. Gently, I pressed my lips to the soft, exposed spot next to his navel. As I gradually increased the pressure, I felt him stir. Looking up, I noted his warm brown eyes, half-closed and long-lashed, shining down at me with sexy complicity. He took my hand and guided it toward the hardness straining his shorts. Then he pushed my camisole up past my breasts and rubbed my erect nipples between the thumb and forefingers of his hands. Pleasurable warmth flooded my sex, and I was tempted to tear away all his clothes at once, but I knew I had to resist; this was a moment to be savored.

We took our time undressing and exploring and tasting the nooks and crannies of each other's bodies. I licked his sweet, full lips, and rubbed my hands against the stubble on his cheeks. Burying my face in his chest hair, I kissed his stiff nipples. I ran my fingers teasingly over his balls and the tip of his swollen penis, relishing the feel of his hardness sheathed within a cloak of soft skin. Kneeling, I flicked my tongue over the head of his cock and deliberately it teasingly. Inching my mouth up and down his slippery shaft, I moaned with pleasure as he stiffened even more in my mouth. My lips didn't release him until I sensed he was ready to come. Then I ran my fingers through the hair on his chest and abdomen, gently tugging as I went. I stood up, caressing his neck, my hands inching their way toward his crowning glory. Finally, digging my fingers into his scalp, I pulled him close to me.

Groaning, Stephan pushed me onto my back across the couch and hovered above me. Nudging my labial lips apart with the swollen tip of his penis, he eased it in and out of my moist slit. I ached to feel him deep inside me, and the sensation of his chest hair rubbing against my nipples almost made me climax. He kissed me hard on the lips, and then began feverishly working his mouth down my body. He didn't stop until he reached my clitoris, pausing there to tantalize me before sliding his hot tongue inside me. It was all I could do to keep from coming now, but I managed to hold myself back, desperately needing to prolong the experience.

Finally, he lifted his wet face and smiled at me as he moved into position, and lunged his hard cock into my cunt with one sure thrust. I groaned with ecstasy as I grasped his buttocks, feeling their muscles contracting with every plunging stroke. When he grabbed my legs and draped them over his shoulders, my entire body tensed and I was at last overcome by an orgasm as I vaguely felt him soaring with me.

We lay on the sofa for awhile. Stephan caressed my body while I ran my fingers through his hair. As it turned out, we spent many evenings in just such a manner during my first year abroad.

Merci, Stephan.

29. Diana — House Sitting

Sandra's instructions were simple, 'Don't pack so much as a toothbrush. Relax, have a good time, and feed Cat occasionally.' She was leaving me to care for her house while she flew out of town for a week. 'And no excuses for not having positively pornographic tales to tell me when I get back. You want to forget that jackass you were married to, don't you? Put on something sexy and head for the airport. Now!' She hung up, leaving me with a handful of dead receiver. I prepared to leave.

Looking in the mirror, I concluded that I liked the way my long, cinnamon hair waved over my tan shoulders. The mirror showed no reason to hide the shapely body I usually disguised with drab, shapeless clothing. Forest-green eyes highlighted a face that could pass for younger than my thirty-five years. I liked what I saw, for perhaps the first time in my life.

I stopped on the way to the airport to buy a skin-tight pair of jeans, a shocking pink blouse, shoes and a purse, dumping all my old clothes into the arms of an obviously perplexed salesclerk. I was beginning to break out of the cocoon developed during the long years spent captured in an unhealthy marriage.

I arrived in fine spirits to find Sandra rushing out of her house followed by a darkly handsome man juggling a cluster of suitcases. She commented approvingly on my 'terrific outfit' and pointed in the direction of her car. 'That's Paul. We'll be back on Sunday. Feed Cat and have a good time. I'll call tomorrow.' She waved, and was gone. Being around Sandra was like getting caught in a whirlwind, but I loved her dearly. Laughing, I picked up the Siamese christened Cat and walked into the house.

The sun was kissing the ocean when I took Cat out onto the deck. I intended simply to rest and enjoy the view, but Cat startled me by jumping out of my arms. Following her back inside, I spotted a very handsome young man standing in the living room wearing only tight gym shorts. Cat was undulating around his tanned, muscular legs.

'Hi,' he declared, smiling to reveal a row of perfect white teeth. 'I'm Gary. Sandra asked me to take care of the lawn... and of you, if you need something done around the place. I'm pretty good at fixing things. I'm going to turn the sprinklers on now. See you later.'

My mouth still hanging open, I stood staring at the stained-glass panel of the door through which he had vanished like a divine apparition. It occurred to me that perhaps I was suffering from hallucinations. But I opened the door to see him standing in the center of the lawn prodding what appeared to be the only sprinkler not spraying water. I heard him mutter 'Damn!' as the errant sprinkler suddenly began spraying cool water all over him. Then he walked towards me, water tracing little rivulets down his darkly tanned body, his laughter vibrating the air and my senses. What could I possibly be thinking? This man was barely half my age. Oh, but he was magnificent – tight ass, long, muscular legs, taut stomach muscles, and hair so blond it seemed to glow in the deepening dusk. I couldn't help noting his tight shorts and his obvious lack of any undergarments. My heart was pounding.

'Would you like to come in for something to drink?' I asked.

'Sure.'

Well that did it. For all intents and purposes I was on my way to seducing what looked to be an eighteen-year-old boy. Shame and desire seesawed in my mind as I led him into the kitchen. Turning away from the refrigerator with two beers, I saw him gazing at me with the appreciative eyes of a man. Seemingly of their own volition, my nipples began stiffening and prodding the front of my pink blouse. My dark aureoles were plainly visible as my nipples got shamelessly firmer, pushing defiantly at the flimsy fabric. When I leaned over to place his beer on the table, he brushed the backs of his fingers across both my nipples lightly, smiling at my sharp intake of breath.

'Felt good, didn't it?' he asked playfully.

I saw his reflection in the mirror over the table. He was inches away, the warmth of his body searing my skin through my thin clothing. His hands lifted my hair, causing my eyes to close as his lips touched my neck at its most sensitive point. My body had already begun to quiver in a way I had forgotten it could.

Raising his head to look at my wide, expectant eyes in the mirror, he smiled and released my hair in a rain of copper. So many emotions flooded me that my knees weakened. Very skillfully, he quickly unbuttoned my blouse and slipped it off my limp arms before I could remember to protest. Then gently grasping my wrists he brought my hands up to my full, round breasts with their jutting nipples. 'Aren't they beautiful?' he whispered. 'Touch them the way you like to be touched.'

Slowly, I watched my hands grasp each of my tits and gently squeeze the nipples as I massaged the rounded spheres.

He stood up, sank to his knees behind me, and tugged down my skin-tight jeans, his lips tracing a burning trail over the cheeks of my ass as I stepped out of them, keeping my high-heeled sandals on. Then he turned me to face him and told me to put my right foot on his knee. The musky odor of my own sexual heat filled my nostrils. Reaching a hand up between my legs, he parted the lips of my pussy even further, revealing my full, purplish slit. Hesitating only a moment, I touched the slick skin around my clitoris to lubricate my fingertips, working my way slowly to my sensitive knob. It felt swollen to twice its usual size as I grasped it between my thumb and forefinger and stroked it like a tiny penis. This excited even the clearly experienced young man pressing his rigid cock against my left leg. I heard him moan, 'Stroke it, stroke it!' and unable to hold back any longer, ecstasy coursed through me in breathtaking waves. A faint scream reached my ears which would have frightened me had I not realized it was my own. Gently, he helped me down into the chair directly behind me.

Once seated, I came face-to-face with the most erotic view in the world. Gary's tight shorts were pulled even tighter by his erection, and I could plainly see the swollen head staring at me from beneath the left leg of his skimpy garment. I leaned forward and licked the big drop of clear pre-cum shimmering from the tip. He moaned, and placing my hands on his firm ass, I could feel his body tensing with the orgasm to come. I yanked down his shorts and sucked and licked his cock teasingly, until I felt him perched helplessly near the brink.

'Come here!' he groaned. He pulled me roughly to my feet and bent me forward over the table. I cried out as he impaled me on his cock, thrusting into me from behind as though gutting me while after wave of pleasure flowed through my pussy juicing and tightening helplessly around his swift, hard dives. I thought I would die his rhythmic pumping and grinding felt so divine. A gravelly combination of a scream and a groan welled up in my throat, and harmonized with his animal-like grunt as I felt spurts of his hot young cum fill my lucky cunt.

30. Sarah –
Better Than the First Time

After fourteen years together and two children, it had been a long time since Neal and I had any time to ourselves. Something had to be done about it. My body missed the frequent lovemaking we had shared. Our wedding anniversary was coming up and I wanted to do something really extraordinary.

It took some thought, but finally I decided the perfect gift would be the ultimate vacation, an extravagant weekend where we'd be waited on hand-and-foot and wouldn't have to contend with having the kids around. I made reservations at our favorite hotel, the one we had stayed at during our honeymoon. I made sure everything would be exactly the same as it was then; I was even able to get the same room. It was sure to be a present and a weekend that neither of us would ever forget.

Friday finally arrived and everything had fallen into place. I had both our bags packed, the kids were having dinner with the sitter, and the limousine was on time. As I climbed in and leaned back against the plush seat, I couldn't help but smile to myself. I couldn't wait to see the expression on Neal's face when I picked him up at work.

When we got to his office, the chauffeur went inside to tell him that his limousine had arrived. A few minutes later, my husband slipped into the luxurious car with me and I flashed him a happy smile.

'What's going on?' he asked, looking astonished.

'Happy anniversary, darling,' I said, leaning over to kiss him.

'You did all this for me?' he asked, amazed. 'I can't even give you your present yet; it's at home.'

'That's okay,' I assured him. 'This gift is for both of us.'

I opened the bottle of champagne that was chilling on ice, pulled two glasses from the bar, and handed him a glass. After I poured the champagne, I said, 'To fourteen more years together, ten times over!'

A few glasses of sparkling wine, and about a hundred kisses, later we arrived at our beautiful seaside hotel. We checked into our room, dropped our bags, and put our arms around each other.

'Stay right there,' I told him as I walked towards the window. 'The first time we stayed here, we didn't go into the nightclub. We stayed in our room and danced.' I pulled the window shades up so we would be dancing in the moonlight. Then I walked over to the stereo, took 'our song' from of its album jacket, and placed it on the turntable. I returned to Neal, who was still standing where I left him. He was watching me with warm, loving eyes. We danced closely and he kissed me tenderly.

'You're the best, Susan,' he whispered. 'I'm so happy I married you.'

I moved behind him and placed my lips below his ear. With soft, tiny kisses, I made my way down his neck. The cologne he was wearing – my anniversary present to him the year before –was driving me crazy. I ran my fingers through his hair, playfully pulling his head back. He had his eyes closed so he could concentrate fully on what I was doing, but now he opened them and turned his head to meet mine. He began kissing the front of my neck and chest, and I could feel my body getting warm all over. As he let his hands run over my breasts, I began unbuttoning his shirt. I tickled his chest hairs with my fingertips then I took his hand in mine, and together, we made our way to the heart-shaped bed.

I helped him slip out of his clothes, and he sat down and reached for me. 'Not just yet,' I said as I knelt on the carpet in front of him. I cupped his large balls in my hands, and gently raised them to my lips. I sucked and kissed them softly, letting my tongue tickle and tease them, while at the same time my pussy got wetter and warmer with anticipation.

I rose and took the head of his big shaft into my mouth while still caressing his scrotum. I slid my tongue over the tip of his cock, and he began moaning with pleasure. I tightened my lips and slowly slid them up and down his erection, flicking my tongue along the sides for good measure. I could feel his balls tightening as he neared orgasm, and I moved my mouth up to his head before taking all of him into my mouth again, even letting the top part of his hard-on caress my throat. He moaned again and grasped my head firmly with both hands as his cum spurted into my mouth.

Contentedly licking my lips, I stood up and began stripping in front of him. When I got down to the lacy lingerie I'd bought especially for this weekend, he just looked at me, smiling, before he indicated he wanted me to take it all off. I did so as he lay back on the bed so I could climb on top of him. He reached for my breasts, taking them into his hands and stroking them lovingly. I rolled over so he was on top of me, and pushed both of my breasts together. He immediately knew what I wanted, and he nuzzled and licked both my nipples at the same time. The sensation was incredible. I pulled him closer to me as he continued sucking my nipples for a while before moving down to my clitoris. I had been wet and ready for some time now, and I closed my eyes, focusing on the pleasure he was giving me as he went down on me with years of experience, knowing just how to please me. As my body began to tremble, I knew I had to have him inside me.

Reading my mind, he slowly stretched himself up over me, and I reached hungrily for his cock. Using my hand, I led his stiff dick down into my grasping cunt. I held his ass in my hands and pushed him down deep inside me. He still had that same sexy ass that had turned me on fourteen years ago. I wrapped my legs around him and pulled him closer, until I could feel all of him filling me, then I placed my hands on his hips and guided him into the rhythm I desired, slow and deep.

'Come with me,' I begged softly, tightening my inner muscles so my sex was snug around him. We pushed our bodies faster and harder into each other's, and reached our climaxes together. Afterwards, I kept holding him tight.

'I want to be like this forever,' he whispered in my ear.

'So was it as good as it was when we were here the first time?'

'Better,' he said.

'I love you so much, happy anniversary.'

We lay in each other's arms and, as we were drifting off to sleep, I thought about how wonderful it was going to be spending the remaining two days of the weekend, as well as the rest of our lives, together.

31. Erin — Voyeur

From the fifth floor balcony, I watched the fiery sun sizzle into the blue ocean. As if on cue, the first stars of the night popped into the sky. I licked the salt air from my lips, absently rubbing against the black iron railing on the balcony as I did so. Tiny grains of sand in my bikini ground against my soft mound, and suddenly my whole body came alive.

Wearing only the skimpy black string bikini, I caught an elevator down to the pool. Two men in the elevator jockeyed for position to get a better view of my breasts, and beyond. I toyed with the idea of slamming the STOP button and peeling off the skimpy suit. This wasn't the normal me; I was being controlled by a lust born of fruity drinks and brightly colored umbrellas, hours in the hot sun and the romance of the Caribbean.

The pool was vast, with a circular bar built into the center. Water covered the concrete stools surrounding it, but no water entered the inner circle where a bartender wearing white shorts and a T-shirt was busy washing glasses. Suddenly he looked towards me and waved, inviting me to join him at the nearly empty bar.

I slid into the blue water and was surprised to find its coolness did nothing to quell the growing heat in my pussy. The water soothed my sun-tightened skin as I leisurely swam across the pool, choosing a seat hidden from the view of balcony onlookers. The water reached just below my nipples as I floated down onto the rough stool.

The bartender spoke directly to my breasts. 'What can I get you?' he asked.

I did nothing to block his view of my erect nipples and ordered a Rum and Coke. Behind me, a blond head bobbed in and out of the water followed by a lean, tanned body. The owner pulled himself onto a stool beside me, and ordered a beer from the obviously disappointed bartender. Droplets of water beaded the newcomer's well oiled shoulders and lean, long arms. A gray bikini brief below the surface of the water strained against its contents.

The bartender grudgingly gave his new customer a beer, and the man took a long cold drink before turning to me.

'Hi,' I said.

His brown eyes answered me by blazing a trail from my lips down to my barely covered breasts and pointed nipples, making me feel naked. His gaze finally rested on the black silk fabric shrouding the obvious focus of his desire.

I arched my back, broadening his view. Goose bumps tingled along the length of my body as hot moisture mixed with the cool pool water made my clit throb against the suit and the rough stool. From the corner of my eye, I could see that the bartender was also staring at my breasts.

The blonde's eyes finally met mine. 'Hi,' he echoed, resting one hot hand on my inner thigh beneath the surface of the water.

Suddenly the pool no longer felt refreshing his touch got me so hot.

He stood up in the chest-high water and stepped boldly between my open legs as I turned towards him. The bartender now had a profile of my body, and I noticed he was still enjoying the view. The blonde's hot hands rested lightly on both my thighs now, and I pushed my aching sex closer, willing his hands to slip beneath the fabric of my bikini. He didn't oblige me, but gently caressed the soft skin of my inner thighs instead tantalizingly.

Lowering my eyes to the gray outline below the surface, I was greeted by the head of my new friend's penis popping above the fabric.

He smiled. 'Do you want it?'

'Oh, yes…' Permission granted I groped below the surface for the object of my desire. Finding it, a small moan escaped my lips. The bartender overheard my inadvertent exclamation, and moved closer. The male bikini brief moved aside easily and his hard prick leapt from the fabric containing it. My hands pumped his shaft hungrily, its head darting dangerously nearer and nearer to my begging pussy. He stepped closer, shielding his member from the bartender's view beneath my breasts. I wrapped my legs around his hips, conscious of the bartender watching my every move. A hot arrow of lust shot through me as I wondered if he knew what was transpiring beneath the surface. The blonde's arms encircled my body and he crushed my breasts against his chest, grinding nipple to nipple. Meanwhile, my hands roamed freely beneath the water, squeezing his tight ass and then his perfectly round, hardened balls, yet always returning hungrily to his hot prick. His slick flesh shark was pointing straight at my wet cave, preparing to gain entrance as I shifted my hips even closer. The bartender also stepped closer, and asked if we needed anything else. His eyes tried to see below the surface of the water, but our bodies were entwined, blocking his view. My voice was frozen in my throat, but my partner answered huskily, 'We have everything we need, thank you.' Reluctantly, and not without a last look, the bartender moved away again.

It was nearly dark now and the vacationers along the sidewalk could see nothing more than two people embracing at the bar. Realizing it was only us and the bartender, my partner brazenly lifted the flimsy material of my swimsuit away from my breasts. They were on exhibit now. He pinched one of my hard brown nipples and I sighed, grateful they were finally being touched by him. Beneath the water, his manhood pushed against the thin Lycra barrier blocking his source of pleasure. I removed it for him, sliding my bikini to one side, and he promptly drove his big cock deep into my tight crevice with one violent thrust, nearly knocking me off the stool. My heart pounded and I bit my lip, swallowing a scream.

The bartender wandered back our way, this time smiling openly at my bared breasts. My partner had a pained smile printed across his face as he, too, was forced not to voice the sounds describing his pleasure. I glanced at the bartender, and wasn't surprised to see a hard-on straining his white shorts. My juices gushed as I realized the bartender knew exactly what was going on beneath the water and was totally turned on by it. Small ripples rocked across the calm dark pool as my partner slowly began a massaging rhythm, aware he wasn't the only man there with a throbbing penis. The cool water rushed against my clitoris, only to be replaced by the friction of his warm dick on the next downward stroke. His hands roamed freely over my body, cupping my breasts as I ached for his mouth to suck and bite my tight nipples. He plunged his swelling erection into my slick hole faster and harder, building the ripples of pleasure into waves threatening to drown my awareness of everything else. He sensed the time was near and slid one hand down until he found my clitoris. Expertly, he milked my hood as I writhed against the concrete stool.

The bartender was openly staring and licking his lips. I watched, mesmerized, as he released his manhood from the white shorts and began following our rhythm with his hand. The sight pushed me over the ecstasy's fine edge and I felt myself starting to come. My partner kissed me passionately and we moaned into each other, but then I couldn't resist looking back at the bartender massaging his prick. I'm not sure, but I think we all came at the same time.

It was a while before anyone spoke, and it was the voyeuristic bartender who finally broke the silence. 'Will there be anything else?'

My blonde lover spoke shakily, 'I think one is enough, for now.'

The bartender smiled and nodded.

My partner left a big tip, and pulled me off my stool. We floated towards the deck side-by-side, relishing the cool water against our hot, sated bodies.

A thin moon peeked out from behind a black cloud as my husband closed the door of our fifth floor room, and we fell wet and laughing onto the bed.

32. Vicky – Rare Find

My best friend and I spent most of our two-week vacation scouting eligible bachelors. Unfortunately, neither of us had much luck. We returned from the Virgin Islands feeling burned in more ways than one.

When I got home there was a message on my answering machine from the owner of a local out-of-print bookstore. He'd managed to locate the volume I'd been searching for, a treatise on John Donne.

Eager to possess this rare find, I made a mad dash for *Ryan's Reading Matter*. I was afraid it would be closed by the time I got there (I was, after all, still contending with jet lag, and my joints were stiff from sitting still for so long) but I reached the dusty hole-in-the-wall with a good quarter-hour to spare.

A broodingly handsome, dark-haired man stood behind the counter. When he saw me, he raised his head slowly from the ledger. His sharp blue eyes and sly smile caught me off guard. I walked over to him and asked to see the store owner.

'Oh, I'm sorry, Ryan doesn't own the store anymore,' he informed me quietly. 'Didn't you notice the new sign as you came in? I'm Nathaniel Johnson, the new owner. How can I help you?'

'I'm Vicky Michaels. I came to pick up a book that was special-ordered for me.'

'Yes, of course, Ryan left me very specific instructions about that. Your book is back in the storeroom. Just follow me.'

We headed for the back of the store, his stride languorous yet confident, my pace a little awkward. Just then the bell at the front door chimed, and two would-be patrons entered. I wanted to kill them.

Nathaniel politely asked me to wait while he attended to what I already perceived as two interlopers. He spoke knowledgeably about ornithology, all the while pointing out books that might be of interest. As he raised and lowered his arm, I took careful note of the way his muscles rippled beneath his white shirt. Finally, my eyes wandered toward the equally attractive lower half of his body, to his firm buttocks and the noticeable bulge in his crotch.

Though the clock indicated only ten minutes had passed, it seemed like an eternity before business for the day was over… and the pleasure could begin. I watched with anticipation as the CLOSED sign went up and the locks clicked shut, separating me, and the mesmerizing Nathaniel, from the rest of the world.

'Okay, Ms. Michaels, now for that book.' He smiled and beckoned for me to follow him again.

Surprisingly, the storeroom wasn't the musty place I had imagined it would be. In fact, the distinct odor of sandalwood mysteriously filled the air. I stood in the middle of the small room, my back to him. My eyes searched the shelves from a distance. Suddenly, I heard the door close. I began to turn around, but before I could face my attractive host, his arms were encircling my waist. I leaned into his half-expected embrace, and my eyes closed seemingly of their own accord.

'Ryan never told me how beautiful you were,' he murmured into my ear, and nibbled on the tender lobe, taking care to unlatch my turquoise earrings. 'Beautiful, so beautiful…'

Opening my eyes with a start, I made a feeble attempt to return to reality. My voice shaking, I said, 'Nathaniel, Mr. Johnson… no… please…'

'It's up to you,' he replied, but he was caressing my breasts now with slow, deliberate squeezes.

'Not here…' I protested weakly.

'Why not? The carpet in here is nice and soft.' He spun me around to face him, and kissed me hard on the mouth. His hands trailed seductively down my sides. My body began to go limp, and I could feel how hard he was. He lifted me into his arms and laid me carefully across the floor. He hovered over me, watching while I strained to unzip his pants. Mission accomplished, I slipped my hand inside them to fondle his straining penis through his underpants. But before I could go further he began undressing me, smiling appreciatively at the front closure of my bra. He unhooked it with his teeth, and kissed my breasts, first tentatively, as if afraid he might frighten me, and then more passionately. I felt his teeth grip my nipple and clutched his head to encourage him. I caressed his soft, wavy hair and savored the warmth of his lips and tongue on my flesh. His right hand traveled downward slowly, enticingly. I opened my legs accommodatingly, and he slipped his fingers into my panties to fondle the slippery folds of my labia, pinching the little pink bud of my clit until I trembled and moaned, scarcely able to control my excitement. Then he yanked my panties down my legs and his tongue flicked tantalizingly along my inner thighs, moving upward to lap at my pussy with a puppy-like energy that was nevertheless devastatingly skillful. I held my breath as he lifted my hips and bent my knees over his shoulders.

Driven wild with a desire I had never felt before as he went down on me hungrily, I summoned every ounce of strength I possessed to slide out from beneath him, and roll him onto his back. Eager to view his full beauty, I undressed him feverishly, delighting in every masculine detail of his body. I rubbed my crotch against his, feeling his hardness growing beneath me. He wriggled impatiently, all the while moaning; practically gasping for air. Placing my knees on either side of his hips, I lowered myself to kiss the very tip of his penis with my sex lips. He raised his hips off the floor and plunged athletically up into my cunt. Then we were soaring like two magnificent birds... yet being only human we needed the ground so we crashed back down onto the carpet, where we fell into an almost unbearably pleasurable rhythm. I forgot all about the book I had come for as we read all each other's secret desires without words.

33. Elena — Correspondence

I looked at my mailbox with anticipation as I walked up the steps to my apartment. For two weeks now I'd been getting letters from a man, unsigned letters, and they were the most beautiful letters I had ever read. I had received seven of them so far, and all were tucked away in the top drawer of my dresser. Even if I never met the guy who was sending them, I knew I'd keep them forever.

I nervously turned the key to my mailbox. As I peeked in, I couldn't help smiling. There was another one. It looked the same as the others – a cream-colored envelope with flowing black script. I put it in my hand, took the letter out carefully, and let myself into my apartment, ready to enjoy yet another of his missives.

My Darling Elena, the letter began as I'd come to expect. *This is my eighth letter to you, and I can't help but wonder how you feel about all this. We have to meet, and soon. Wait for my next letter, I'll explain when and how.*

My heart was pounding as I realized I was finally going to meet my mystery man. I wondered what he would look like. Was he tall? Was he on the short side? How old was he? What kind of man would write love letters to a woman he may never even have met? I sighed as I prepared dinner and went about my nightly routine, trying not to get too excited.

Yet when it came time for bed, I knew I couldn't help thinking about him. Many of his letters had hinted about the things he want-ed to do to me sexually, and they all sounded appealing. I wasn't dat-ing anyone, and it had been a while since I'd indulged in lovemaking that left me weak and made me want to scream at the same time. I thought about this as I lay in bed and my hands made their way down between my thighs. I was wet; ready. Still thinking about him, I closed my eyes as my fingers began probing my sex lips and stroking my sensitive clitoris as my other hand caressed the soft fullness of my breasts. I was imagining what it would be like to have a hard cock where my fingers now explored... with a shudder I quickly brought myself to orgasm, and then drifted off to sleep.

***

Nothing happened for a week. I was puzzled. What about his hint that we would finally meet? I watched the mailbox every afternoon, and stroked myself at night. I had to admit that if this was a game of cat and mouse, he was doing a great job at keeping up the suspense.

Then it arrived. A letter. *The* letter. Not even stopping to let myself into the apartment, I ripped it open in front of my mailbox, and scanned it eagerly. There it was... *At last we'll meet. Be in front of The Buoys Restaurant at 7 p.m. this Friday night. I don't want to intrude by asking to meet at your apartment; you don't know me and I don't want to scare you. But I want to see you, face-to-face, I can't wait any longer. Until then.*

Still no hints as to who he was. I knew, however, that he was considerate – he didn't want to scare me by meeting me at my apartment. But then another thought hit me. What was I going to wear? Once inside, I looked through my closet until I found a pale-blue silk dress with a scoop neckline. Sexy, yes, but sedate enough that he wouldn't think I was ready to jump him, although, of course, I might do just that.

***

It was five to seven, and I didn't know whether I should go into the restaurant or wait outside. But he knew me; I should go in. I turned and was about to push through the heavy swinging doors when a man pulled it open for me. A handsome man... Carl! He worked at an office downtown next to the shopping center I went to. I had bumped into him once, dropping my heavy bags, and he had helped me gather up my spilled cans, boxes and containers. We had talked for a few minutes.

'Hi Carl,' I stuttered, confused for a moment. 'What are you doing here?'

He looked at me and continued smiling.

I could feel my face go white, then red. It was Carl. It had to be Carl. We stood there for a few more moments just staring at each other. I couldn't help but notice he was wearing a forest-green sweater that brought out his eyes, and his longish blond hair was slightly tousled. I wanted to touch him very badly. 'It's you,' was all I could say, and then felt stupid.

'Yes,' he confirmed. 'Come inside. I have some things to tell you.'

As it turned out we had a wonderful dinner. After a shy beginning, we soon loosened up, and we talked and laughed our way through a two-hour meal. As we sipped our last cup of coffee, Carl reached for my hand and squeezed it. I returned the pressure. 'Elena,' he murmured.

I felt my body react immediately; my stomach tightened up and my juices began flowing. Even my breasts seemed to get fuller, straining against the pale silk of my dress. I squirmed, wanting more of his touch but not sure how to get it. I was ready to take him home with me, and I wanted him to know it.

He was thinking the same thing, although he didn't pressure me. 'What do you want to do next?' he asked, raising my hand to his lips.

'I want to get into my car with you and take you home with me,' I replied.

Half-an-hour later, we were nearly naked on my bed, Carl murmuring in delight as he uncovered my black bra and panties and matching garters. (Dressing that night, I had wanted to be prepared for anything.) He was rubbing my breasts through my bra, and I helped him take it off. He immediately buried his face in my cleavage, and then caressed my nipples with his warm, slightly rough tongue. The sensation was so incredible I let out a moan of pure pleasure and pushed his face hard into my breast. I looked down. The tip of his penis was peeking out of his briefs. I quickly pulled them off, sliding my body up and down his, marveling at his firm, taut belly, his broad shoulders and his strong legs, which until now I had never really noticed.

We kissed and groped each other for what seemed like hours, and then he gently pushed me down across the bed and silently parted my thighs. I thought he was about to enter me and groaned in anticipation, but his tongue traveled down my belly and began probing my pussy. I relaxed as his tongue circled and teased my clitoris.

'Mm…' I heard his murmur from between my legs and his eagerness made me even hotter. Very soon I felt an orgasm welling up inside me and gladly surrendered to its exquisite undertow, shuddering and bucking my hips uncontrollably.

I wanted to give him the pleasure he had just given me, so I rolled him over onto his back and began sucking his cock, playing with his balls and flicking my tongue up and down his beautifully veined shaft. I took his erection completely into my mouth, pumping him with one hand while gently squeezing his balls with the other. A few minutes was all I thought he was going to be able to take of this attention, so I slowed my ministrations, and then kissed my way up his body, pulling him on top of me.

He immediately thrust his erection into my pussy, and I groaned as his thick hardness probed my innermost depths. He felt so good, so warm, and we fell into an easy, steady rhythm. He looked down at me, smiling. 'Are you going to come again?' he asked, intensifying the depth of his thrusts, and before I had time to answer, I cried out as another climax swept me away, forcing me to bite his neck to brace myself. My pleasure sent him over the edge as well and he thrust harder and harder, until he finally collapsed on top of me.

He stayed inside me for a few minutes, and then rolled off me, cradling me in his arms. It felt so right I couldn't believe I hadn't known him all my life. 'It was your letters that did it, you know,' I murmured. 'How could I resist?'

'Keep watching your mailbox,' he said, kissing me. 'You haven't seen anything yet.'

34. Janet – After the Concert

He lay in a heavy sleep as I quietly entered our bedroom and set down my violin in the corner beneath the window. The concert, a sell-out performance, had gone into overtime and I was coming home much later than usual. I had phoned him during intermission to tell him I would be home late and that he needn't wait up for me. Obviously, he had taken my advice.

As I removed my shoes and hung up my black concert dress, my eyes began adjusting to the darkness of the bedroom. I thoroughly surveyed every inch of my beloved man's body, which was totally naked; the night was too warm for blankets. A warm, sexy feeling permeated my body as I watched his chest expand and contract with each breath.

I put my things away, and then settled into the comfortable leather chair next to the bed to observe him. His head, adorned with dark curly hair, was not quite centered on the fluffy satin pillow. His face, usually animated and expressive, was placid in sleep. His long eyelashes fluttered over his cheeks, and his nostrils were flared, allowing for his deep, rhythmical breathing. His full lips were slightly parted. At that moment I was sorely tempted to awaken him with a long, wet, warm kiss. I restrained myself, however, remembering how tired he had been lately and realizing he needed his sleep. I had a strong impulse to take one of his hands in mine. It took every ounce of will power I could muster to let him sleep. Yet despite all my efforts to leave him in peace, I felt a growing desire for him.

All of a sudden he changed position, moving ever so slightly toward the left side of the bed, but his sleep remained undisturbed. How I wished he would wake up! I was beginning to feel very aroused looking at him. My eyes drifted down to his crotch. His exquisite penis was at rest. I studied it hungrily for several minutes. His cock was beautiful, from its thick base to the delicate opening at the end of the full head.

I couldn't stand it any longer. I had become hot and moist and I desperately needed to release the sexual tension that had built up inside me. Not wanting to wake him, I spread my legs apart and inserted the index finger of my right hand into my pussy as far as I could. My inner parts were warm and lubricated, so I used my juices to moisten my aroused clitoris. I worked my finger in tiny circles all around my sensitive little seed, luxuriating in the deep pleasure taking root in my pelvis as I kept my eyes on my sleeping lover.

After only a few minutes my orgasm began cresting. It started slowly, and then gradually increased in intensity until my whole body was suffused with ecstasy. By the time it was over, I was winded, flushed and, in a way, sorry – I knew he enjoyed watching me pleasure myself.

After my climax, most of my sexual tension had been released. My nipples, stiff and sensitive only moments ago, were now soft and supple again, and I felt the tension slowly ebbing inside me. Still, I wanted my man. I needed to touch him, to taste him, to feel him. I slid out of my chair and positioned myself on the edge of the bed, sitting next to his sexy body.

I gingerly picked up his hand, and drew it up to my lips, kissing the sensitive palm and drawing circles with the tip of my tongue. I slid his index finger into my mouth until it lay on top of my warm tongue, and began a slow sucking motion. I repeated this with each of his fingers, drawing them in and out from between my pursed lips with passionate care.

Gently, I reached for his flaccid penis and held it in my hand, delicately stroking it. I watched my lover's face as his eyes began to open, and suddenly, his penis stiffened to attention. He raised his hand and rested it on my knee. From the stillness of his body, I could tell he was tired, but he began caressing my thigh in a way that said, 'I want you.' I looked down at his cock, and with the same index finger that had just produced my ecstasy, I swiped up the drop of pre-cum glistening at its tender tip.

I slid my leg away from beneath his hand and knelt beside him on the bed, positioning my face in line with his genitals. I took his cock into my mouth, and knowing he was still barely awake, I sucked him gently, reveling in his taste, texture and aroma. Aroused by the strong sensations of pleasure I was giving him, he emitted small groans of encouragement while stroking the back of my neck as I sucked him, more vigorously now. He was on the edge… he squirmed and gasped softly and before long I felt a familiar tightening in his balls, which I held cupped in one hand. When I felt his thigh muscles tense, I knew he was about to come. And he did, quickly, spurting a large amount of love fluid into my mouth with a few powerful contractions. I held on to him the whole time, licking and sucking him until his pulsing had subsided and his eyes closed again, this time with fulfillment rather than exhaustion. He snuggled me against him gently, and smiled sleepily. 'Was that your idea of an alarm clock?' he teased.

'Sorry to wake you,' I apologized with mock regret. 'I promise I'll never do it again.'

His smile widened. 'I think I'll forgive you, and you'd *better* do it again.'

35. Janice – Reunited

Facing an old lover has to be one of the hardest things in life, particularly a first love. Joel and I had met when we were both eighteen-years-old, and we dated all through college. We lost our virginity together and thought we would be a couple forever. Things change, however, and the relationship ended after graduation. But tonight, for the first time in five years, we were going to be face-to-face again.

I had been flitting around the apartment for hours. Everything was in order – the wine was chilling, the appetizers were ready, and beneath my clothes I was wearing new lingerie I had purchased in anticipation of our night together. I knew it was going to happen; these things you can just feel. I had been wet and deliciously anxious all day just thinking about his lips on my breasts... about his dick sliding in and out of my pussy... we had made love all the time when we were in college and it had always been fresh and exciting. I wondered how it would be between us after five years.

I was checking my hair and makeup in the mirror when I heard his knock. I opened the door, butterflies in my stomach, and saw he was as handsome as ever. I wanted to press myself against him right then and there.

'Hi, Janice.' His voice was husky.

'It's been so long,' I said softly, and then gave him a friendly kiss.

We settled on the sofa and began talking about old times. The conversation led from the past to the present, and we spoke for hours until we ran out of things to say. That's when I began feeling nervous. My body had been craving his for hours, and my desire for him finally out-weighed my anxiety. 'Come here,' I said, pulling at his arm and moving closer to him. 'Do you feel the same?' I asked, brushing his cheek with my lips. I moved my face closer to trail my tongue against his lips, and as we kissed, I felt five year's worth of passion about to be released.

He kissed both my cheeks, and his hands wandered over my back and down the front of my silky blouse.

My fingers trembled as I slid the buttons of his shirt through their holes and gently pulled it off, my fingertips caressing the crisp curly hair of his chest I had missed so much. I moved closer so I could brush my tingling nipples against his firm flesh. I kissed him again, marveling at the subtle but intense pleasure he was giving me. His warm tongue moved down my throat to the erect tips of my breasts through my blouse, and I could hardly wait for his lips and tongue to kiss my nipples.

'Joel ...' I whispered.

'Tell me what you want,' he murmured.

'You know what I want,' I whispered urgently. It was time. Wordlessly, we shed our clothing with the ease of long habit, and then we looked a little nervously at each other. I could see him admiring my sexy red teddy and was glad I had worn it.

'I've waited for this so long,' he said, smiling. 'And now we're here. Together.' He pushed me gently down on the couch and his hands moved across my body, massaging my breasts through the flimsy satin, and reaching beneath me to squeeze my ass cheeks before caressing my thighs. Meanwhile I was busy running my hands over his muscled flesh, and stroking his long, hard penis with one fist while my other palm lovingly cupped his balls. I was aching to be licked, sucked, and fucked senseless!

He pulled me up so my back was resting against one of the high arms of the couch. I knew what would come next as he snapped open the damp crotch of my teddy, and my breathing grew heavy as his tongue teased my clitoris. His lips took its tiny length into his mouth and sucked on it gently. I held onto his hair as I felt my thighs begin to tremble. It wasn't long before the skilled working of his tongue had me ready to come, and sensing my imminent release, he pulled back.

'You're going to come around my cock,' he commanded, inching his way up my body to rest on top of me.

I looked at his cock. It was as big and hard as I remembered it.

Very slowly, he slipped his glorious hard-on inside me, his eyes shining with delight as he penetrated me. I moaned as his erection filled my pussy, stretching my innermost flesh open around it. He pushed deeper and deeper into my body and my vaginal muscles clamped down around on his cock as hard as they could. He moved in and out of me with slow, hard strokes as I writhed against him, struggling to get closer and closer to him even though it was impossible; his cock-head was already kissing my cervix with every thrust. Suddenly, his mouth moved to my breasts and he began sucking hard on my nipples, knowing full well this would send my senses spiraling into a climax. He fucked me faster and harder, sucking on my tits the whole time, and I began climaxing, arching my back and shoving my tits up into his mouth.

Afterwards, he lay beside me on the couch. 'Feels like old times,' I said, stroking his hair.

'We could make it new times,' he replied, pulling me even closer.

I kissed him. It felt like the beginning of something beautiful.

36. Maryanne – Good Neighbors

My eighteen-year-old neighbor, Alex, was always a joy to behold as he worked in his parents' yard. He was usually shirtless and in tight denim shorts that showed off his firm round buns to good advantage. As an older divorced woman, I indulged in a sex life that pretty much consisted of watching him work and imagining him at play.

One Saturday afternoon my doorbell rang and I opened the door to find him on my porch. I'd seen him doing yard work earlier and now here he was, gleaming with sweat and holding my cat, Muffy, in his arms.

'Your cat was stuck up in the tree in our yard,' he said. 'I thought I'd better get her back to you.' I could tell he was surprised to see me still in my nightgown at four o'clock in the afternoon, but I was interested to note he seemed truly impressed by my appearance. I may be a mature woman, but I'm still a looker.

'Well, Alex, how sweet of you,' I cooed. 'Won't you come in and let me fix you a nice cold drink?'

He barely hesitated before stepping into my foyer.

I invited him into the kitchen, and poured him a cold beer, smiling to myself as he jumped when my breast grazed his arm as I served him. Normally, I'm a very reserved woman; no one who knows me would imagine I could take a teenage boy by the hand and lead him into my bedroom with the intention of seducing him, but that's exactly what I did, and he seemed grateful not to have to ask.

When we were in my bedroom, I slipped my nightgown over my head and reclined alluringly naked across the bed. He seemed unsure of what to do next, so I said, 'Baby, take those shorts off, please, I want to see what you've got for me.' He was trembling with excitement or maybe first-time fucking anxiety, but he complied readily, and I was rewarded with the sight of a tremendous hard-on. It had been a long time since I'd seen a real one, and I almost literally purred with pleasure.

Suddenly, he began to masturbate, making no move to join me on the bed. I didn't mind in the least since I was finding it exciting as hell just watching him jack-off. I felt a powerfully sweet warmth between my legs that began spreading throughout my entire body as I watched him stroking his cock.

'Oh yeah,' I murmured, 'yeah, baby that's it, go for it.' His knees were slightly bent, his mouth gaping open, and I could tell he was in the throes of a sexual frenzy unlike anything he had ever known before. I looked into his eyes, and saw the depth of his arousal. He was so exposed, so vulnerable, and yet the overriding emotion he was feeling was unbridled sexual lust. He wanted me to see his erect throbbing cock, and as he rhythmically stroked it with his fist, I could tell he wanted me to see him come. I wanted that, too, and was already so turned-on by all of this sideline activity that my desire to fuck him had diminished. As Alex's pumping increased in urgency, I spread my legs and began writhing my hips against the bed.

'Oh, shit,' he muttered. 'Goddamn… it's too good…' He slowed his strokes while his other hand caressed his balls.

'I want to see you come,' I said. 'I want to see you shoot your load, baby. I want you to come all over me. I want you to just stand there and come and come and come.'

My dirty talk did him in almost at once. With an almost angry stance, thrusting his hips out towards me, he pumped his cock directly over my naked body. His eyes glazed over and he spread his legs just a little wider, looking like he was taking aim for my breasts.

'Okay, baby, you want it, you'll get it!' he gasped. 'I'm going to give you all I've got!' He threw his head back, groaning with pleasure, and I loved every second of seeing him so sexually aroused. He was slamming his cock furiously with his fist. 'Goddamn, it's good… Goddamn…' Then with a whistled intake of breath, he looked down at himself and watched his engorged dick and hips moving back and forth in a fucking motion.

I don't think I've ever been so wet. Not even my greatest lays compared to the excitement I felt watching this young, inexperienced man beating his meat for me.

'Oh, shit, here it comes,' he growled. 'It's gonna shoot… oh, shit, I can't stop now, it's coming…' With a deep groan he planted his feet firmly on the carpet and stood there stroking himself as a stream of spunk shot out of his cock and onto my writhing hips. His eyes rolled back into his head as a second, third, and then a fourth jet of hot semen burst forth from his pulsing head.

As the first wave of his pleasure landed on my body, I, too, began feeling the inevitability of what was happening. I looked up at his naked, sexy body and felt the beginning tremors of my own orgasm. 'Oh, God, baby, me too,' I whispered as the waves of pleasure overwhelmed me. I clamped my legs together feeling each spasm of pure ecstasy slice up through my body. I never knew coming could be so good without actually fucking.

I'm looking forward to more afternoon delights with my young neighbor. Maybe I can introduce him to a few new pleasures, too.

37. Joyce – Intimate Strangers

My ex-husband relished diversity in his sex life morning, noon, and night – on the bed, on the floor, on the kitchen table, on top, underneath, sideways – he loved it all. 'Variety is the spice of sex,' he would quip repeatedly. Unfortunately, he was applying this theory to his needs alone. We only fooled around when, and how, he wanted to. Ours was not an equal-opportunity love life, and that's why he's my ex.

A year after our divorce, I was still searching for an unselfish lover. At a party one evening, my friend Nancy and I were fantasizing about which of the men there might be great lays and which were probably lousy ones, the kind we were used to. We were giggling as an incredibly gorgeous guy walked in, and my imagination ran amok. I heard my own sharp intake of breath as Nancy whispered, 'Look at that face, at that body! Are those jeans tight, or what? I can see every inch of his…' Her words faded as my pulse pounded in my ears. I could practically feel his mouth on mine, his hands slipping into my panties…

His kisses started soft and sweet at my earlobes and moved down my neck to devour my cleavage. Pressing closer to my compliant body, he pried my lips apart with his hot tongue. Large hands sent shivers down my bare arms, and I felt my knees buckling. He fumbled with my zipper, and moments later my dress crumpled at my feet. His kisses left a wet trail on my neck while both his hands cupped my breasts, his thumbs circling my hardening nipples. His blonde head slipped lower, following the generous curves of my flesh as he pressed me back onto the bed. His blue eyes met mine as he began to strip slowly. His cock, big and hard, sprang out from between the loose folds of his zipper. He gripped it in his strong hand so only his swollen head was visible and began masturbating right in front of me. And while his fist moved slowly up and down his erection, he smiled and said, 'Tell me when you're ready for this.'

Entranced, I stared at him as he pleasured himself. My hands couldn't help but creep towards my own lap as I lay spread-eagled on the bed in front of him. Then he knelt, and pushing my knees even further apart, he used his mouth and the fingers of his free hand to open my slick pussy lips. I writhed in uncontrollable pleasure, my hips following his every lick. He inserted three fingers into my creaming hole and kept up the rhythm of his tongue against my clitoris, the deep moans emanating from his chest telling me he was loving this as much as I was.

With my fingers buried in his hair, I climaxed, every nerve-ending in my body seemingly centered in my pussy and in the clit that swelled against his lips while my juices filled his mouth. I experienced one of the most intense orgasms of my life, and as my heart and breathing slowed, I think I murmured, 'That was the best I've ever had.'

To which he replied, 'Well, if once was good, twice will be even better.' And he proceeded to go down on me again, until I wanted him inside me more than anything else in the world...

'Joyce, have you heard a word I said?' Nancy hissed, invading my daydream. 'That fox is still staring at you! Do you know him or what?'

Smiling, I watched my awesome Adonis threading his way through the crowd towards us, his sexy eyes penetrating into mine. As I rose to greet him, I answered my friend, 'As a matter of fact, I know him very well.'

38. Jeannine – Wild Ride

It had been a bad two months all around. Feeling very much over-worked and under-appreciated, I decided to visit a friend in Dallas who had been begging me to come and see her. When I arrived, she told me she had made plans for us to spend a relaxing week with a rancher friend. We took a quick trip to a local store, and I emerged appropriately attired – boots, hat and gingham dress.

The trip to the ranch was uneventful, just miles and miles of endless grasslands. Pulling into the driveway, I was surprised to see it wasn't a cattle baron's estate, but a small private ranch. Don, the owner and operator, strode out into the blazing sunlight. Dark-haired, boasting an old-fashioned bushy mustache, he wore a broad smile and tight jeans. Mm… six feet of solid muscle!

He greeted both of us, but his eyes were clearly focused on me. I could tell he was reading my mind, and I was doing my best to send him a message regarding everything I wanted to do with him. Moving smoothly and swiftly as a hawk swooping down on its prey, he helped us unload the car. Then, having told us to make ourselves at home, he went back to work.

Dinner was plain but good, though I kept thinking about how delicious *he* must be. Hours later I went for a walk, and straddling the threshold of Don's private room, I said, 'Hello.'

'I've never believed in long introductions,' he replied. Coming from anyone else it would have sounded like a snarl, but that was his voice, husky and suggestive. He took me in his arms and gently pushed me back against the edge of an old luggage truck, lifting me up onto it. Then he raised the skirt of my gingham dress and began caressing my thighs. He hooked his thumbs into the waistband of my panties, and in an instant yanked them down over my boots, tossing them away carelessly. He spread my legs, stepped in between them, and expertly began rubbing his bulging denim-clad crotch up and down against my moist pussy. He maneuvered it so the fly of his pants rode directly between the sensitive lips of my labia and I was heating up fast knowing I was about to realize what had been a dream since my girlhood – to be made love to by a real cowboy.

Abruptly, he moved away, and when he saw how wet the crotch of his jeans were, he grinned. Throwing a blanket over his broad shoulders, he said, 'Come on, let's go outside.'

I smoothed down my dress, and followed him through the small woods behind the cabin. We stepped into a wide open pasture. Overhead a full moon lit the expanse of grass so brightly I could have read a book by that light; however, that was not my intention. Other than our muffled footsteps and breathing there wasn't a sound in the world.

Don spread the blanket on the ground and called me over to him. Taking me in his arms again, he kissed my waiting mouth and lifted the dress up over my head. He unfastened my bra, and let it fall. Feeling quite foolish for a moment I just stood there stark naked except for my boots in front of a fully dressed, horny cowboy. Crouching down, he helped me off with my boots.

'Lie down,' he commanded.

I obeyed him as he knelt beside me. My breasts, exposed to the cool night air, were warmed by his work-roughened hands. He played with my sensitive nipples, first lightly and then more firmly, skillfully rubbing and pinching until the small dark circles of my aureoles became hard and round as pebbles beneath his calloused fingers. Then he began kissing me passionately, beginning with my lips and moving down my neck to between my breasts and across my belly. He moved even farther down, and I spread my legs open for him. His bristly mustache tickled the inside of my thighs as he thrust his amazingly hard tongue into my cunt. It squirmed inside me, pliant and sure, his thumbs working to spread open my moist lips. His technique was incredible – flicking and sucking, sucking and flicking. He kept at it until I thought I would scream with pleasure, and I didn't just think I would, I did, the blood pounding in my ears like thunder as I climaxed.

We lay there for a moment surrounded on all sides by the woods and empty grasslands. The stars shone like spurs above us in the black velvet sky. Then I realized he was still fully dressed, and that he hadn't yet come. I looked at him questioningly. Silently, he unbuckled his belt and unfastened the buttons of his fly. I spied the splendor of his erection, and gasped. Don was uncut, with a foreskin that still completely covered the head of his cock. Grinning, he took his penis in hand and began working the skin forward and back, first exposing the dark head then covering it again. The sight of this man's dick left as nature intended it literally made my mouth water. I felt like I was going crazy; I couldn't figure out what was taking so long for him to get inside me.

With me still lying on my back and him still fully clothed but exposed now, he knelt between my legs again. He pulled his foreskin forward so the head of his hard-on was covered again, and then leaned over me. His aim was perfect; he sank slowly all the way into my pussy, and then slid back out and penetrated me again with the same patient ease. After that the rhythm of his strokes varied, alternating between fast and slow, deep and shallow, ever changing while his lips and hands sought out my heaving breasts. He seemed tireless; his thrusts going on and on as I came again, this time even more fiercely. Few men had ever brought me to two orgasms so quickly. As the mists faded, I realized this rugged male animal was still inside me and still fully erect.

He pulled out of me, stood up, and slowly stripped off his shirt, boots and pants. The distended veins of his cock were clearly visible, highlighted and shadowed by the bright moonlight. I asked him how he liked to come, what I could do to please him, and with his dark eyes almost glowing in the silvery darkness, he let me know what he wanted. Pulling the skin back behind the head of his tireless erection, he said, 'I want to ride you like a pony.'

'What?' I gasped.

'I'll show you. Get up on your hands and knees.'

I started to protest, but he insisted. 'It'll be real good for both of us,' he assured me, so I did as he asked, and he knelt behind me.

'Bite down on this, my little filly,' he instructed, and I could scarcely believe it when I felt the hard length of his thick leather belt thrust between my lips and press down on my tongue. I moaned, shocked and totally turned on at the same time, as I bit down on the leather just like a bridled pony. Gently, he pulled my head up as far as it would go, forcing me to dramatically arch my back and thrust my naked buttocks towards him invitingly. I moaned again, straining all the muscles in my body to sustain that seductive pose as I felt him guiding the flaring mushroom head of his penis into my pussy. I bit down on the belt as he rode me, banging his cock into my cunt from behind with all his strength, keeping my body totally and helplessly open to his violent thrusts with gentle but firm tugs on the belt. I let myself go, thrilled by how forcefully he reached forward and squeezed my breasts, bobbing wildly back and forth as his erection charged in and out of my clinging sex. He was deep in the saddle, riding the range. I heard him repeat, 'Yeah, yeah, oh, yeah!' over and over again like some chant to a pagan god. His breathing became ragged and short, and suddenly he shouted, 'Here it comes!' his penis pulsing and jerking deep in my pussy. He shot his load way up inside me, and under the big western sky, I climaxed again. That was a new experience for me, and I loved every minute of it.

When I could think clearly again, I was lying in his arms. His big, capable hands were fondling my exhausted body and he was licking my nipples as if seeking to quench a terrible thirst. The coarse stubble on his chin felt like the caress of a cactus as he nibbled gently on my 'rosebuds' as he called them. He wanted to know how long I would be around, and I had to tell him it would only be a week.

'That's enough time,' he said, fingering my damp pubic hair. 'I've got more kinky pastures to show you.'

39. Susanne – License to Love

While standing in line at the Department of Motor Vehicles Driver's License counter, I spied a man two people behind me who took my breath away. I forgot about renewing my license as I took in his animal magnetism. Wearing what I hoped was my most seductive smile I casually turned and looked into his expressive brown eyes.

He grinned back at me, waving his expired license in my face. 'Aren't birthdays a bitch?' his deep, baritone voice drawled.

My eyes studied his lustrous brown hair, rugged features and muscular physique. Smiling up into his face, I replied, 'They're just one of life's little hazards. I'm going to be a year older myself next week.'

He introduced himself. His name was Perry. He casually rested his hand on my shoulder and spoke for my ears only. 'The worst part is spending a birthday alone, and a Saturday, at that. At least on a working day I could stay busy and forget I'll be forty-two.' A twinkle came into his eyes as he added, 'I'll bet your man's going to blow your mind after you blow out your candles. No such luck for me.'

My mind was reeling. This beautiful man, who certainly did not look forty-two, had just handed me my heart's desire on a silver platter. I shook my head and answered, 'No, there's no man in my life at the moment.' A wicked little smile crept onto my face and I whispered in a teasing voice, 'Why don't we just blow each other's mind with a joint birthday party?'

He grinned. 'I can't wait to get out of here so we can plan our party.'

After we were both in possession of our new licenses, we stopped at a Diner for coffee. Although the next hour of intense eye contact and conversation had my pussy wet and hot, I was determined he was not getting into my panties until party time, for I had plans. Before he could make a serious move, I said, 'Sorry, but my schedule is unreal today. How does three o'clock tomorrow afternoon sound for our big bash? I like to start early, don't you?'

Obviously disappointed, he just nodded in agreement, but after all, he did have the promise of tomorrow.

I jotted down my address, and handed it to him. 'I'll be waiting,' I said, winking. 'Remember, perfect timing is essential. Your birthday cake will be done precisely at three.'

'Can't you get away for just a few minutes today?'

Instinctively knowing that at any moment I would weaken and confess all I had to do for the next twenty-four hours was get ready for our party, I glanced at my watch and exclaimed, 'I'm running behind already! Tomorrow at three o'clock sharp!' and with a wave, I was gone.

I literally flew home. Turning him down had been hell, but it was my birthday, too, and I planned to have the most satisfying one ever – my own favorite fantasy coming true. I would blow his mind as well as his dick.

It was a good thing I had a lot to do, for I knew I would not sleep until Perry brought me to orgasm, many, many orgasms. I kept bursting into fits of silly giggling as I turned my apartment into a harem and thought of the erotic escapades that lay in store.

The next day as I waited naked in excited expectation behind my closed apartment door, I knew exactly when he reached each of the signs I had placed out in the hallway. I heard a small chuckle when he read the *Happy Birthday, Baby, 42 Looks Good to Me* and a belly laugh when he saw, *Mature Men are Better Lovers.*

As he approached my front door, I became a little edgy about his reaction to my decor. But when I opened the door, giggling with a mixture of nerves and excitement, the expression on his face changed from apprehension to astonishment to pure joy.

I led him to the bed, over which a large sign said *Let's Eat!* I was going to be his birthday cake. Whipped cream and cherries were at the ready. I squeezed the sweet cool cream onto my breasts and belly, and demurely looked up into his face. 'Come and have a piece, of cake, I mean.'

That's all he needed to hear. Quickly, he began nibbling the cherries balanced on my already erect nipples, and I moaned as his tongue caressed my breasts. He lapped up the whipped cream on my chest and abdomen, sending erotic sensations throughout my whole body. My hands relished the feel of his muscular physique, his clean-shaven face and that magnificent head of hair. When his mouth reached my pussy I was in heaven, for his tongue stroked and teased my clit in just the right way to please me. I watched him making love to my pussy with his skillful mouth and an orgasm engulfed me.

'Mm,' I breathed, 'that was nice, but now it's your turn, birthday boy. Quickly into your birthday suit!' He obliged me with alacrity, and I playfully pushed him onto his back and grabbed the can of whipped cream. I giggled as I sprayed him all over. Starting with his neck, I enjoyed every sinful calorie as I licked his chest, teased his erect nipples, tongued his navel, and slowly ate his cock. My mouth fit his dick like a glove, and the longer I sucked, the hotter my pussy got.

'You really enjoy my dick in your mouth?' he asked.

I grinned up at him with a whipped-cream-smeared face and answered, 'No, I *love* your dick in my mouth.'

'Well, let's see where else you love it,' he said, and rolled me over onto my back, whipping my feet up onto his shoulders. The intensity of the sensations as his dick plunged deep into my vagina took my breath away, and the sweet fire of ecstasy overwhelmed me again as he thrust while massaging my clit with his thumb.

'Are you coming again?' he asked, watching me with liquid eyes.

I was panting too hard in the throes of a climax to answer, but I reached up and pulled him down against me as I basked in the afterglow of intense pleasure.

'Let's see how good it feels with you on top,' he muttered thickly. I knew he was as hot as I was, and it felt great being in control; riding his powerful cock with a slow, rhythmic motion until I felt the pulses of his orgasm deep within me. I held on for dear life as exquisite sensations all came devastatingly together in my third and best climax of the day.

As I lay spent in his arms, I whispered, 'That was the most satisfying birthday present ever. Mature men *are* better lovers.' I planted a gentle kiss on his cheek.

'Thanks,' he said sleepily, playing with a strand of my hair, but then he startled me by suddenly sitting up and looking at me with a dead serious expression. 'Do you have a calculator?' he asked.

'A calculator?'

'I need to know just how many times forty-two can go into thirty-two.' He had noticed the date on my driver's license.

I pulled him back down and molded my body to his. As I nibbled on his ear, I breathed, 'As many times as he likes!'

40. Sharon — One Plus Two

I was flattered when Neal and Anne invited me to their cabin for the weekend. They were the attractive couple who sometimes graced our Friday night singles dance. Whenever they arrived, word spread quietly through the group. They were the Count and Countess of the realm. Neal was magnificently handsome and dark, and Anne was a pert, petite, lovely blonde. Just the sight of either one of them made my heart beat faster.

One Friday night I found Anne standing beside me on the dance floor more than usual. It was almost as though she had chosen me as a lady-in-waiting. When I told her my name, I wished I could have said 'Sonya' or something more mysterious and romantic than Sharon.

After that night, we talked often. Conversation moved smoothly because of Anne's charming nature, and one night I was pleased when she complimented me on my dress. I muttered something about wishing my looks were as good as my clothes.

Anne's blue eyes widened. "Don't be silly,' she declared. 'Neal thinks you're one of the most attractive women here.'

If my heart had cared before, it now did a flip-flop in shock. Neal had noticed me? Well, my looks weren't actually bad. My hair, which I sometimes described as mouse-brown, was really soft, light-brown with glistening highlights. I thought of my nose as being too small, but I suppose it could be called cute. My body? Proportionate. Legs? Long and curvy. I suddenly felt good about my looks and stood taller.

Neal was approaching us with a drink in each hand. As he handed one to Anne, a spark of something passed between them. Neal handed me the other drink, and his smile enchanted me. My knees felt weak as his hand brushed mine. 'You take this, Sharon,' he said, 'I'll go get another one.'

I was warm with happiness; Anne's attention, and Neal's touch, had me glowing, and it was almost overwhelming when I heard Anne say, 'Neal and I are driving up to our cabin tonight. Why don't you come up Saturday afternoon and stay until Sunday?'

I accepted eagerly.

***

I arrived at the cabin after four o'clock. It was deep in the woods on a hilltop overlooking a valley of oaks and pine trees. Anne greeted me wearing a light-blue silk robe. She showed me to my room, and told me to get into my swimsuit and join them at the pool. Then I had to face putting on my new bikini. I looked at myself in the full-length mirror. Was it too little? Did my breasts bulge over the top of the tiny bra too much?   I carefully tucked my pubic hair into the panties, turned and spread the narrow piece of cloth in back as wide as I could, and stepped out the door to the pool area.

I took a deep breath. I felt as if I were on Mount Olympus; I felt free in my near nakedness. A gentle, warm breeze was bathing my body and I felt a tingle of sexual excitement.

Before me spread the forest, and at my feet were the pool and spa. There were half-a-dozen pool-side mats, a padded bench, a glowing barbecue, and two padded deck chairs.

Neal was at the barbecue and Anne lounged on a deck chair. One look at her told me my bikini was not too daring. She was wearing a satin-looking white something that barely covered her pubes, and she made no attempt to conceal the outline of silky hair which showed she was a natural blonde. The dark circles of her nipples were easily seen through her white top. I sensed her sexiness from fifty feet away.

I walked across a soft poolside mat to settle on the deck chair beside hers. As she reached to lift a bottle of chilled white wine from an ice bucket, I turned my eyes toward Neal. He was busy at the barbecue, so

I could stare openly. His broad shoulders moved with a masculine grace and his back muscles rippled. His light-blue silk bikini hugged his narrow hips and tight buns. I was in a trance, and only came out of it because Anne chuckled. She was offering me a glass of wine, smiling.

'Would you like me to lend him to you?' she asked casually.

Neal turned, and the thin material of his bikini clearly outlined his penis within it. I had a vivid mental picture of him both with and without the bottom, and I tried to decide which was the sexier. Finally, I grabbed the glass Anne was offering and took a sip. 'Look out,' I smiled, 'I might take you up on that.'

The three of us chatted, and I found them extremely inquisitive about me. Yes, I had once been married for a while. No, I didn't have a steady boyfriend. I was a secretary taking evening courses toward a teaching degree.

Anne said, 'Sharon has doubts about her looks.'

Neal seemed surprised as he turned his dark eyes full on me. 'Sharon, you are not only attractive, you are the liveliest, most sparkling person we've met in a long time.'

That, coming from Neal, was enough to boost my ego for the rest of my life. Then, when they added that they hoped I would come visit them often, my heart sang. I think I was in love with them both.

When Neal served the hamburgers, we sat up on the deck chairs to eat. Anne and I were side-by-side on one of them and Neal sat across from us. Was it purely by habit that he sat with his knees wide apart? I kept my eyes moving toward the few lights that had come on in the valley below, but I still caught glimpses of Neal's firm pectorals, the rippled knots of muscles nestling above his navel, and of course of the soft tube pressing against the light-blue silk cloth.

When darkness settled, Neal rose to light the Tiki torches and their orange-yellow flames threw shadows that accentuated his body and made him look like a Polynesian god.

Anne nudged my leg with her thigh and murmured, 'Something nice to have around the house, hmm?'

I was grateful for the suggestion we dive into the pool, but the water was warm and did nothing to cool the pleasant yet uncomfortable erotic flames subliminally licking my body, uncomfortable because I saw no way of satisfying the desires steadily building within me.

We played with a beach ball and finished in a corner with our bodies slithering against each other's. The contrast of Anne's smooth, soft flesh and Neal's firm muscles made me forget the ball, and I let it bounce away from the pool.

We settled into the spa, where the tingling, bubbly jets of water pummeled our bodies. Both of them had their eyes closed. Anne's pointed breasts in their small bra floated on the waves and streams of bubbles rose between Neal's thighs.

Anne rose from the water. She murmured, 'Massage me' and spread herself face-down on the padded bench. Neal knelt beside her, and his strong hands began sliding up and down her back. I moved my body so the water jet was washing against my back. When he squeezed gently just above her knees, and began working his hands slowly upward, the water swirled on the backs of my legs and I could imagine Neal's hands there.

Anne turned on her back, and Neal swept his hands across her smooth skin before pressing his fingers into her armpits and slipping his thumbs under her top. His palms moved slowly down, hovered at her hips, and then moved lower to stroke her belly and thighs. I squirmed in the jet just as his fingertips coursed upward and touched the white satiny cloth of her bikini bottom. I heard her catch a quavering breath before she rolled off the bench and said to me, 'Your turn.'

I tried not to look hurried, but I immediately placed myself on my back instead of face-down. Neal's hands began at my ankles and worked slowly upward. He bent my knee, and squeezed up and down the soft flesh of my thighs. Each time his hand crept upward, I instinctively wanted to raise my hips and my breaths came faster. Then there was another softer, gentler touch... Anne's delicate hands were stroking my arms, moving up to my shoulders and circling my breasts. I pulled my shoulders back. Her hands slipped into my bra, and I welcomed the touch of her fingertips on my nipples. I didn't realize I had spread my legs and lifted my hips until Neal's hands slipped into my panties to explore my wetness, and I quivered.

I squirmed, and felt my panties and bra being removed. Then I was lifted and placed on a soft mat. I opened my eyes, and in the light of the flaming torches I saw that both Anne and Neal were naked now, too. Anne's small conical breasts jiggled slightly as she moved, and the golden bush of blonde curls at her cunt seemed aflame in the torch-light. Neal was on his knees beside me, and his erection was so stiff it seemed to throb. I reached out to curl my fingers around its warmth and began stroking it, touching the tender tip with my thumb. He pressed his hips forward as Anne's fingers found my clitoris and vibrated, sending thrills through my body. I raised myself up onto my elbows so I could take the top of Neal's prick into my mouth and twirl my tongue around it. He moaned and Anne lowered her head between my thighs. I felt her hair tickle my skin and heard wet sounds as her tongue fluttered over my clit. I couldn't hold my hips still as I sucked to get more of the warm flesh of Neal's cock in my mouth. Anne took my clit between her lips, making soft sucking sounds.

Neal withdrew from between my eager lips and positioned himself between my thighs as Anne took hold of his shaft. She was not only lending him to me, she was guiding his cock into my pussy!

I watched him enter me, and cried out as he thrust his full length hard into my slick warmth. He kept his body straight, looking down at where we were joined together and Anne's fingertips were working my clitoris. I gasped, making small animal sounds as I writhed uncontrollably. Neal plunged his cock in and out of my hole and Anne kept on vibrating my clit. I was ready to come, and when she leaned over to suck on one of my nipples, there was an explosion in my pelvis that went on and on; it didn't diminish, spreading up my spine and down my legs as I suffered one searing orgasm after another. When Neal moaned and humped his hips faster, I knew I was taking his thick juices into my body, and that was one last glorious thrill before I lost consciousness.

***

Anne tucked me gently into bed and slipped a sheet over me. She kissed me and whispered, 'We didn't intend for that to happen, but I'm glad it did. It was beautiful.'

I slept heavily until the first rays of dawn penetrated my room.

They woke me, but I dozed back to sleep and dreamed... I saw Neal plunging his cock into Anne's pussy while I watched and fingered myself. I was almost coming as I swam up out of my dream and discovered my hand was sticky. I dozed again, and this time it was my turn... Neal fucked me while Anne's hand worked her soaking cunt in its nest of thick golden hair as she watched us...   I woke on the edge of an orgasm and finished myself off with my fingers. Finally, I was wide awake, and there was all of Sunday still ahead. Were my dreams a premonition?

I dressed quickly, wrote a note saying I had just remembered an important Sunday morning appointment, and left.

Back in the city, I managed to get in touch with a number of the members of my single's club and casually asked them if they knew of anyone ever being invited to Neal or Anne's cabin. No one ever had been; I was the only one they had ever invited.

Later, I received a note from Anne. She said she was sorry I had had to leave so early Sunday morning, but that she and Neal thought I was a wonderful person and hoped I would come up to their cabin the following weekend.

I'm still debating about going. What would you do?

41. Rachel — Mystery Caller

It was over two years ago. The time we had together had been short, but so very sweet. Suddenly, it was over. He didn't call, and none of our mutual friends seemed to know where he was. He had quit his job and vanished from the face of the earth. I thought about him a lot, but gave up all hope of ever seeing him again, and then I met someone else and got married.

The day started on a dreary note, with heavy, threatening, overcast skies. But these same skies had produced a glorious sunrise, and a small, hidden part of me felt chilled, as if it was an omen. Of what, I had no idea, at least not then.

Although the weather showed no signs it would improve, gradually everything else did. My workload was light, and I took a leisurely extended lunch with a colleague by the local waterfront. It had been good to relax, and any earlier apprehensions were forgotten.

When I finally returned to the office, I was almost immediately hit with several back-to-back phone calls. During what I hoped was that last of these, I was told there was yet another caller on hold. I answered with my standard pleasant greeting, 'Thank you for waiting. How may I help you?'

The reply was, 'Do you know who this is?'

The voice did sound vaguely familiar, and the slight feeling of recognition I experienced for some reason made me uneasy. Since I had taken the call at another phone, I suggested he hold while I returned to the privacy of my own office. I used the opportunity to try to regain my composure, which I had noticed was fading fast. It can't be, I thought. I went into my office, closed the door, took a deep breath, and picked up the receiver. 'Hello?' I said tentatively.

The voice asked again if I knew who he was. When I replied that I thought I might, but that I didn't want to venture a guess until I was sure, he said, 'Think back to about two years ago.' Needless to say, I was right, and it was a good thing I was sitting down. He hadn't disappeared after all. I guess I could have been a little nicer when I finally spoke, instead I yelled, 'Where the hell have you been?'

'Is that all?' he asked. 'I thought you'd be ready to kill me.'

Some months ago I might have been; however, I explained that even though I was hurt and bewildered when he stopped calling, I was also smart enough to realize that if he didn't want to be found, maybe it was for the best, and I did what I could to forget him. It was surprising how easily I managed to cover the sudden surge of excitement churning in my stomach.

We talked for nearly an hour, during which I informed him of the fact that I was now a married woman, yet he still asked me when we could meet. I told him I'd call him when I got home, as I had some things to do after work. He gave me his number, and we hung up.

My errands were completed in record time, and when I called him, we decided to meet about an hour later. We chose a local shopping center as a meeting place, so as not to arouse the suspicion of my nosy neighbors.

When I got into his car, I could immediately feel the intensity of his coffee-brown eyes gazing at me from behind his sunglasses; his stare burning right through my shape-hugging shorts and T-shirt. Before I could even say hello, my juices were flowing. I knew that, despite the amount of time that had passed, and the fact that I was now a married woman, the passion that had existed between us before was as strong as ever.

We stared at each other for what seemed like ages, and then finally he began driving with no particular destination in mind. We simply meandered for a while, filling each other in on our lives. He did most of the talking, since a lot had happened to him, whereas my own life – apart from my marriage, of course – remained relatively mundane. He never explained why he simply vanished from my life one day, and for some reason, I didn't press him, sensing by his tone that he regretted it.

Eventually, we decided to stop for sodas. We sat in the parking lot for a while as he continued telling me his stories. I watched the look in his eyes change from pain to anger to hurt as he related several different situations that had arisen while we had been apart, and I realized he still held a very special place in my heart. Then suddenly I became aware of the fact that I had lost all interest in talking. I leaned over, my eyes meeting his, and said, 'Shut up.'

He returned my gaze with a mischievous smile. 'Did you just tell me to shut up?'

My answer was to cover his lips with mine before he could say anything else. We clung to each other then, our tongues probing and our bodies producing a heat so intense it was quickly very warm in the car despite the cool evening and the open windows. Too soon he broke away. 'Can we go somewhere?' he asked quietly. 'I want more.'

Knowing exactly how he felt, I began pondering possible locales for our lovemaking. I thought carefully, because it had to be somewhere special as well as discreet.

As we drove away, he remarked casually, 'You know, I still have a blanket in the trunk.'

Immediately, I knew our destination. The sun was gone, the stars sparkled, and in no time we had arrived at a small park that was always deserted after dark. It was the perfect spot.

We left the car outside the park gates and began walking through the picnic area, the air heavy with the scent of newly mowed grass. We quickly found a small, isolated grove of trees with a clearing into the center. Jay spread out the blanket, turned, and took me in his arms. As our lips met, we seemed to melt into each other. He ran his hands slowly down the curve of my back, firmly grasping my buttocks and pulling me even closer so I could feel his hardness pressing into my belly. The rest of the world seemed to vanish, and I lost all sense of time and place as my legs grew weak with desire. It took a moment for me to realize he had spoken.

'Can I ask you a question?' he whispered. When I had trouble finding my voice, he asked, 'Why are we standing here?' We both knew the answer.

I allowed him to lower me onto the blanket and once again take me into his strong embrace. We rediscovered each other, our hands and tongues exploring as if we had never been together before. Even through my clothing his touch set off a charge that warmed every inch of my body. He had always had an instinct about how to make me respond, and it was wonderful to know some things never change.

As he began removing my shorts and panties, I reached around to unhook my bra and release my breasts. His mouth moved away from mine, making its way first to the hollow of my throat and then down to my erect nipples. He greedily sucked each one in turn while his hand found its way past my thatch of blond curls to the hot wetness between my thighs. He only teased me at first, but then two of his fingers entered my slick sex as he teased my clitoris with his thumb. Every nerve ending in my flesh seemed to fuse into one glorious longing and he had no difficulty bringing me to orgasm just with his hand.

I decided it was time to reciprocate. I laid my hands gently on his chest and urged him over onto his back. I paused to marvel at the size of his erection before placing my mouth over it and sucking him lovingly. He moved with me, arching his back to match my rhythmic movements as I took him deep into my throat. When he tried to pick up the pace, I stopped and just teased the tip of his cock with my tongue. I was in charge, for now.

Although I had not allowed him to touch me while I pleasured him, by then I wanted him inside me so badly I ached. Finally I mounted him, descending a little at a time so as to relish every inch of his thick length penetrating me. I paused for a moment, and then began moving up and down slowly, the memory of the old fire between us flooding me. Soon he was matching my strokes, and our pace quickened until I cried out. He took control then, and I had no will to resist. Gripping my hips he thrust up hard inside me and for the second time that night subjected me to a shattering climax. Just when I thought I could take no more, he gently placed his hands on my waist and rolled me over onto my back. He entered me again and we moved together as if possessed. He continued plunging deep into my hole with an unbridled passion I didn't think was possible, and at last we came together, both of us shuddering with the intensity of it all.

After lying exhausted for what felt like an eternity, we forced ourselves to return to reality. We dressed slowly, saying little, not wanting the evening to end. Our stroll to the car and the short drive back to the shopping mall were equally silent, as if speaking would turn the evening into no more than a dream.

When the time came for us to part, he looked at me tenderly. 'Call me,' he said, and then vanished from a life again, this time forever.

42. Candice – Please Come Again

It was evident that our waiter, Steve, was flirting with me throughout the entire meal. As he set my orders on the table, he made every effort to casually graze my hand with his. Another course, another graze, another smile... Was he serving me dinner or trying to seduce me? My folks could sense it, too, as I made desperate attempts to prolong the dinner.

Finally, none of us could eat another bite; we had to leave even if I had no desire to. Steve asked if we wanted anything else, flicking his eyes over me again.

I flirted back, sliding my tongue over my lower lip. 'No thanks,' I said, 'just the check. And I'll take it.'

After a moment, he returned. 'Have a good night,' he declared cheerfully, then added a little more quietly, 'hope to see you again soon.'

My legs quivered beneath the table as I placed my credit card on top of the bill. As I did so, I noticed something unusual about the check. The words, *Please Come Again* were underlined, and next to them, Steve had written, *I get off work at eleven.*

When I got home, I changed into some shorts and a tank top and thought about Steve. I decided I'd go for it.

My heart racing, I pulled up outside the restaurant at ten-forty-five. I checked my face in the rear-view mirror, and feeling confident slipped out of my car and walked into the restaurant. I didn't see him right away, but soon I spotted him coming out of a back room.

'I wasn't sure you'd come,' he said, making his way towards me.

'I wasn't sure I'd come either,' I joked. My nervousness soon eased, however, for I could see he was a little nervous himself. We spoke for a few minutes before he suggested we go over to the bar.

The bar was in a separate room. Steve and I wanted to touch each other, but for now we had to contain our lust to the dance floor. Our bodies immediately drew together, and I inhaled his masculine scent as I draped my arms around his neck. We moved even closer. I could feel his erection pressing against my crotch. His cock felt big, and I longed to be this close to him without clothes between us. I longed to have his naked body touching mine. Five minutes more and we knew it was time to leave the bar.

I followed Steve to a door marked *Employees Only* and he whipped out a key to let us in. I really didn't know what to expect, but I was hoping for the best.

We made our way to a couch and sat down, our eyes locking. He put his hands on my shoulders, and then moved them up to my hair, gently brushing it away from my neck.

I could feel my panties moisten with anticipation as he slowly moved his hand down to my pussy. While he caressed it through the fabric of my shorts, he grabbed my chin with his other hand and softly kissed my lips.

I pulled him toward me and we lay down on the couch side-by-side. I nestled my warm pussy against the promising bulge in his pants. I moaned with pleasure as I kissed his neck and moved my hand down to between his legs. He gasped softly as I slowly explored the length and girth of his cock through the cloth. The anticipation was getting to be too much to bear; I stood up to pull off his pants, and following my cue, he helped me remove mine.

When we were finally naked, he stared at my breasts. 'You're so beautiful,' he whispered.

By way of reply I cupped my breasts in my hands, flicking the tips of my thumbs over my nipples until they hardened. I then took his hands and placed them on my tits, and he immediately buried his face in my cleavage. It was the perfect time to push him down onto the edge of the couch and slowly lower myself onto his penis.

A few minutes of grinding my pussy around his cock brought me to an unbelievable climax, but from the tense expression on Steve's face, I could tell he was not yet there himself. His erection felt thick and hard inside me as he moved frantically, achieving his own release with his fingers digging almost painfully into my hips.

After a few minutes, I gently eased his penis out of me, and sat down beside him.

'That was incredible,' he said.

I smiled. 'I hope you'll come again.'

43. Marjorie – The Groupie

It all began three years ago this Halloween. I went to see Slug perform. It was the first time I'd seen them live, and they immediately became my favorite band. Besides the raunchy rhythms, lustful lyrics and basic all-out professionalism, I could feel something special in the air.

By some stroke of luck, I was able to meet the gorgeous singer, Anthony, right before the show. (My favorite uncle is buddies with their road manager.) He possessed more than just plain star quality. I had met a couple of rock musicians before, and none of them made my panties damp just from shaking hands. His incredible blue eyes seemed to hypnotize me; I knew I would do anything he asked of me. Since that first fateful meeting, I kept having dreams (both night and day varieties) about Anthony. Whenever I was doing anything boring, I would escape to my fantasies. In that magical state, unreal but totally intoxicating, I felt him deep inside me, penetrating my eager, yielding flesh the same way his sapphire gaze had pierced my eyes. Recently, I got a chance to live my fantasies...

After a show where my seat was second row center, a security guard approached me and asked me to follow him. I was still in a heady state from all that grinding music, plus his resonating voice, which seemed to call out to me and me alone. Nervously, I wondered what might be wrong. I was pretty much in a daze, but I was glad to have a guide lead me away from the cheering crowd. For one second I looked back, and was amazed at the sight – a heaving sea of denim and leather.

The security guard, silent and protective, led me out to the band's bus, and discreetly disappeared. I stepped into the bus, and realized with a shock that Anthony was the only group member present. Wow! Whenever I had watched him on stage, he seemed to be reading my mind. Now I knew, without a doubt, that this was true, and he had decided that tonight was the night he was going to put all my wildest fantasies into very spirited action.

He motioned for me to take a seat next to him on a couch. I sank into the deep, leopard-skin cushions, already in another world. We chatted amiably for about half-an-hour, and then suddenly he stood up and crooked his finger at me, smiling wickedly. 'Follow me, young lady,' he said in his sexy baritone. Even though I thought my feet were going to melt into the floor, I managed to make it to his bunk way in the back of the bus; nice and secluded.

'I want to make love to you right here, right now,' he told me, not giving me a chance to think, as if I wanted to. His long, able tongue plunged deep into my mouth, discovering sensations I didn't even know were possible all through my body. It felt so good I couldn't believe even more was to come. The next thing I knew, he had pulled off my T-shirt and unhooked my black lace under wire bra. He bent his head down to my right breast and began sucking on its almost painfully erect nipple. When I let out a loud moan of approval, he switched to my left breast. The guy knew how to turn me on; I was juicing with excitement, ready to go down on my knees before this master of music-making. But I had to wait. He was still fully dressed, completely zipped up. He guided my hand to the bulge in his skin-tight black leather pants, and I gladly helped him peel them off along with his shirt, and last to go were his tiger-striped briefs. So many times watching him writhe in sensual performance, I had imagined how perfect his cock must be, and now it throbbed before me, long, thick and hard and totally real. I licked my lips with an eagerness I had never felt before. I wanted to please him in that special way.

I sank to my knees before him, and his warm hands rested gently on my head as I sucked him down passionately; fervently licking his gorgeous love muscle like a cat worshipping him. Its slight salty taste was a treat I had waited for far too long. On and on I sucked, my saliva mixing with the pre-cum flowing from his magnificent pump.

Almost roughly, he pulled me up by the shoulders. 'Hey, I'm the one who's supposed to be doing the seducing here,' he teased. 'Now I'm going to have to teach you a lesson you'll never forget.' He yanked down my mini skirt and panties, swept me up into his arms, and laid me down on his bunk. Then he put his face between my thighs and his long, pointed tongue went to work on my clit. I gasped with pleasure and he looked up at me for a second with his intense blue eyes. In that confined space, far from the throng of the concert hall, his eyes were magnificently alive and close-up. After a while, he started finger-fucking me gently, and then a little more forcefully. I pleaded with him to use his cock, but he smiled that mischievous smile again teasing and fingering me until I groaned in frustration. At last he stood up, and grabbing my hands, he pulled them up over my head.

'I'm in charge here,' he said, tying my wrists together, and then attaching the silky cloth to a metal loop in the wall. I was totally help less now, and it turned me on so much, I thought I was going to die as he joined me on the cot, and penetrated me slowly, so slowly I thought I would lose my mind. And once he was inside me, he kept moving against me at that same slow, tortuous pace.

'Oh, God, fuck me!' I begged. 'Fuck me hard!'

He granted my wish and began rocking his hips hard and fast between my open thighs, gyrating them just he way he did on stage. I tightened my vaginal muscles around his driving cock and felt my clit opening up like a bud ready to bloom into a beautiful orgasm. He whispered in my ear that I should just relax. I made an effort to obey him, and the head of his erection must have found my G-spot as he banged me because suddenly I suffered a series of explosive little climaxes that had me crying out and begging for mercy. The shattering ecstasy in which he eventually joined me with his own explosive orgasm left me drained and yet mysteriously longing for more just like his throbbing, pounding, heart-felt music.

44. Kristina – What She Wants

Men lay bruised and battered, twisted arms reaching toward a distant and brutal God, wincing under the thunderous cannon bursts and blinding explosions of a humanity gone mad, absolutely mad... Enough, I thought, closing my history book. I removed my glasses and stretched, reveling in the sensual pleasure of alleviating the tension in my muscles.

I closed my eyes and let my thoughts drift back to the wounded and bleeding soldiers... men, sensual creatures, hard muscles sculpted to marbled perfection, rugged features twisted into expressions of exquisite torture, pleading, helpless, raw need, calloused hands that once caressed delicate, sensitive feminine flesh... I sigh, my clitoris rising urgently in its fleshy hood, straining against my panties. I spread my legs slightly, and touch the demanding wetness between them with my fingertips. Slipping a hand into my loose sweatpants, I fondle my own slippery folds, turning my thoughts once again toward the soldiers...

Suddenly there's a knock on the door. 'Kristina? It's Eric.'

Study night with Eric. 'Coming!' I yell, and then giggle to myself. 'Or at least I was until you showed up,' I mumble. I open the door.

He leans against the frame, eyebrows raised. 'Are you okay? You look a little... uh... you look a little flushed.' He smiles uncertainly.

His left thumb is hooked into his belt loop, and tucked beneath his right arm are two heavy history textbooks.

I stare fixedly at his long fingers; I can see them, I can feel them, sliding deep inside me… 'I've been exercising,' I say quickly. I look down, avoiding his eyes, only to realize I'm staring at his crotch; I can't take my eyes from it.

He smiles. 'Whatever you say.'

I turn, and start looking for my note cards on war strategies.

Eric closes the door, and comes up behind me. He must have put his books down, because I feel his left arm encircle my waist as his right hand plunges into my sweatpants and cradles my hot pussy in his hand.

'What are you doing?' I gasp, but make no move to resist his searching fingers.

'What do you want me to do, Kristina?' His voice is low and sweet in my ear, his hot breath sending chills down the nape of my neck. 'Do you want me to stop?' He kneads my breasts with his other hand, pinching a nipple through my t-shirt. He kisses the side of my neck lightly, gently sucking my earlobe. He smells like soap and cologne, a clean, manly smell.

My hands reach behind me and clutch his thighs. 'Eric…' I whisper helplessly.

'Yes, Kristina?' he asks gently. 'What do you want me to do?'

I can't speak; all I can think of are his hands, his fingers, and his hard-on pressing against my ass.

'What do you want me to do?' he asks again relentlessly, his voice low and husky. His breath is coming faster and his body is tense against mine.

'Everything!' I breathe, turning to face him.

He gently pulls my sweats down over my knees, and they fall loosely to the floor. I shiver as I step out of them watching him push his own pants and underwear down to his knees. His hand cups my cunt again, and all four of his fingers – those long, smooth fingers – work skillfully inside me, at first slowly, carefully opening my tender folds up around their conical hardness, and then faster, thrusting deeper as my juices flow out of control. With his free arm he encircles my waist and lifts me up until my toes are barely touching the floor. I cling to his broad shoulders and wrap my legs around his hips, kissing and biting his neck. I utter a small cry as he pulls his hand out of my vagina, and gripping the back of my thighs swiftly wraps my pussy around his cock. His erection lodged deep inside me, he walks over to the couch and spreads us both down across it.

'You're so beautiful,' he whispers. He sucks on my nipples, and my sex tenses around his driving strokes and I dig my nails into his back with unbridled passion.

Afterwards, as we lie panting and caressing each other, I say, 'I think I've learned a lot tonight, but there are still a few things I'm a bit unclear about.'

He laughs. 'It may have to be a late study night, you know.'

I smile. 'Well, the more you study, the more you learn.'

45. Gloria – Jackpot

I work in a food processing plant. Practically everybody in my town does. We're unionized, so we get pretty good benefits, and we all feel close, almost like a family. Still, the long hours can get to you, even when you're young and healthy. And sometimes they get to you because you're young and in need of a good lay.

Since I broke off with Joe a few weeks before, I'd been feeling kind of down. I have to admit, not having a regular guy to snuggle with left me feeling sort of unattractive; I felt dumpy and dowdy, and I sure dressed the part. During times when I was away from the plant, I found myself almost wishing I had another set of uniforms – off-duty uniforms. Now that just wasn't like me at all; hardly the spangle-and-spandex good time gal all my pals were used to.

My first Saturday off in months was coming up, and I really need-ed to get away and relax. So I made plans to take a little trip across the border to Reno. I've always enjoyed going there; it's a place just made for good clean fun.

With that in mind, I made a bonfire of the 'old maid' duds, scaring the heck out of my neighbors in the process. I stashed a few cute and sassy outfits into a suitcase, got the tank of my car filled up with gas, and curled my eyelashes. I was ready to go.

Heading down the road, I hollered, 'Hallelujah!' to no one in par-ticular.

I pulled into the parking lot of a cozy, out-of-the-way motel. Much as I enjoy the attractions of Reno, when it's lights-out time, I like to drift off to dreamland far from all the noise and glitz. The traffic had seemed heavier than usual, and I was a little tired from the drive. Time for a long, relaxing shower...

The water trickled over my pert breasts and down my slender thighs. As it ran over my pretty little mound with its lush pubic hair, I started feeling sensual and alluring again. My nerve endings were coming alive, and I decided to hit the town and see what kind of fun could be had.

Now I've never been a big gambler. To tell the truth, I don't have the funds of some of the folks I've seen in Reno; I can't just piss away cash like that. I usually play the slot machines; the dollar machine suits me just fine. But after playing the same machine for three hours, I was really getting discouraged. It paid one thirty-dollar jackpot, and I put almost all of it back into the game.

'I'll play one more time,' I reasoned with myself. I don't give up easily, and besides, I knew I was looking good in my all-red get-up – red mini dress, lace stockings, high heels, and velvet hair bow. Suddenly, like a message from beyond, bells started ringing. I had actually hit a thousand dollar jackpot! My luck was changing, that much I knew.

A short middle-aged man, almost totally bald, appeared out of nowhere. He was writing on a piece of paper and asked me to wait for the casino host, the person who would hand over my winnings.

I glanced up from my lucky machine, my head practically spinning with excitement. A tall man with a full head of wavy brown hair introduced himself as the casino host. He had enough hair on his head to share with the other guy. That struck me as so funny, I had to stop myself from giggling. But when I realized how attractive the host was, I quickly switched from my little-girl mood to my lustful-lady one. I smiled coyly, and saw how his eyes sparkled back at me like jewels, or better yet like stars in the sky. And I could have sworn those eyes detected my nipples hardening beneath my skin-tight dress. The material was hugging me the way I wanted to be hugged by him. I gazed hungrily at his tanned and muscular body, especially admiring the bulge in his pants.

'Hope to see you again,' he said, handing me my booty.

I returned to my hotel room, happy to have won so much money, but tormented by thoughts of the handsome casino host. Damn, I hadn't even gotten his name! Oh, well, I was only there for the weekend. I lay down on the bed, exhausted. I closed my eyes, but couldn't fall asleep.

The phone rang. I snatched up the receiver, wondering who on earth it could be, and to my amazement, it was the casino host. In a low-pitched, sexy voice, he explained he had found my wallet containing a receipt from the hotel in which I was staying. In my excitement over winning, I had left it at the machine. Now he was asking if I could go back to identify it.

I drove back into town at a breakneck pace, more eager to see him than my poor old left-behind wallet. I felt a rush of adrenaline; I wasn't tired anymore.

When I returned to the casino, its inspiring host was seated at the bar. I ran up to him, out of breath. His name was Dan, he informed me, and lo-and-behold, his shift had just ended. Handing me my wallet, he asked if I had eaten dinner yet. The thought of food hadn't entered my mind all evening, but I wasn't going to pass up a chance to spend a little time with him.

We chatted aimlessly through the meal, wasting time with small talk. We couldn't take our eyes off one another. When he asked what I would like for dessert, I make absolutely no effort to disguise my true intentions. I let my eyes wander down to that precious area below his belt. He squeezed my hand and suggested we go up to his suite for an after-dinner drink.

Luckily, no one shared our elevator or our wandering hands would have met either with disapproving glances or with voyeuristic stares. His tongue slid in and out of my mouth so tantalizingly I thought my knees would give way. Scarcely able to control myself, I only managed to stop myself from unzipping his pants by reminding myself where we were going. I stroked his tight ass and the backs of his thighs with the kind of animal passion I hadn't felt in a long time. He ran his hands over my breasts, pinching the nipples and making me gasp. If that elevator had been a cage and he had been my keeper, I would have remained happily in captivity 'til the end of my days.

Once inside his suite, I unleashed the full force of my desire, and he in turn showed me just what kind of man he was. When he asked me what I wanted to drink, I replied with a long and lingering kiss. Meanwhile, my nimble fingers unzipped his pants, slipped into his briefs, and found his cock. I worked his head, circling it over and over again, my thumb and forefinger shaped into a ring feeling the drops of pre-cum jewelling on the tip.

He moaned and scooped me up in his arms, surprising me with his strength. He carried me out to the balcony, where the view was probably fantastic, but I scarcely noticed it. He set me down and unzipped my dress, yanking it up off over my head. My black lace panties went next, leaving me in just my stockings and high-heels. He knelt before me, and flicked the top of his tongue between my sex lips, gently penetrating my pussy.

Then it was my turn to sink to my knees and pull down his pants, my hands clawing wildly at the fabric covering his legs. I wanted his big cock deep in my throat, and I got it. I sucked him good and hard, making a shameless amount of noise as I greedily enjoyed the taste of his skin and semen.

'I want to be inside you now, baby,' he whispered. 'Please let me come inside you. You don't know how much I want to.'

My yearning mouth reluctantly let go of his cock. I stood up, and let him bend me forward over the railing. I cried out as he entered me from behind with a hard, sure thrust while below me all of Reno watched.

46. Barbara – Flying Lessons

I love private planes. They look so exciting from the ground, and I had always wanted to fly in one. Quite by accident, I was introduced to the owner of a small local airport in our city, and I told him of my fascination with small planes. Because his airport did local rush-hour traffic reports for several radio stations, he offered to let me go up during the traffic reports. I was elated when he said he would have the pilot-reporter phone me to schedule a time.

A week later, the phone rang at my office. It was Allen, who introduced himself as the pilot and traffic reporter for a local radio station. 'Well, Barb,' he said, 'I hear you want to go for a plane ride.'

'I'd love to,' I replied, taking note of his sexy voice.

Allen said he would take me up the next day at 4 p.m. and told me to meet him at the airport. I had butterflies the entire night thinking about how exciting it was going to be.

The next day, I was waiting for Allen to pick me up at the airport. All of a sudden out of nowhere I heard a faint humming in the sky and saw a small turboprop plane flying toward me over the runway. Five minutes later it landed, coasted right up to me, and the man behind the controls opened the passenger door, motioning me in. 'Hi, I'm Allen,' he yelled over the sound of the motor. 'Let me buckle your seat belt.'

'Hello, I'm Barb,' I said awkwardly as he reached across my lap to strap me in. Our eyes met, and I noticed the brilliant blue of his irises and how dramatically they contrasted with his black hair. He was gorgeous! I could feel my heart skip as we exchanged smiles. There wasn't any time for me to be nervous; as soon as I was locked in, he cruised down the runway and took off.

We had only been up in the air for about an hour when it was time to head back for the airport. He asked me if I'd like to fly again, and I declared, 'I'd love to!' I wanted to see him again and to get to know him much, much better. When we arrived back at the strip, he promised, 'I'll call you' and still feeling ecstatic, I headed for home.

Allen did, indeed, call. In fact, he took me flying three more times in the next three weeks, and each time I was with him, I could feel the electricity building between us.

Our fourth flight together was an early-morning one. The weather was cool and crisp, and we had only been in the air for about ten minutes when he suddenly reached over and rested his hand on my leg. His touch literally sent chills through my flesh, and I could feel my temperature rising. We looked at each other, smiling, both of us knowing this was not going to be any ordinary flight.

Efficiently working with one hand, he pushed my sweater up above my waist and caressed my breasts. I helped him free them from my bra, and bit my lip as his fingertips brushed across my nipples. How he was able to control the plane while bending over to kiss and suck my tits was a mystery, until I found out later he had put the plane on auto pilot.

Allen's delightful nipple-sucking was making my pussy almost painfully hot and juicy. I was more than ready for this dangerously daring experience when he suddenly unsnapped my belt and pulled me over onto his lap. I felt his hand slide up into my skirt and shove the flimsy layer of my panties aside. I clung to the back of his seat as he cupped my pussy in his hand, and then hungrily thrust two fingers up inside my slick sex. He boldly explored the innermost depths of my cunt as I writhed against him, desperately wishing it was more than just his fingers working inside me.

I whispered in his ear, 'Would you like me to frisk you now?'

He squeezed my mound and panted, 'Oh, yeah!'

I reached down, pulling slightly away from him so I could unzip his bulging fly even as I licked my juices from his fingers, moaning at how sweet I tasted. His hot, hard, cock sprang out at me, pushed up by his underwear as he tugged it down out of the way. His erection was beautiful. I stroked it up and down with one hand, forming a ring around the swollen head with my thumb and forefinger. He was breathing heavily, his eyes begging me to suck him. Carefully, I slipped off his lap and back into my own seat, from which I happily obliged him. I licked his cock all over, sliding my tongue up and down and flicking the tip against his head.

'Oh, God,' he groaned, 'this must be heaven!'

His sounds of pleasure drove me to slowly glide my tongue over his tender balls, and then to fill my mouth with them. I licked his scrotum gently, feeling it ready to burst with pleasure. I longed for him to fuck me, but I was afraid we would crash if we went at it in such a cramped space. I stroked the inner side of his thighs through his pants and his muscles became even tauter. Taking my time, I slid my mouth back up to his swollen penis. His cock was on fire as I sucked him hard and fast, until he suddenly ejaculated. I swallowed all his bittersweet cum, wanting to impress him, and felt my pussy aching to make love with him.

His eyes were closed as he said, 'You were just incredible, but I won't be happy until I make love to you full and proper. I want you to feel as good as I did.'

'I can't think of anything I'd like more,' I agreed.

Fifteen minutes later, we were back at the airport, but this time we didn't leave the plane. Instead, we glided onto the runway, and when we came to a stop he put his arms around me, pressing me to him and kissing me passionately. He stripped off all my clothes, then sat back and smiled at me as I squirmed with anticipation in the passenger seat, turning towards him and leaning against the door as I spread my legs as far apart as I could so he could bury his face between them. I was ready to come after only a minute, and moaned in anticipation as he sat up, shoved down his jeans and underwear, and spread himself over me. I don't know how he managed it, but he suspended his body over mine as he rammed his cock inside me with all the lust in his heart. He jammed his erection deep into my hole, banging against my clit as I squeezed my vaginal walls tight around him; making him groan with pleasure every time I grabbed his cock with my inner muscles. We made love for what seemed like an eternity, and then at last I felt my pussy contract with an impending orgasm. We came together, both of us moaning with satisfaction.

Afterwards, we both sat up and kissed gently, letting our hands wander over each other's bodies. I guess this is what they mean by 'friendly skies.'

47. Lauren — Flat Tire

I'd known for a long time that the tires on my Saab were too old; nevertheless, I stood cursing the flat. I was somewhere just south of Flagstaff, Arizona. The sky was darkening and it was bitterly cold for April. The air smelled like snow. Well, there was nothing to do but try and change the tire. I opened the trunk and pulled out the spare, then put my head back in to look for the metal contraption that turns the nuts. It wasn't there. Neither was the jack. Trying to remain calm, I counted to ten and cursed out loud.

Two or three cars had gone by since I pulled over, but none had even slowed down, much less stopped to help. It was getting darker, and I couldn't see any cars coming down the highway now at all. Panic setting in, I opened the hood and got back in the Saab. What if no one stopped? Could I walk to the nearest exit? Little white flakes were falling on the windshield and I realized I had nothing but a windbreaker with me; it had been over eighty degrees in Tucson.

Just as I was conjuring visions of frozen death by the side of the road, a Chevy Blazer pulled over and parked in front of me. I jumped out of the car to greet my rescuer, and got a very pleasant surprise. The man climbing out of the truck was dark-haired, of medium height, with broad shoulders and muscular arms outlined against his plaid flannel shirt. His gray eyes had little laugh lines at the edges, and they crinkled in a smile as they met mine.

'Anything I can do to help?' he asked.

I explained the problem, and he quickly got his tire changing equipment out of the Blazer. 'You must be freezing,' he observed, pulling a lambskin jacket off the front seat to give to me.

I took it gladly.

In no time at all he had the tire changed. 'Your spare's not in very good shape,' he told me. 'Why don't you follow me? There's a gas station at the next exit and we'll see if we can get you a new one.'

I thanked him and introduced myself. 'My name's Lauren,' I said.

'I'm Tai,' he returned the favor, and smiled again.

I followed the Blazer up to the station, thinking it would be fun to get to know my rescuer better.   It was dark when we got there, and we were just in time to see the attendant get in his car and leave.

Tai came over to my window. 'You really shouldn't drive on that tire. Listen, my house is just down the road. You could stay with me if you'd like and get a new tire in the morning. How about it?'

It looked as if I would get my chance to know him better. I thanked him for his kindness, and followed him to a rustic log cabin nestled back in a pine-covered valley.

Inside, it was warm and cozy. I sat on a couch before the fireplace and took off my shoes. Tai brought two cups of hot chocolate from the kitchen, and sat down beside me. As he settled on the cushion, his knee brushed mine and I looked into his eyes. Deftly, he took the hot chocolate from my hand, set it down next to his on the coffee table, and gently began pulling off the coat he had leant me. Then he kissed me, his tongue almost politely exploring my mouth. It was all so sudden, so unbelievably exciting, I couldn't resist him.

My hand wandered to this crotch, where I felt a very promising bulge beneath his jeans. I had them unzipped in a matter of seconds. I knelt down to take his cock in my mouth, licking up and down the sides of his beautifully engorged organ while both his hands caressed my breasts through my t-shirt. He pulled back suddenly and urged me to spread myself across the couch. Gently but efficiently, he stripped off my clothing. When I was completely naked, he caressed the insides of my thighs, moving one hand up to cradle my pussy while his other hand fondled my breasts. I could see his erection growing larger, straining for action, and I spread my legs wide to take him. 'I want you!' I gasped. 'Please…'

He quickly stripped off his own clothes, then spread his body over mine, bracing himself on his arms as his hard-on sank slowly into my welcoming depths. I grabbed his ass and pushed him in as deep as he could go. He took the hint and began thrusting fast and hard. It wasn't long at all before we came together, our bodies straining to merge into one.

After several moments of satisfied silence, I kissed him on the mouth. 'Flagstaff isn't as cold as I thought it was,' I whispered.

48. Terry – Private Party

Because of my husband's profession – he's a successful corporate attorney – we are often invited to large dinner parties. Although the parties are always pleasant, they had long ago become repetitious to me – always the same food, drinks, topics of conversation and people. I don't know what made me spend two weeks looking for the perfect dress and three hours getting ready for the latest of these parties. I wore a classy yet somewhat sexy black dress I thought would turn a few heads, and Stef confirmed this suspicion with a lustful whistle when I emerged from my dressing room.

We arrived at the party and after the usual greetings and formalities, Stef and I settled into our respective cliques. He chatted amicably with his colleagues while I mingled with the 'abandoned' wives. This standard operating procedure generally took up the better part of the evening.

I was halfheartedly listening to a conversation when a familiar voice sent shivers down my spine.

'I see your favorite drink is still white wine,' said Tony Riley, the sexiest man on campus during my college days. We were outrageously attracted to one another and had had a brief and wonderful relationship until he transferred to another school and I met Stef. If there was any specific man I fantasized about during my marriage, it was Tony Riley.

The other women halted their conversation and suddenly put on their most sultry smiles as they sized up the mystery man behind me.

I turned to him, and was immediately entranced by his intoxicating good looks and piercing, deep brown eyes. I managed to mumble a shy, 'Oh, hello!'

'I was afraid this was going to be one of those stuffy dinner parties where the only women I knew would be colleagues, but this is a wonderful treat,' Tony said. 'You look incredible.'

The conversation became totally comfortable after a few minutes of chit-chatting and filling each other in on the details of the past few years. Tony had always been the most attentive man I had known, and it didn't take him long to notice that Stef was wrapped up in an ongoing discussion, leaving me to find my own entertainment.

'Terry, we've got some catching up to do,' he said with a tantalizing glint in his eyes. 'Stef doesn't seem to be keeping an eye on you. Let's have our own dinner party.'

It was now or never, I thought. I was so excited by the anticipation of fulfilling my fantasy, I was hardly aware that we were sneaking out through the kitchen, picking up a tablecloth and some silver for our own evening's activities on the way.

The party was on a large estate, and we made our way to a clearing illuminated by the full moon. Tony spread out the tablecloth and then walked over to me, gently kissing my lips. I ran my fingers through his brown hair and pulled him close to me as our illicit passion quickly escalated. I couldn't believe I was doing this, yet I couldn't stop. Our tongues were deep in each other's mouths and the desire was growing stronger between us. I wanted to go wild and do everything with him, and I could tell he felt the same.

'This is a gorgeous dress,' he spoke breathlessly as he unzipped the back and pulled it gently down off my shoulders, exposing my breasts. 'I want you so much.'

'Tony,' I gasped, 'you don't know how many times I've dreamed of this!'

He let go of me for a moment to pop open a bottle of champagne, but instead of filling two glasses, he poured some of the cold bubbly liquid over my erect nipples, and then licked and sucked them until I felt intoxicated with pleasure.

'Make love to me, Tony,' I begged. 'I've waited so long...'

'Not yet. Come here.' He pulled me down onto the blanket with him and shoved my dress up around my waist. He spread my legs, and baptized my hot pussy with some more cool champagne. Then he set the bottle aside, knelt between my thighs, and began licking and sucking my clitoris. His tongue was so big it engulfed my entire vulva when he lapped it hungrily. I squirmed and moaned as I never had before, not even with my beloved husband. He slid two fingers inside my tight and tender slit while still sucking on my clit, subjecting me to the most unbelievable sensations I had ever experienced. It was as though he knew my body so well he could hear my thoughts and all I desired.

'Oh, Tony,' I groaned as a climax arched my spine and I fell back across the blanket.

He worked his way back up to my mouth, kissing me deeply and passionately. 'I want to be inside you!' he said desperately, and promptly entered me with a well-aimed thrust. His thick cock filled me to bursting, and I squirmed in the throes of an excruciating fulfillment. 'Oh, God, you feel incredible!' he breathed. 'I can't hold back…' We bucked wildly against each other and had simultaneous orgasms.

We lay beneath the moonlit sky catching our breath without saying a word. Then we got up and dressed and headed silently back to the house, sharing the remainder of the champagne and making sure we looked unruffled. Before we went back inside, we kissed one last time and agreed we would never think of dinner parties in the same way again. And since we'll be attending the same ones often, I've started looking forward to business affairs.

49. Annabel – The Masseur

After my skiing accident, a bone specialist put me on massive doses of a powerful painkiller. It relieved the pain in my limbs, but left me extremely depressed. Where once I had skipped and sung, purposeful and exhilarated, I now dragged myself through the slog of daily life; I had become a prescription drug addict.

It was with a sense of horror that I recognized my predicament. Having always been something of a news junkie, I was in the habit of watching documentaries. One evening my local public broadcasting station presented an alarming program concerning the negative effects of certain medicines. Chronic depression was listed as one of the consequences of taking too much of the very substance I had been ingesting daily, and, even more frightening, with every swallow I had taken myself farther down the road to dependency.

Luckily, the day after that revelatory broadcast, the first appointment on my schedule was a session with Ariane. This industrious psychotherapist worked alternate Saturdays. Since the work week generally found me pressed for time, I often found it convenient to start the weekend by scraping a few scabs off my heart.

Ariane's frizzy dark head nodded as I related to her the contents of the television program. If she hadn't been such a proud, almost regal presence, I would say her head positively bobbed up and down. She agreed I should stop seeing the bone specialist, and didn't seem concerned that I didn't know of anyone else who could treat me.

'Don't worry,' she insisted, pulling her lack leather jacket snug against her body (she had opened the window to let in some crisp morning air) and gulped some coffee from her mug. 'Annabel, my silly one,' she went on condescendingly, 'just go cold turkey, and for those joint and muscle pains, go see this marvelous masseur I know, Sam.'

My brow became furrowed; my nose crinkled. 'Is that Sam as in Samantha or as in Samuel?'

'You'll see,' she smiled.

***

I arrived for my first massage appointment feeling vaguely self-indulgent. I was also a little anxious, since I suspected I was to be handled by a strange man. But I was determined to go through with it in order to get well, and to partake of a new experience.

In the tiny cubicle, I was told to remove my clothes and spread myself face-down on the massage table. I made sure my nose poked through an air slot, and the attendant then covered me with a crisply starched sheet, placing warm packs on my back, neck and shoulders. Then I was left alone, and the heat gradually entered my tight muscles. I seemed to sink into the table, and was nearly asleep when the door opened quietly.

'Hi, I'm Sam,' said a deep, gentle voice. 'How are you?'

I mumbled vaguely that I was not great, and that I hoped this treatment would do at least some good. Out of politeness, I looked up. I really hadn't cared what the masseur looked like, but now I saw how handsome he was.

He clicked on a cassette player and eerie, strangely hypnotic New Age music filled the cubicle. He removed the warm packs and the sheet covering my back, and his strong, sensitive hands began working up and down my spine, smoothing the muscles to either side of it. Gently but insistently, his fingers coaxed away the tension much as a hot iron dissolves wrinkles. Almost my entire body was yielding to his healing touch. Yet I was intensely aware that the source of this comfort was a man, and a stranger at that. It occurred to me that Sam knew my body more intimately than most of my lovers ever had. Some of them had only been interested in what was between my legs, scarcely caressing me elsewhere...

As I awakened from this mist of bad memories, I slowly became aware of subtle but unmistakable sensations… at the end of each stroke, those strong, masterful hands were lingering on my skin ever just slightly, and when he leaned against me, I could have sworn I felt an erection.

His magical hands slid beneath me and gently squeezed my breasts, delicately pinching my nipples and jolting me into a long-delayed recognition of my own physical and emotional needs. I wanted to be an active participant, so I rolled over and looked him straight in the eye. I placed my hands on his broad shoulders, and pulled him down to kiss me. No other man had ever touched me so firmly yet so tenderly and tantalizingly, and I knew as his head sank between my naked thighs that I was about to get the best oral massage I had ever had in my life.

50. Melissa — Desert Heat

Stay with me,' I implored, shyly drawing back my nightshirt to reveal my right nipple. 'I have some things to show you.'

Damien blushed despite himself, and his hand rose from the doorknob to my naked flesh. 'How can you be so soft?' he whispered in wonder. 'There's nothing as soft and fine as you.' Then he bounded through the door with a mock cry of guilt, his hands elaborately shielding him from my offending breast. He made for his bicycle, leaped astride it, and then turned back towards me with pained dignity, 'Ye have tempted me sorely, my love, but the desert is a jealous wife and I must submit to her bold caresses.'

I pouted.

His face and voice softened. 'I shall return to my true love 'ere long and shower her with kisses,' he intoned, 'with extra measure for the softest spots.' Then he leapt off the bike again and returned to kiss me full and long on the lips, his chest fragrant with the scent of his maleness and sunscreen.

I took off my lavender bandanna, and tied it around his neck. 'A token for my champion,' I said, 'lest he forget his lady love.' Then, in lower tones, as my hand strayed to his thin bicycle shorts, 'Hurry back and you shall be as silk in my hand.'

He smiled and laughed, and I watched him pushing his bike down the cactus-lined path to the deserted blacktop below. He waved, his legs pumping vigorously, his blond hair swept back by the wind.

I didn't begrudge Damien his time alone. It did us good to be apart, he flying down some remote piece of road and me bent over easel and paints, alone in the desert. But I allowed myself a moment of reverie as I changed into a thin cotton dress imagining the play of Damien's hands over me. I stepped out into the warm morning, and hungrily inhaled the desert's clear fragrance. Everything looked sharp and hard, guarding itself from the sun's draining heat. Yet the morning wind caressed everything, playing across my bare arms and calves; fingering my hair.

***

I had lost myself in colors and textures when the crunch of tires on gravel announced Damien's return. The sun was high in the sky and heat glowed from his skin. He admired my painting, his palms resting on my shoulders, his long fingers caressing my neck and throat.

He went inside to take a bath, and I followed him a few brush strokes later. As he splashed and chattered, I silently observed that his bicycling hadn't done him much harm. A few calluses, to be sure, but his riding had also given a pleasing and visible strength to his long legs, and his upper body was lean and taut and hard. These features were of course known to, and admired, by many, but I alone knew Damien's softness; the fact that the skin stretching over his muscles and bones was warm and velvety to the touch. Like me, he responded to a gentle hand, and he returned what he received. No lover was more sensitive or deliberate than Damien. In our every embrace he found a new shape to trace or texture to caress.

He rose and stepped out of the tub, his flexed quadriceps rippling beneath his tan. He reached for a threadbare towel – too rough, I thought, for such fine skin – and dried himself. After he finished, I firmly grasped both his hands. He offered no resistance. I led him to our tiny bedroom, and pushed him gently onto the bed, running tender hands over his warm, still damp body, moving slowly toward his groin. He didn't say a word, but his eyes and smile became soft as he lay stretched out before me.

I cradled his pliant but hardening sex in my hands, and gently kissed his mouth. My tongue played over the softness of his lips before straying down to his neck, licking it first lightly and then deeply and close-ly, sucking his skin and warming him with my affection.

'I adore you,' I whispered. 'I love you with all my strength.' I stepped back and he lay there proudly naked as I slid my fingertips across him, all the way from his hands to the undersides of his arms to his chest, down to his belly, his hips and his legs. I felt all of him using my palms, my knuckles, the slight down of my wrists, even the length of my arms. He sighed with pleasure, stretching himself like a sleek cat before a fire on a cold night.

As the sun inched westward I moved closer. I brushed my mound against his thighs, my face buried in his neck, my breasts gently crushed against his muscular chest. My nipples sought and found his, the pairs eagerly rising to each other. My thighs offered themselves to his, and he raised each upper leg in turn to receive mine. I petted his quivering shaft, running first my fingers, and then my slick vulva, up and down its rigid length. He blushed at my touch, his desire growing harder and heavier. I kissed him full on the mouth again, tonguing him deeply, and then sank down over his erection, letting the mushroom-like tip slowly part the lips of my labia. He thirsted for more of me, I knew, and soon his shoulders, abdomen and corded thighs flexed, his cock inching high, straining to fill me. I rose with him, deftly holding him just where I wanted him. All of his strength seemed to flow to his rigid cock, and his thick desire clung suspended amidst my tender sex lips. When his hips slowly sank back down toward the bed, I almost, but not quite, let him slip free. Then I lowered my mouth to his again and repeated the tingling, inch-by-inch journey down around him. He soon lost himself, emitting long groans of unspeakable pleasure min-gled with frustration.

I sank a few fractions of an inch lower around his erection, and I could have had him then; I thought hungrily of his hot flesh and wet-ness impaled deep inside me. But stronger than this lust was my desire to lengthen and intensify my beloved's yearnings. I slipped from him, and quickly knelt beside him so my mouth could play teasingly over the head of his penis. His quiet moans intensified as I licked it, suck-ing on his velvety tenderness, resting my mouth only when I felt his passion threatening to burst. In those delicious intervals, I held his hard-on motionless between my lips until I felt his muscles slacken, delaying his orgasm. And he offered me his quivering organ willingly, no longer seeking to thrust. Only then did I straddle him again and draw him fully into me, gripping his full length with my tight sex.

He lay utterly still even as he filled me with quick, delicious throbs and warm streams of cum. I heard him softly call my name again and again as he slowly grew small and cool within me. Then he pulled me down into his arms with a sigh and held me close, the afternoon breeze wafting the white curtains gently into the room.

I awoke to the feel of the breeze on my belly. Damien was sitting up, and when he saw my eyes were open, he laid my head on his lap, spreading my black hair across his thighs. He cradled me, bending low to kiss my brow and eyelids, nose and lips. Then I felt his hands on my face studying its every plane, savoring the shape of my forehead, throat and cheeks. His fingers traced the lines of my jaw and chin and the curves between eyes and mouth, and I felt my skin grow ever more sensitive to his wandering touch.

His hands ranged farther, caressing my neck and shoulders and slowly running down the length of my outstretched arms before sliding back up to again stroke my hair and face. His palms then moved to lovingly across my ribs before slipping down to my waist. My torso grew warm and languid, my nipples large and hard. Then his gentle hands cupped my breasts, pressing and shaping their softness. I moaned and my hips began rising and falling. He kissed my brow and lay down beside me, turning my body towards his so he could slip his erection between my yearning thighs. Our sexes touched in a shy first kiss, and I felt myself open and part to contain his passion, its swollen tip again binding us. We lay there for what seemed like hours, our bodies utterly still in that close embrace as we softly kissed and watched each other. Then he gently pulled his head out from between my labial lips and slipped three fingers inside me. I twisted and turned with pleasure, yearning to feel his touch deep in my innermost flesh, my sex stretching and quivering around his penetrating fingers. A glow awakened inside me, spreading through my pelvis and up through my torso, and still his tongue and free hand caressed my neck, arms, and breasts, intensifying my rising desire. The warm wetness between my thighs became achingly hot; my writhing more hungry. There was no restraining what I felt and no wish to restrain. My passion yielded itself wholly to him and increased to a pulsing, vibrating torrent that swept away all thought and memory.

Damien's hands slowly stilled upon my flesh, yet still he cradled me against him, holding my pussy in his hand, his deep eyes gazing into mine. My sex was liquid heat cupped in his palm as he kissed my face everywhere with moist, light lips. Then he moved down slowly, and I sighed as his tongue found my most private recesses, gently licking and sucking their moist tenderness. His fingers opened me up with care now and I gave myself to him. My legs gripped his head, my hands burying themselves in his fair hair, my sex clenching helplessly and deliciously around his hard licks and thrusts. At last, after blinding heights of pleasure reached on the wave of his tongue, my juices flowing helplessly into his mouth, I urged him up into my arms and rested my head against his chest.

Outside the fierce desert wind stilled to a whisper as the crimson sun sank into the western mountains.

51. Lois — Over the Edge

After graduating with a degree in biology, I landed a job working as a ranger in a national park. Since I was just starting out, I didn't get one of the glamorous parks, the kind you see in *National Geographic*, but I was assigned to a nice little place nonetheless. It's great working outdoors in a low-pressure job, although it can get a little boring at times. My partner, Hal, is a nice guy, but old enough to be my grandfather.

Last week Hal and I were driving through one of the more isolated areas of the park when we heard a cry for help. We stopped, got out of the car, and looked down a steep ravine. We spotted a jogger who had fallen over the edge.

'I'll go get a stretcher and a trauma team,' Hal said.

'Okay. I'll stay here with him.'

I quickly slid down the side of the hill, calling down to the injured man that help was on its way. When I landed on even ground, I noticed how attractive the victim was. He had an aristocratic nose and full, sensual lips set in flawless mahogany-colored skin. He pulled away his headband, and spilled midnight-black curls over his forehead. 'Does it hurt bad?' I asked gently.

'Not as long as I don't move my ankle,' he replied. 'I think it's definitely sprained.'

'Well it could have been a lot worse,' I observed, and then we sat in silence for a while, waiting for Hal to return with medical assistance. I kept catching his eyes drifting over my body.

'So what's your name?' he asked me.

'Lois. And yours?'

'David. My friends call me Dave.'

'Pleased to meet you, Dave.' I sat near his head, and suddenly I realized I was leaning over him slightly, trying to inhale more of his tantalizing masculine fragrance. Then suddenly, yet as naturally and as casually as if he had done it a thousand times before, he grasped my honey-colored hair and gently but firmly brought my mouth down to his. He tasted my lips with pleasure, almost sipping them as if they were a fine wine. His skillful kiss left me breathless enough that I didn't protest when he abruptly thrust a hand up my khaki T-shirt. My pulse raced as he caressed my breast through my bra, my nipple stiffening in response. He started to roll over, but the instant he moved, his whole body stiffened and he groaned out loud.

'Your ankle,' I said.

'I'm okay,' he assured me. 'The movement just startled me, is all.'

Just then we heard the sound of a truck coming to a stop at the top of the incline. We gazed at each other wistfully.

'I think you're going to be laid up for a while with that ankle,' I remarked. 'I'll have to come visit you and keep you company.' I smiled thinking about all the wicked things I planned on doing to him secure in the knowledge that his beautiful athletic body wouldn't be able to run away.

52. Sherry – The Maintenance Man

It was a typical weekday afternoon. I was sitting in my neighbor Margie's apartment staring at the flowered wallpaper, only half-listening to her idle prattle. The subjects of her aunt's gallstones, and the daily doings on the soaps, weren't exactly riveting my attention. No, that had been grabbed early on by the splendiferous sight of a maddeningly muscular stud muffin. Toiling and sweating beneath the pipes of Margie's kitchen sink, Joey was only partially visible to my heavy-lidded eyes. I was still practically half-asleep (having spent most of the previous night tossing and turning) but my senses were being awakened (as in aroused) by this vision in blue denim.

I proceeded to give him a thorough once-over. In doing his job, the maintenance man stretched and strained his beautiful physique. His tall, lean, hard body was everything I could have wished for. Now here was a guy with a build! The rolled-up sleeves revealed arms strong enough to embrace a full-figured woman (and that's what I am). Though large, his hands appeared quick, nimble… Mm, what heaven it would be to feel them all over my skin. I saw no need to censor my thoughts, and when I saw him kneeling beneath the old porcelain basin, stuck in the middle of all those rusted pipes and cans of abrasive cleanser, I didn't stop myself from fantasizing about seeing him in that position stark naked. I couldn't even see his mouth too clearly, but there was something magnetic about this guy. Somehow I knew that when I did get a good look at his face, I would want to do more than just look.

Margie kept up her monologue, even though by now she had clicked on *Days of Our Lives*. She and the TV droned on; I could hear the incessant buzzing in my ears, but none of the words registered in my consciousness... my neighbor's head kept bobbing up and down as her thin lips made funny shapes in the air, and the chic characters waved their arms as they floated across the little screen... my mind had drifted off to a magical realm far away overflowing with vivid fantasies of a decidedly carnal nature. Meanwhile, my pussy had readied itself for action.

'Done!' the plumber announced.

I was startled, but Margie knew the guy was talking about the old sink. He'd managed to repair the thing in record time. Damn! I hadn't realized how expeditious those fingers would be at such boring tasks and now he was getting ready to leave.

I walked the hard-bodied handyman to the door, explaining to my neighbor that she should remain seated in front of her favorite program and not bother herself to get up. I started rambling to Joey about some fictitious problem I had with the pipes beneath my bathroom sink, when of course what I really wanted was for him to get under my skirt. He looked me straight in the eye, and his chiseled face, with its proud and perfect bone structure, caught me completely off guard. I lost my balance for a second, and he reached out to steady me. So this is what they meant by falling in love at first sight...

'I'm sorry to say my schedule is full for the day,' he informed me, 'but if it's really urgent, I can come over after work.' The tone of his voice was completely serious and businesslike, and his forehead was a little furrowed, as though he might be worried. But the slight twinkle in his eye seemed to hint at good things to come.

I suggested he arrive at my place at six-o'clock.

He nodded curtly, his eyes burning into mine and seeming to make promises I intended to see he kept.

I waved a hasty goodbye to Margie, dodging her questions as though they were spears. By her knowing smile and the amused tone in her voice I could tell she was more than just a little suspicious. After all, why hadn't I mentioned my plumbing problem to her earlier? Oh, well, I thought merrily, Margie's just jealous.

'Two's a party, three's a crowd!' I giggled, pushing up my unfettered breasts with my hands before dashing down the hallway to my own apartment, eager to prepare for the evening's entertainment. Margie stood in her doorway and watched me nearly trip on a shredded part of the carpet. Her uproarious shrieks of 'Shame on you, you little slut!' and 'Don't forget to go to confession!' echoed like the voice of conscience in my ears and were most probably heard by tenants two stories away. That Margie! She always has to have the last word, no matter what, but I didn't care. I was happy as a clam.

I showered with my new musk-scented bath gel, confident it would bring out the beast in my virile maintenance man. After a ridiculously slow search for a suitably eye-catching ensemble, I finally settled, a little reluctantly, on a black lace teddy (a gift from an ex-beau) and a pair of acid-washed denim shorts. I wasn't really too sure how they looked together, but I hoped I wouldn't be keeping them on too long, anyway. As for my feet, I slipped them into a pair of rubber beach thongs to complete my 'casual' look. I was ready, ready, ready... my sweet love juices were already dampening my black lace panties, and my nipples were fairly popping through the sheer top.

Finally, I heard two knocks on my front door. Joey! Beneath my breath I said, 'Handyman, be horny, horny as hell!' Chanting isn't really my thing, but practically anything's worth a try when a good fuck is at stake. My heart was pounding like an anvil. I pushed the stray hairs away from my eyes and opened the door wide. The sight of him waiting there for me – his handsome face shaved clean, his incredibly desirable body wrapped in fresh clothing like the ultimate present – almost knocked me off my feet.

'Why don't you show me where the problem is, Miss?' he said hesitantly. His dark, wavy hair was all slicked back, so that his prominent cheekbones were better revealed, high and sharp enough to chop down trees, I thought giddily.

'Call me Sherry,' I said seductively, letting him into my apartment and brushing past him as I closed the door behind him. 'And the problem,' I swung my arm around his shoulder and gripped the back of his neck with my hand, 'is definitely not under the kitchen sink.' By now my wicked little tongue was dancing lightly against his lips, tentatively teasing, aching for a swift reply. I didn't have long to wait. The minuscule distance between our bodies was electrically charged. We stared into each other's eyes a second, and then let our hands and mouths continue the conversation. We actually French kissed with our eyes wide open for a good ten to fifteen minutes. It was just like being on a sensual rollercoaster, what with that big bulge in his pants rubbing up against my denim-clad cunt, first slowly, as if we were waltzing at a tea dance, and then harder and faster, aiming straight for my center of gravity.

I unbuttoned his shirt with my peach-polished fingernails, and inhaled deeply. He had obviously showered before coming over, and he had even dabbed himself with some kind of after-shave lotion or cologne. Pushing my nose further into his impressively wide and hirsute chest, I realized I wasn't the only one with a preference for mysterious scents; he was wearing the same musk scent I had on, only a masculine version. Through his shirt I teased his nipples with my fingertips as he cupped my heavy breasts in his hands, and squeezed hard. I let out a little squeal, letting him know I liked that sort of rough treatment just fine. We fondled each other all over, our touches mirroring each others. Our motions, our emotions... it was like being in a dream.

'You don't have to tell me,' he whispered in my ear, taking a little love-bite. 'I already know... you're already wet down there, waiting for me, waiting patiently.' He slipped the loose straps of my teddy off my shoulders and slid one of his warm, strong hands down toward my pussy. He stopped just short of my mound, obviously teasing me. My pants were still zippered up; he hadn't even unsnapped the waistband.

'I thought I'd just about drop down and die before you got here,' I sighed, stifling an impatient groan. (Margie always said I was a little hysterical about sex.) My hands had reached his glorious cock and balls and were kneading and rubbing him, over and over again, through his slacks. His breath was getting uneven, and it was delightfully apparent he was prepared to do his job.

In a kind of fever of desire, we managed to get each other undressed, and every time a body part was uncovered, that part would get kissed and caressed. If one of us wanted to lick and suck some more before going on to the next area, that was okay, too.

Then he gave me a big surprise, suddenly scooping me up in his arms and laying me down right there on the carpet in front of the door. We were totally naked now as his nimble fingers slid inside me while his thumb stroked my clitoris, rubbing back and forth, up and down, driving me to the brink of glorious madness.

I reached out and grabbed his shoulders, pulling his straining cock down inside my warm and clinging depths. We took turns being on top, thoroughly enjoying the seemingly endless waves of sexual sensation we roused between us. From the corner of my eye, I could see the old porcelain sink in the kitchen and the pipes beneath it, which were working just fine.

53. Liz — Guilty As Charged

I was tired and irritable as I dragged myself to the jail to interview yet another client. I am a probation officer. Often my day is just beginning at five o'clock in the evening, when normal people are speeding home to their spouses.

On one particular occasion, as on so many previous trips to the county courthouse, I was wearing a serviceable but dowdy suit, a pair of sensible dark gray pumps and my 'schoolmarm face' as I describe it to my friends. The prison system is a grim environment; definitely not pretty. Being a woman, I can never let down my guard, not even for a second, or the inmates won't respect me. And respect is what I demand in all my relationships and encounters.

The cold marble staircase led me to the county jail on the tenth floor. The iron door clanged behind me, heavy and foreboding. To be sure, I'd heard that sound a thousand times before, but that time it actually made me shiver.

Before long the night guard appeared. He was there to search me, as though I had done something wrong. First he went through my purse with a sickening thoroughness to make sure I wasn't trying to sneak in a gun, maybe, or an ice pick. I sometimes fantasize about slipping a monkey wrench in there, right under the tampons, just to see what kind of reaction I might get. Even a can of ginger ale becomes suspect in that milieu. Prisoners aren't allowed to share sodas for fear they might spit drugs into the liquid. I always feel somewhat embarrassed when the guard checks through my personal belongings. My purse is my private life, and it's this stranger's official duty to invade it.

Next it was time for the metal detector. He moved it over my body very slowly, fearful he might miss one square inch of flesh. Truth to tell, there have been times I actually enjoyed this ritual, finding it perversely erotic. Once again, as with the handbag inspection, there was that undeniable element of trespass, of forced entry. As the scanner moved lightly over my body, I felt a tingle in my belly. I tried to clear my mind for the job ahead. And all the while this intimate contact was going on, the guard and I avoided eye contact, as usual. When it was all over, I rounded the corner to meet my waiting client.

At twenty, Devon already had an impressive record. His wry, bittersweet half-smile and offhand manner indicated he had been through this routine many times before. The not unusual nature of his crime – armed robbery – and his record – extensive – was of great interest to the prison psychologist because of Devon's high IQ and articulate way of expressing himself. For example, 'I have committed no crimes against humanity' had been noted early on. His case was given a remarkable degree of attention. He, himself, you can bet your ass, was treated like pond scum.

The first thing I noticed was his eyes – deep, intense, penetrating and violet-blue, sort of like Liz Taylor's eyes. Except, of course, I've never seen hers in person, and I've seen Devon's eyes, and everything else of his up close where it counts. His powerful chest strained against his jailhouse uniform, a jumpsuit, no less. I couldn't stop myself from imagining what it would be like to get him out of it.

At first there was a total lack of expression on his face and in his voice; he was a regular zombie. When he finally realized after about half-an-hour that I was genuinely sympathetic and not just another functionary, he became animated. His eyes sparkled, iridescent; the anger and hostility of his full lips softened and disappeared. He looked even younger than he was.

We talked late into the night, sharing furtive smiles and confidences. There was a wide gap between our life experiences, but our fears and hopes were very much alike. And somewhere along the way, he had managed to acquire a sensitivity I had never before encountered. It nestled, radiant and pure, in some crevice of his soul unclaimed by the streets. Still, he had the defensive part to him; it pushed me away with the occasional sarcastic remark, 'I'm here for the free room and board' or brusque mannerism. It challenged and annoyed me. Having discovered goodness, I knew there must be more.

I yearned to see what other treasures – the physical kind – lay hidden beneath the surface. Despite years of professional experience (and previous sessions with attractive inmates) this time I just couldn't help myself. When he glanced out the window and caught sight of a tiny dead bird lying on the sill, a piteous expression came over his face. I ran over to sympathize, to comfort. Then, as if controlled by an external force, my arms encircled his taut, muscular frame and my mouth met his.

Years of martial arts training stood him in good stead. Lickety-split he had me high off the ground and deep in his overpowering embrace. He carried me over to his narrow bunk. There any traces of brute rebellion were transformed into ineffable tenderness as we coiled around each other on the regulation covers. He lifted my skirt around my waist and tongued me through my underpants, lightly touching my clitoris with every lick. My breathiness urged him on, and aided and abetted by myself, he yanked off my brassiere. We caressed and undressed each other in that dreary cell, the two of us against the rest of the world. Somewhere in the distance, a group of inmates harmonized through *Amazing Grace* and *The Midnight Special*. Amidst it all we went at it panting and perspiring, every sensory organ alive and kicking and free.

He rolled me over onto my stomach. His hands slipped up my skirt and cupped and squeezed my ass. The thought of those fingers opening so many forbidden sensual locks excited me in a way I would never have thought possible. Now his fingers had thrust themselves into my panties and were toying with my snatch. This foreplay was simultaneously tantalizing and tormenting, and I loved every second of it. He shuddered and let out a primal moan, almost as if he'd just had a terrible fright. Then he slipped off my panties and shoved my skirt up out of his way. Gripping my hips, he lifted my buttocks into the air and penetrated my pussy from behind. I gasped as he pumped his cock deep inside me, and I moaned feeling his erection growing thicker and stronger with every thrust. We made love throughout the night and into the morning, two waylaid dreamers.

54. Clarissa – Out for a Drive

As a schoolteacher in a one-horse town, I had learned to be extremely discreet in any romantic entanglements. My recent dates with an upstanding science instructor from a neighboring burg met with approving smiles from the locals. I was even reasonably satisfied with our relationship, until his mother arrived for a visit. That was three months ago, and she showed no signs of leaving.

I dialed his number, and was greeted by the perpetual busy signal. 'Damn!' I muttered, slamming down the receiver. The science instructor's mother was no doubt arranging his appointments these days, and they didn't include any rendezvous with me.

Then I heard a knock on the door. It was Nicholas. A recent divorcé, he had returned to his hometown to lick his wounds. Though I had only spoken to him briefly at his father's candy store, I knew all the facts via the old reliable grapevine.

'I was taking a walk and noticed your lights on,' he smiled warmly. 'May I come in?'

I gave a careless shrug. 'Why not?' My hair and clothes were disheveled, but since I didn't see him as important, I didn't care.

We both had a beer, and we were chatting about inconsequential matters when he suddenly stood up and announced, 'Look, I'm feeling pretty hemmed in right now. What do you say we take a drive?'

As Nicholas drove his pick-up through the countryside, I had the chance to get a good look at him for the first time. To my surprise, he was quite handsome in an understated sort of way; I didn't recall him being this attractive before he left town. His hair had a tiny bit of gray near the ears, and a dimple ornamented his right cheek. The light breeze from the open window tousled his hair, giving him a slightly rakish appearance, and I found that tinge of possible wickedness undeniably attractive.

He slowed the car to a crawl. 'Well, where are we going?' he murmured, his eyes penetrating mine.

Suddenly inspired, I gave him directions for a place I knew well. We turned onto a dirt road that was little more than two tire ruts that came to an abrupt stop at the edge of high weeds. I tugged at his arm, indicating it was time for us to stop, too. After he helped me out of the truck, and I smoothed down my wrinkled clothes in a ladylike manner, I took the lead, escorting him through the high grass. Our destination was a dilapidated dock with barrel floats extending out into the river. 'Don't worry, it's safer than it looks,' I promised, stepping onto the dock.

Nicholas slipped off his shirt and spread it over the weathered boards. Then he turned to me and kissed my lips lightly, hesitantly slipping his tongue between my teeth. I replied by flicking my tongue up much the way a fish might flip its tail. We kissed again, this time more passionately, and he occupied his hands with the buttons of my blouse. As his tongue moved further into my mouth, penetrating deeper into that moist cavern (a prelude to the delicious doings to come) his warm fingers tantalizingly brushed against the tips of my exposed breasts; I don't believe in bras. Then he pinched each one delicately but firmly enough to make me gasp in the middle of a particularly deep kiss.

I had to pull away from him for a moment just to catch my breath. He chuckled softly, and adroitly slipped off my blouse. The balmy air felt good on my naked skin. I reached for him and he pulled me into an overpowering embrace. I knew our total union was inevitable, and I sighed blissfully as he laid me down gently across his shirt. He murmured in my ear, telling me he wanted me; telling me he needed to feel the weight of his body against mine. My eyes closed. I felt the pressure of his mouth on my nipples, the palms of his hands curved around the undersides of my breasts. I stroked his back and his chest, mussed his hair, and reached for the region below his belt. There was a distinct hardness there; he was responding to my touch just as I knew he would.

We were both moaning with pleasure. It was time for the lower halves of our yearning bodies to be exposed to the cool breeze of the evening and to each other. He pulled off my shorts and panties and tossed them aside. I then helped him off with his khaki pants and white briefs.

'Hurry,' I whispered, the sound of my own voice surprising me.

Even more of a surprise was the sound of a barge approaching. It startled both of us, but I was accustomed to hearing such noises. 'I come down here to watch them at night sometimes,' I said hoarsely. Reluctantly, I started to get up to retrieve my clothing, but Nicholas held me back and kissed me on the mouth again. I succumbed, letting the thrill of seduction supplant my common sense.

While the barge lights rounded the bend, coming closer, he stroked my inner thighs and probed my moist mound. Triumphantly, he found the object of his search – my sweetly aching clitoris. He replaced his fingers with his equally able tongue, coiling it like a snake, stimulating that already palpitating spot and causing my love juices to flow.

'Oh, yes, more, more, please,' I gasped, 'don't stop, don't ever stop...' Stimulated by the soft breeze and the unrelenting motion of his tongue and fingers, my pussy pulsated with longing for his cock.

The barge's powerful motor was clearly audible now. It had rounded another bend and its workers could surely see us by now. But I was only heedful of my own bottomless desire. I straddled my lover's erect dick and rode him wildly, lost in a frenzy of lust. I could hear the men on the barge hooting and hollering, but I refused to stop until Nicholas and I came together, collapsing in a happy heap.

55. Emily – Coffee Break

Throwing my pen down in dismay, I sat back in my chair and stared at the remaining freshman essays I had left to grade. I found myself looking aimlessly around my office, trying to see if maybe there was something, anything else with which I could occupy myself. Just as my eyes began to study the bookshelf nearest the door, I saw Mark Beardsley pass by in the hall, and stop.

Mark is a fellow English teacher who has the look of one of those stereotypical, old-world professors. He comes off as very serious, but I've always wondered what he's really like inside. He's a very good-looking man, and it's been a kind of quest of mine to find out more about him.

'Good morning, Elizabeth.'

Before I could reply, I felt an excitement beginning to grow inside me. I always got nervous around him, but this time it was worse. Even though it was only a 'hello' we had never spoken one-on-one before; we had barely nodded to each other at teachers' meetings and faculty Christmas parties. The sweet odor of pipe tobacco brought me back to the present.

'Hello, Mark,' I said casually. 'I was just about to take a break. Want a cup of coffee?'

'Sounds great,' he replied, and then added, 'I have some brewing in my office, so we won't have to settle for the stale coffee downstairs.'

'Great,' I declared calmly, although I couldn't believe what I was hearing. The two of us in his office alone? I certainly couldn't let this opportunity pass me by. I got up, straightened the papers on my desk, and followed him.

His office was just down the hall and around the corner, but it seemed like an eternity before we reached it. I looked around me. The small space was filled with books and posters and knick-knacks, but I didn't see a coffee pot.

I heard the door close behind me. I was about to turn around when I felt a pair of hands on my shoulders. They were so warm as they moved up my neck to caress the soft spot behind my ears that I didn't protest.

'Mark,' I said, and then stopped. I wanted him to continue, but it had happened so fast.

As if reading my mind, he whispered, 'I'll stop if you want.'

'No,' I whispered back, 'please…' I closed my eyes. My nipples were tightening and the moisture between my legs was beginning to dampen my panties. His hands slid over my blouse across the contours of my breasts, and I could feel his hardness against the small of my back. Every nerves ending was sensitive to his gentle touch and my body began to ache for his.

No longer subtle, Mark began rubbing my breasts more firmly and I felt my nipples poking through the lacy bra beneath my blouse. 'Touch me,' I begged, turning to face him and caressing his penis through his pants. In reply he groaned softly, and quickly undoing the buttons of my blouse, he unfastened my bra in front. He parted the cups and took my naked breasts in his hands and nibbled first on one nipple then the other, moaning through mouthfuls of my soft mounds. The touch of his tongue combined with gentle nips of his teeth aroused me even more. I was falling into a dark abyss where everything my body desired was permitted and where every touch was an irresistible invitation to pleasure…

I took off his sweater, and with trembling fingers unbuttoned his shirt. His tongue was still worshipping my breasts as I unzipped his slacks. Then he slipped a hand inside my skirt and into my panties, moving urgently to my wet pussy. Two large, strong fingers slid inside me, and as they moved back and forth rhythmically, I could not hold back my moans.

'Emily... God, you're so beautiful!' He carefully leaned me back against his desk. He glided his hands up and down my inner thighs, then parted my legs and his palm gently cradled my wet sex. 'I know you're going to taste so good,' he whispered as he sank to his knees. I shivered as he parted my labial lips with his fingers, and then inserted the tip of his tongue in the entrance to my body. He traced a path around my vulva as I moved to his rhythm. His tongue probed deeper and I thrust my pussy into his face as his lips and tongue nestled into my sex. It wasn't long before my hips were bucking as his tongue brought me to the edge of an almost unbearable pleasure. I cried out as I felt my vagina contracting, listening as if from very far away to Mark's moans of satisfaction as I climaxed.

Now I desperately wanted him inside me; I needed to feel his hard cock in my slick cunt. He seemed to sense this because he muttered, 'You're mine now' as he stood up, shoved down his pants and underwear. 'Turn around and bend over,' he commanded, and thrust his erection up inside me. He fucked me deep and hard, until I didn't know where his body ended and mine began. His breathing quickened, and then I felt him tense as he bucked like a wild horse against me, releasing himself inside me and groaning my name.

Much, much later, when we had put on our clothes again and returned to the real world, he smiled and said, 'I never did offer you that cup of coffee.'

'You owe me one.'

And since that amazing day, he has offered me much more than coffee. As they say, all work and no play would make me a dull girl.

56. Stephanie — First Date

It was nearing eight-thirty and the butterflies in my stomach were getting bigger. I had had a steady boyfriend for so long that I was no longer accustomed to dating. But it had been three months since Matt and I broke up, so I figured it was time, both to date and to make love again. I still missed Matt, but I was so filled with frustrated desire I was ready for almost anything.

At eight-thirty on the dot, a car honked outside. I took one last look in the mirror. I not only wanted to impress my date, John, but his friends as well. John was taking me to a party.

When we arrived at the door, we were greeted by Bob, our host. John had talked to me briefly about him. 'Hey, John, how ya doin'?' said Bob. 'Glad you could make it. And who is this vision of loveliness?' he asked, looking at me.

'Bob, this is Stephanie. Stephanie, Bob.'

Bob stretched out his hand. 'Nice to meet you,' he said, but before I had a chance to reply, his attention shifted to the guests arriving behind us. 'Everyone's down in the basement,' he told us, reaching around me to grab someone else's hand.

I followed John downstairs. The basement was empty enough for us to make our way to a couch in the corner without encountering too many people. I sat down and John sat beside me.

'Do you want something to drink?' he asked.

'No, thank you,' I said. I didn't want him to leave me alone. He picked up my hand, and held it in his lap. His hands were strong and warm.

'Do you want to leave?' he asked, sensing my discomfort.

'No,' I answered as if I really meant it. He put his arm around me, and I melted into his side. It was, of course, only our first date, but I felt totally comfortable with him, and loved the feeling of his arm around me. I looked up into his face. His eyes were staring into mine. Our lips moved closer, and we kissed for the first time. It was a simple kiss, but it made me yearn for another one. We kissed again, and this time I could feel my nipples getting hard. He moved his hand up the back of my shirt, and began pressing his fingers lightly across my back in a sweet sensual massage.

'Let's have a more private party,' he whispered in my ear, and I nodded eagerly.

A few minutes later we wandered upstairs in search of an unoccupied room. Finally, we moved into a bedroom. As we sank down onto the bed, he caressed my breasts through my shirt. I wasn't wearing a bra, so he was able to gently tweak my nipples. I let out a little moan. He unbuttoned the top two buttons and reached in to cup one of my tits, rubbing the nipple between his thumb and forefinger. My pussy was getting warm and wet. I reached out and boldly stroked his crotch. I could feel his dick growing hard against my hand. As I rubbed his hard-on through his pants, he lowered his head to my breasts and began sucking gently on my teats. My pussy was really hot now. I began rubbing my pussy rhythmically against his side while I unzipped his pants. Reaching up beneath my skirt, he moved my panties to one side and thrust a finger into my slick hole.

When all my clothes were off, he sat me on the edge of the bed and parted my legs. He kissed my clitoris, and then thrust the firm muscle of his tongue into my cunt as far as he could while I caressed the back of his head. He increased the pressure on my clit with his thumb and continued rubbing it as his mouth fucked my pussy. He made me come that way in record time.

'That was wonderful,' I murmured as he raised his head and smiled at me with shining wet lips.

'At your service,' he replied teasingly. He stood up, and at once I began helping him peel off his clothes. This time I sat him on the edge of the bed, his rock-hard cock staring straight at me as I knelt before him. I grabbed his erection with my hand and rubbed it slowly as I teased the tip with my tongue. The taste of his dick made me hungry for more. I sucked slowly on his head as I continued caressing the shaft gently with my fist. The further his cock went into my mouth, the tenser he got. He grabbed my head, moaning, and I began sucking him furiously.

There was a knock at the door.

We scrambled frantically to get dressed, and John opened the door. Standing before us wearing a teasing smile was Bob.

'Oh, sorry,' he said, and backed out of the room.

I couldn't help but laugh.

'Where were we?' John said as he locked the door behind us.

57. Eva — Dancing Lessons

Lying on my back in the sauna, I opened the thick white towel covering me from chest to thighs. The dry heat was intoxicating; making me feel mellow and sexy. I could barely move. I didn't want to. My skin grew moist and prickled as though it was being teased by a thousand ghostly kisses. I felt my nipples hardening. The pleasure of just letting go and relaxing after a good workout washed over me. I parted my legs and my pussy lips opened slightly. The rush of air felt like the tip of a hesitant tongue caressing my cunt, and just my finger brushing lightly against my clit would surely bring me off. Yet even though I could come with a quiet gasp, I was afraid someone would see me through the hazy mist. Masturbating would have to wait for later.

Later... later was an empty apartment, a spinach soufflé in the microwave, and old movies on TV. That's the pattern my nights had taken since Larry moved out. The days were frantically full down at the Ad Agency. I liked my job and my co-workers, but a long, hard day at the office was usually followed by a long, hard night with a vibrator.

Although I am not unattractive, it isn't easy for me to meet guys. I guess I'm pretty shy when it comes to that. I try to keep busy and go to the gym a few times a week, but I wanted to do something else, something frivolous, silly; something exciting. Maybe I was watching too many old movies and was waiting for someone to sweep me off my feet.

Rousing myself out of daydreams, I realized I was caressing my thigh with one hand and absentmindedly exploring my moist labia with the other. It was definitely time to go home.

After a quick shower, I noticed something of interest on the billboard in the locker room. Dance classes, Latin dance classes. Now that sounded wildly exotic. I always loved Spanish dancing. I copied down the number.

Once back at my apartment, I stripped off my corporate business suit. With a frozen dinner sizzling in the microwave, I plopped onto the sofa and dialed the dance class number. A sultry male voice answered. Luis gave me the details about the classes, but I found it difficult to concentrate on what he was saying. His deep, melodic voice was making me melt inside. Did he know I was sitting naked, fingering my pussy as he spoke?

'My last pupil quit,' he explained, 'so I'm open.'

'So am I,' I told him, stroking my mound. 'I mean, I'm free Thursday nights.'

***

Later that week, as I climbed the stairs to the second-floor studio, I tried to picture my new dance instructor. It was a large room. Two walls were covered with mirrors and the other two with windows. Five pairs of teachers and students moved around on the scuffed wooden floor. A dark, handsome man worked his way toward me.

'Eva?' he inquired.

It was Luis, and he was more attractive than I had fantasized. Tall and slim, he was molded into tight chinos showing off a perfect ass. I could count every rib and muscle through his tank top. His full lips and dark eyes smiled at me, taking me in with great interest. I was wearing a sheer silk dress and sneakers. 'Latin dancing should be done in high heels or barefoot,' he informed me with mock sternness.

'I left my heels at the office,' I explained.

He sank gracefully down on one knee in front of me and unlaced my Reeboks. Then he peeled off my socks. 'Pretty feet,' he said, cupping my foot in his palm. 'Pretty lady.' He smiled up at me.

Suddenly feeling weak, I clasped his hand in mine and helped him up, as though he needed my help.

He talked his way through the cha-cha-cha in that delicious, melodic voice of his. I tried to listen, but I couldn't help drifting off into sensual daydreams. I wondered how that sexy voice would sound begging me to suck his cock or crying out as he came deep inside me...

'One-two, one-two-three,' Luis was whispering in my ear.

'Fuck me!' I wanted to whisper back.

Every Thursday morning I laid out my sexiest undergarments and my most feminine business wear. And every Thursday night was the tortuous tease of being held in Luis' arms. Moving close against him, his warm breath would caress my neck. I wondered if the firm hand pressed against my spine could feel the lacy bridle of my garter belt. Did he notice my nipples hardening against his chest, a silent message of seduction? The quick flash of his tongue against his teeth told me he did. In a close embrace, I could feel the outline of his cock against my thigh. Was it hard? He always twirled me away before I could guess a wicked smile on his lips.

After five lessons, I was frantic with desire for him. Our chaste mating dances were driving me crazy. I started having the most bizarre dreams. In these dreams we never seemed to get around to making love, but there was endless foreplay, and I heard Luis' voice say, 'Latin dancing is always done in high heels.' I'm wearing red stiletto heels. He is lying naked on the wooden floor as I straddle his face. 'Like this?' I ask. In reply, he buries his tongue in my pussy. Sultry guitar music plays in the background as the other students and instructors move around us, oblivious to our passion. I dance on Luis' face, gently moving my hips and pumping my pussy against his sucking mouth. His tongue searches out my labial lips, licking and lapping hungrily. Grasping my ass, he pulls my wet cunt even harder against his handsome features. He nibbles on my clit, taking it into his mouth and circling it with his tongue. Looking down, I watch his fiery eyes watching me. In seconds, I am having a throbbing orgasm…

Last week we learned the Meringue. Maybe it was being hip-to-hip with my lusty Latin and rubbing bellies, but that was my favorite dance. He was as distantly flirtatious as ever. My knees were weak as we slid across the floor.

After the lesson I was in such a fog that I forgot my briefcase. By the time I went back to retrieve it, Luis was alone in the studio. Shyly, I told him how much I loved the Meringue.

He smiled. 'That's not the real Meringue.'

'What's the real Meringue?' I asked breathlessly.

'It's like Spanish dirty dancing.' He stepped closer. 'Do you want to learn?'

I nodded. He put on a tape, and took me in his arms. We swayed as we had before, but this time he held me closer, so close I was sure now he had a hard-on for me. 'In this Meringue, the woman slides down on the man's leg.' He wedged his knee between my thighs, hiking my tight skirt above my knees. 'Go down on it,' he instructed.

Keeping the rhythm, I moved my hips from side to side and slowly slid down his hard leg, rubbing my pussy shamelessly against it.

'That's it,' he said. 'Now come up.'

I gladly did as he said, and the second time I descended, he held me down longer, gently pumping his leg beneath me while I squirmed ecstatically against it. When I was up in his arms again, he kissed the side of my neck, and then my mouth. He held my blonde curls in his hands and dipped his tongue between my lips. We sank down to the floor as one. Finally having him in my arms the way I had longed to for so long, I caressed his chest, his highs, and his tight ass. He fumbled with the tiny pearl buttons on my blouse, and my nipples were already hard and straining through my lace undergarment. He buried his face in my exposed cleavage and undid the front closure of my bra. My tits fell into his hands like ripe fruits. Lapping on the rosy pink nibs, he teased them as I moaned. Whipping off his tank top, he rubbed his bare chest against mine, making me ache to get my hands on his equally hard cock.

'Oh, *mi besso*,' he murmured.

Unable to resist, I rubbed his dick through his pants.

At once he peeled off his dance pants and spread himself on his back on the floor. I knelt beside him, my tits dangling in his face as I touched the bare skin of his penis pulsing gently in my hand. 'You tease!' I said. 'I've wanted you for so long!' I bent forward to dip his cock into my mouth. I sucked him down for a good long time, making noisy slurping sounds like a little girl relishing a big chocolate ice cream cone.

'On your hands and knees,' he instructed abruptly, and the instant I obeyed him his cock slid easily into my begging pussy. I watched our fucking bodies in the many mirrors, my vagina passionately hugging his erection.

'Look at us,' I whispered.

He looked, and we both watched as he lifted me roughly up by the hips and thrust his dick even deeper inside me. My orgasm meshed with his, our senses and sensations dancing seamlessly together. Trembling, I couldn't hold myself up any longer and slumped onto my elbows, my cheek resting against the smooth, cool floor as he pumped his hot cum into my throbbing cunt.

***

In the taxi home, I couldn't help but smile. So that was the real Meringue. I couldn't wait to learn the Tango.

58. Stacy — Midnight Dip

As I lay beneath the sun on my favorite Caribbean island, I started thinking about how lonely I was. It had been almost six months since I broke up with Tony. I figured this trip would be a good way to take my mind off of him, but instead I started missing him even more. Nevertheless, I wasn't about to mope around while I was on vacation.

I began getting into what nightlife the island of Montserrat had to offer. Night after night I'd meet man after man, but none of them had what I wanted, until last night...

I was standing near the dance floor when I spotted an intriguing man at the beachfront bar. He had brown hair, a well-defined body, and was wearing a navy-blue tank top and shorts. He looked good enough to eat.

I went over and stood at the part of the bar where he was and ordered a drink. I didn't speak to him, but I did look at him and smile. Feeling a little shy, I turned around and walked toward the beach with my drink. I sat down in a wicker chair, and much to my surprise, the handsome stranger followed me.

'Hello,' he said as he sat down beside me. 'I'm Charles.'

I took a deep breath. 'It's nice to meet you, Charles, I'm Stacy.' We talked about where we were from and what we did, and I could tell he was getting horny by the way he looked me. I was wearing my bikini with a wrap-around skirt, and I kept catching him looking at the slit in the skirt tied loosely around my waist.

When the bar closed, he asked if I wanted to go for a walk. Although it sounded tempting, I thought of a better idea. 'I'm a little hungry,' I said. 'How about coming back to my bungalow for a snack? My fridge is stocked.' He accepted my invitation willingly, as I knew he would.

We entered my bungalow from the back porch, where we paused to kiss. I led him inside, and told him to make himself comfortable while I prepared us something to eat.

I walked back into the living room to bring him a glass of wine, and I accidentally dropped his napkin. As I bent down to pick it up, he pressed his hardness against my ass and caressed my soft cheeks with his hands. I leaned back to press harder against him, and he wrapped his arms around my waist. I knew what he wanted – and I wanted it too – but I didn't want to rush into anything just yet.

'Shouldn't we eat something first?' I asked.

'Mm,' he moaned, 'I know just what I want to eat.' He slipped a finger through the slit in my skirt and into my bathing suit, and I closed my eyes and didn't move. Slowly, he stood up, his finger still probing the inside of my pussy. He leaned into my ear and whispered, 'Let's go swimming.'

It was close to midnight, we were all alone in my bungalow, and he wanted to go swimming? My eyes opened in amazement, yet on second thought, it sounded like fun. I pulled off my wrap-around skirt and was ready for the ocean. Charles pushed down his shorts, but he had no swim trunks underneath them, and I gasped at the sight of his erect penis.

We ran hand-in-hand down the beach, and submerged ourselves in the deliciously warm water. I came up behind him, slipped my arms around his chest, and kissed the back of his back. He took one of my hands and placed it on his cock. He sighed as I rubbed it, and grabbed my arm and swung me around to face him. I lifted one leg and wrapped it around his waist. I kissed him, savoring the wonderful feel of his tongue inside my mouth. I felt a rush of desire blaze through my body. To tease him a little, I broke from his hold and dove into the water. When I came up, I saw that my bikini top had fallen and exposed my breasts. My first instinct was to cover myself, but I didn't because he was staring appreciatively at my full tits. I waded over to him and looked up at his face. Beneath the water, I took hold of his hard-on and began pumping it. I wanted to keep jacking him off, but I also wanted him inside me. He caressed my bare breasts, and then with one swift motion yanked the bottom half of my bikini down.

He entered me slowly, and the sensation was everything I had hoped it would be. It had always been a fantasy of mine to make love in the water, and now it was coming true, and I was coming, too…

Afterwards, we decided to stay in the water a while longer, swimming around and trying to splash each other. I couldn't stop laughing as I watched him try oh-so-hard to do a handstand, and I couldn't stop thinking how glad I was I had finally taken a vacation.

59. Mireya — Lube Job

I'd had my car for over a year, so I figured it was time to give it a good tune-up. As I drove to the local garage, I remembered the new mechanic I had met the last time I brought my car in for an oil change. His name tag said 'Wayne' and he had sensual hazel eyes and broad muscular thighs. That's all I knew about him, but it was enough to make me wet whenever I thought about him.

I pulled up to the part of the garage where Wayne was standing.

'May I help you?' he asked invitingly. My perfect fantasy man, standing inches away in skin-tight jeans and a ripped shirt, was asking if he could help me.

'I hope so,' I answered, admiring him from head to toe. I wanted him to 'help' me in more ways than one, but for now, I thought, I'd better stick to business. 'My car needs a good tune-up. Are you the one to do it, Wayne?'

'I sure am.' He leaned so far into the window of my car I could feel his warm breath on my face. 'As a matter of fact, I can do it so well, you won't be disappointed.'

Was my car overheating or was it just me? The smell of sweat from his body was driving me crazy. I had to say something before I became too flustered to utter anything intelligible. 'Where should I leave my car?' I asked.

He motioned for me to pull up where it said *Service Zone* without once taking his eyes off me.

After I parked, I went back to Wayne, but he turned around and started walking away. It looked as though he was going outside when he stopped at the door to the garage and grabbed hold of the handle.

'What are you doing?' I asked.

'I don't want anyone to disturb us.' He pulled the garage door closed. 'I'm going to give your car special service.'

Just as I was beginning to absorb the implications of his words, he asked me to pop the hood. I reached in and pulled the lever. He looked inside, poking around the engine with a tool from his belt.

After five minutes, he called for a coffee break and we went into a small room. I sat on an old decrepit sofa while he poured us some coffee. As he placed the cup in my hand, he leaned toward me. 'I've noticed you here before,' he said quietly, his eyes slowly devouring my body.

I was so turned on I knew something was going to have to happen. What I felt for him was too strong to let pass. I found myself somewhere between aroused and confused. After all, Wayne was quite different from the clean-cut guys I'd gone out with in the past. His hands were dirty, and I couldn't imagine what on earth we'd have in common. But I think that's what I liked about him, the fact that I'd be a 'naughty' girl for fooling around in a garage with some mechanic I barely knew. It would be such a change from the typical pasteurized sex I was used to.

As he was setting his cup on the table, he placed his left hand on my thigh. His touch was like electricity running through my entire body. He stroked my legs, making his way up to my pussy. The caress of his rough hand felt as good as I had imagined it would. I wanted to grab him, rip off his clothes, and let him fuck me until I was exhausted. But I had to remain calm; I wanted to take things slow. I didn't know him well enough to be uninhibited.

He took the cup out of my hand and slowly moved his up to my blouse, carefully unfastening each button. He was sitting pressed up against me, and I could feel his erect member against my belly. He pulled off my blouse and draped it carefully across the arm of the couch beside him.

'You have no idea what you're doing to me,' he muttered. He

reached behind me and unhooked my bra. His mouth gently engulfed one of my small breasts while his other hand started undoing my pants. Momentarily standing up, he removed them along with my panties. Those were all my clothes. I thought maybe I should now remove his to touch him and excite him the way he was exciting me, but I loved the way he was making me feel and I didn't want to interrupt his momentum.

Kneeling before me, he pulled my hips towards his face, and I could see his tongue darting in and out between his lips as he teased my clit. I felt like I wanted him to lick me that way forever and wondered how long the pleasure would last. He buried his entire face in my wet sex with an abandon I had never seen before in a man, and I could feel myself irresistibly building up to a climax. He sucked and licked me while his hands massaged my breasts, and then he stopped just long enough to stand up again and pull off his jeans. Seeing his erect cock spring out at me immediately made me ache to have him inside me.

He bent over and gave me a long passionate kiss as he rubbed his stiff penis between my tits, bunching them up around his shaft to caress himself with their soft mounds. I reached for his balls, and carefully squeezed and caressed them. I spread my legs, inviting him to enter me as he knelt before me again, but first he teased me by just inserting the head of his cock between my labial lips. Slowly, he drove his erection into my pussy, and the sensation was intoxicating. He thrust in and out of me with the hard, even rhythm of a piston, and I could feel his balls tightening. He was going to come very soon, right when I did…

Afterwards he said casually, 'You were great. Thanks.'

'Thank you,' I replied politely.

That's the last time I'll wait a whole year before getting a tune-up.

60. Katie – Hunting Season

The day was extraordinarily warm for late October, even in Tennessee. I had a trying morning loading beef calves to be sold at auction, so I decided to take the afternoon off and have a private picnic at a quiet stream on a remote part of my farm.

In the lazy afternoon sun, I fell asleep on a blanket in the shade of a tree. When a shadow was cast over me, I awoke instantly to find a tall, bearded stranger standing over me, a shotgun slung casually over his arm.

My alarm must have shown in my eyes, because he immediately apologized for startling me. 'I'm sorry I disturbed you,' he said politely. 'But you just made such a lovely picture lying there in the sun. The gun's not even loaded. I only use it as an excuse to tramp through the hills and hollows and admire the fall colors. Farmers look at you rather strangely if you ask to walk their land, but they'll readily give you permission to hunt.'

'Well, you didn't ask permission to hunt on this farm,' I chided, though my smile told him I meant no ill-will.

'How do you know?' he asked, smiling in return.

'Because I'm the farmer,' I laughed. 'You're welcome to hunt, but even more welcome to just enjoy the scenery, as long as you don't have an eye for my cattle,' I added.

'That's fair enough,' he said. 'I like my beef in smaller servings.'

I noticed him looking at the wine and the glass left over from my lunch. 'Would you like some?' I asked, gesturing towards the bottle.

'I'd be delighted,' he replied, 'but if you don't mind, I'd like to borrow the glass first, to drink some water from the stream. Tramping these hills is hard work in weather like this, and this is the sweetest water in the whole country.'

'Oh, so you've been here before,' I observed.

'Well, I thought this field was just another part of the farm on the other side of that peculiar-looking barbed-wire gate, but if I'd known it wasn't, and that the farmer was so pretty, I'd have come asking permission a long time ago.'

'That barbed-wire gate is called a fence gap. Most of the farmers around here have a gap in their line fences to bring back their bull when he goes wandering. I guess my fences are in such bad shape you wouldn't know it was a line fence,' I said ruefully as I watched him lean the shotgun against the tree and pick up the wine glass.

He walked gracefully through the dappled sunlight to where the crystal-cold stream cascades down a series of rock shelves into a small, clear pool. The sun shone on his sandy hair and glinted off his bronzed, well-muscled arms where the waterfall splashed him. This stranger was handsome, rugged in manner, with a full but neatly trimmed beard. As he turned to walk back, the sun shone in his slate-gray eyes, making them seem bottomless.

With a charming mixture of confidence and courtly diffidence, he sat on the blanket beside me. 'I wouldn't mind a glass of wine now. Will you join me?'

'Well, since I wasn't expecting company, I only brought one glass. It may not be too clean,' I added as I poured him a glass of Portuguese rosé.

'No matter, the wine will sanitize the glass, and besides, you look the picture of country health. I've heard about these beautiful farmers' daughters, but the farmers must have been hiding them from me.'

'I can certainly see why,' I teased, 'with your slick city charm. But I'm not really a farmer's daughter. I fled the city myself, permanently, a few years back for the peace and privacy and beauty here.'

'My name's John, by the way.'

Somehow names hadn't seemed important our meeting was so natural. 'I'm Katie.'

'It certainly is private here,' he remarked, handing me the glass. I became conscious of his glances at my light cotton top and skimpy cutoff jeans. Instead of embarrassing me, however, they had a more stimulating effect even than the nice weather. I began feeling deliciously wicked.

When I handed the wineglass back to him, he leaned forward to take it, and in a smooth motion continued forward to kiss me. Then, without breaking the kiss, he set the glass behind us and brought his arm around to pull me closer. He tasted of sweet wine and spring water, and his smell was clean and masculine. Gradually, his kisses grew more passionate, exploring my mouth, nipping softly at my lips, and finding the sensitive spot behind my ear and at the nape of my neck. His oral attentions were so artful I couldn't help but respond to them.

My cotton top was held up by thin straps tied in a bow and buttoned down the front. As John kissed my shoulders, he teased open the bows with his teeth like a playful puppy, and then slowly unbuttoned my top, kissing the smooth skin between my breasts as each button revealed more to him of my soft, swelling flesh. Because of the heat, I hadn't worn a bra, and when the last button was undone, he reverently peeled each side of my shirt back, glancing up into my eyes to gauge my reaction. I was thoroughly enraptured. Casual sex is not my thing; I hadn't been with anyone since my divorce the previous year, but I felt bewitched by the wine, the lazy day and this gorgeous specimen of a man.

As he sucked my nipples with his skillful mouth, I ran my fingers through his thick hair and massaged the muscles rippling along his sturdy back and arms. Soon I felt his hands exploring the snap and zipper on my cutoffs. As he deftly helped me out of them, he smiled mischievously at my red lace bikini panties.

'Are you sure you weren't waiting for me?' he teased.

'I think I was,' I replied huskily.

Instead of removing my panties, he suddenly slid lower and used his teeth to nip at me gently through the fabric, just barely catching my skin in his teeth and driving me wild. With his lips, he pulled gently at the pubic curls escaping from the lace crotch of my panties, and when he gently nibbled on my clit through the porous fabric, it nearly sent me careening into a climax. A few minutes of this was all I could stand. I sat up and began undressing him.

I unbuttoned his shirt to find, as I expected, a tanned muscular chest. He stood up to undo his jeans, and step out of them, but when he went to pull down his jockey shorts, I insisted on helping him. Tugging downward a couple of inches revealed a magnificently long, thick cock. I ignored it momentarily and slowly pulled his underpants down, caressing his muscular legs in the process. He stepped out of them, and I returned my attention to his glorious hard-on. I clutched his tight buttocks and kneaded them with my fingers as I kissed away a tiny drop of semen pearling at the tip of his penis. He tasted clean and salty and whetted my appetite for more; I couldn't resist sucking and licking the whole length of his erection, letting him stimulate himself with my throat. He groaned quietly and caressed my hair, but soon sank down on the blanket beside me. Gallantly, he helped me lie back across it and removed my panties with the air of being awarded a rare trophy. He spread himself above me, and very slowly filled my pussy with his rampant cock. After a few slow, tantalizing thrusts, he accelerated his pace, quickly achieving a vigorous rhythm, and already aroused to the breaking point, I climaxed with such violence that I cried out helplessly. I pleaded with him to come with me, but he kept on vigorously riding my hole, and to my surprise I became even more turned on. Then his face took on an almost pained look and I knew he was close to orgasm, but with heroic self-control he slowed his pace, and then stopped moving inside me completely. He lifted my right leg as though he was going to throw it over his shoulder, but instead he raised it straight up in the air. Again he began thrusting even more deeply, the sound of his balls slapping against my vulva resounding in the clear, crisp afternoon air. And in an uncanny display of coordination, he nipped and sucked at erotically sensitive areas I never knew existed – behind my knee, at the crest of my shoulders – while all the time he kept pumping his cock into my pussy with a fierce energy that had me moaning with gratitude at his generous virility. Beads of sweat broke out on his forehead and I was panting, not from exertion but from a series of orgasms each mounting in strength. At last, when I felt I was about to faint from the sheer intensity of it all, he ejaculated deep inside me, groaning in sweet agony.

When he finally caught his breath and looked down at me, his face registered alarm. 'Are you all right?' he asked gently. 'You look pale.'

'I'm fine,' I whispered weakly. 'It's just been so overwhelming... I think you'd better rest a minute yourself.' He was still breathing heavily.

He lay down beside me, and smiled as he propped his head up on one arm. 'I hope I didn't hurt you. I mean, I don't usually...' He seemed at a loss for words.

'I loved it,' I assured him. 'Don't apologize.'

It was autumn and the sun had begun setting. Even though the day had felt like summer, a chill now settled in, forcing us to put our clothes back on.

'Do you live by this stream, my woodland nymph?' he asked me, smiling. 'Or is there a tree nearby you call home?'

'There's a big tree at the head of this hollow I call home,' I laughed, 'but after our workout, I don't think I want to climb into it on my own.' I whistled, and then asked him if he could ride bareback as my two horses, grazing across the gully, came trotting up. 'The colt is very gentle, and though I don't have another bridle, if you'll just hang on, he'll follow the mare anywhere.'

His smile deepened. 'And so will I.'

ABOUT THE EDITOR

Maria Isabel Pita is the author of seven erotic novels, Thorsday Night, Eternal Bondage, To Her Master Born (re-printed as an exclusive hard-cover edition by the Doubleday Venus Book Club) Dreams of Anubis, Pleasures Unknown, Recipe For Romance and The Fabric of Love. She is also the author of the non-fiction book, The Story of M... A Memoir, a vividly detailed account of her first year of training as a slave to her Master and soul mate. Maria lives with her beloved Master, Stinger, and their dog, Merlin. She is currently working on part two of her memoir, Beauty & Submission, coming soon in hardcover. You can visit her at www.mariaisabelpita.com and www.thestoryofmamemoir.com